Kim,

Thank

Support. I appreciate you.

Blessings Always,

Avery Goode

DISHONEST

A NOVEL

BY

AVERY GOODE

Published by Goode Gyrlz Publications, LLC

P.O. Box 311822 Atlanta, GA 31131

This novel is a work of fiction. All names, characters and incidents occurring in the work are either the product of the author's imagination or are used fictitiously, as are those fictionalized events and incidents that involve real persons. Any references to real people, events, establishments, or locales are intended only to give the fiction a sense of reality and authenticity.

ISBN-13: 978-0-9975164-1-8

ISBN-10: 0-9975164-1-0

ACKNOWLEDGEMENTS

Since the initial release of Dishonest in 2011, I am so glad to say that I have grown as an author and more recently, as a publisher. This re-release is a blessing. Especially because it is released by my company, Goode Gyrlz Publications, LLC. This is the first of many.

God has truly been Goode to me and He is worthy of all praise. Thanks go to Him first and foremost. Next I'd like to thank my wonderful children, Kenisha, Tory, and Tree. You all are my air. Jah'vyon, Azauriah, JaLynn, and Brooklynn, you guys are my wings. To my mom, Rida and my dad, Toots, you are the best. I love you. Thanks for being supportive parents. To my sister and her crew, I love you guys. Special thanks to Tressa 'Azarel' Smallwood for being such an empowering mentor. Thank you for your support, advice, prayers and for setting such a great example to follow. To Susan Fox, you are the epitome of a hardworking woman. Danyelle Cooksey, thank you for investing in me and my family and for featuring Dishonest as your book clubs' selection. Who knew that that great day would lead to such a wonderful sisterhood. Nikki Segar, thank you for helping me sell and market all of my books. You are a magnificent friend and event planner. To all of the editors, graphic designers, photographers who have helped me along the way I thank you all immensely. The industry needs creative people like you! There are entirely too many people to list by name but for those of you who truly support me and the Goode Gyrlz movement, I thank you from the bottom of my heart.

–Avery Goode

PROLOGUE

Dear Diary: The game is getting real crazy. Bitches snitching and nigger's dying. It's time for me to let this shit go. The money is so damned good though. I don't know if I can stop.

Money. That's my drug of choice.

CHAPTER ONE

I was found lying between the bodies of my decomposing parents, the little girl thought. They had been dead five days before they were discovered. Honesty Mitchell was wedged under her daddy. She could not get up and didn't want to. Moving would take her away from the people she loved the most. She would be alone. In her mind she knew they were gone but she wanted to be with them as long as she could. Her senses were numbed. She could not see. Could not hear. Could not feel.

Kim, her mother's best friend was the one who found them. She and her boyfriend were the only friends of her parent's who had a key to their house. They were very close. The first day Kim did not talk to her friend she was cool. She knew that her girl was planning to have her man on lock down and she knew what that meant. But when she didn't hear from her on the second or even third day she began to worry. Day four put her into panic mode but she decided to chill before making something out of nothing. Her concerns mounted because no one had seen or heard from either of her friends.

Kim's husband, Leo, had told her that he felt something bad in his spirit. She believed him but didn't know what to think. He was always *feeling* something because he thought himself a clairvoyant. But this morning was different. *This* morning, Kim felt something too. Five days with no communication? Hell no! In her terrifying dreams, her best friend, Silver, called out to her. The cries she heard were audible. Like she was in the same room with her.

At dawn on the fifth day, Kim got the spare house key out of her nightstand, dressed quickly, and made a mad dash across town. She prayed the whole time she drove. When she pulled up in front of the house, everything appeared to be normal. Exhaling the breath she had been holding since turning her car off, Kim got out of her vehicle and approached the house.

Her heart pounded hard in her chest. There was a loud thud in her ear. Boom, boom, boom, boom. She reached out to touch the door knob. Her palm was sweaty and her hand shook like a leaf. Her key would not go into the hole. She dropped them on the ground.

Now I see how women get killed in movies, she thought as she fought to regroup.

She took a few deep breaths, inserted the correct key, opened the door and walked inside. Immediately a foul odor hit her in the face.

What the hell is that? She thought as she walked through the house towards the kitchen.

As much as she wanted to check to see if something had spoiled, she needed to find her friend. Everything else could wait. While she was close to the garage she checked it. There was nothing out of the ordinary. All four cars were there. *Did he take them on a trip and use the airport shuttle instead of driving? Take a taxi?* He had done that before and not let anyone know.

I hope that's what he's doing this time, she thought as she continued to search the downstairs.

She called out everyone's name as she checked the rooms. No answer. The odor intensified the closer she got to the stairs.

The smell was so pungent that as she ascended the staircase, her eyes began to water. She used her shirt sleeve to cover her nose. The odor was getting stronger. The shirt was not enough. She held her breath. One thing that she noticed was that the house was quiet. Too quiet. Like the power was shut off. She flipped the hall light switch to see if it worked. It did. She had never experienced this type of silence before. A quiet so loud it was deafening.

Her stomach lurched violently, showing signs of rebellion. The odor was coming from the master bedroom. She approached the door and stopped, placing her sweaty palm on the knob. Before twisting, she prayed again. The same prayer she had been praying all morning.

Lord, please let them be alive. Prepare my heart for what I am about to find.

But nothing could have prepared her for this. Lying in a pool of blood were her best friends, Golden and Silvia Mitchell. She was taking in the scene of what had obviously been a massacre. At first, she couldn't move. Her legs felt like led. Although it was obvious they were gone, false hope had her check for pulses anyway. She had to make sure.

Golden, a.k.a., 'Goldie', was lying on his stomach. The bullet entrance on the back of his ear was visible. There were other bullet wounds in his head and his back. Whoever did this wanted to make sure that he was dead. His rotting flesh looked like a cheap fur coat had shed on him.

Silvia or 'Silver', died with her eyes open. Even post mortem, her eyes told a story. Not only had she seen the shooter, she *knew* who did it. Her flesh was rotting too. Blood from her head had dried in her hair causing it to stick to her face. She looked like a zombie. Her once beautiful gray-blue eyes were sinking into the sockets.

It did not dawn on her that the couple's little girl could have been in the room. She was six years old after all and even though she was small for her age, the child was a firecracker. Very independent and outspoken for someone that young. Honesty Mitchell was the spitting image of her mother in looks but had her dad's mannerisms and temperament. He loved his privacy. She did also. Kim was about to leave the room but as she turned she noticed that the sunlight bounced off a shiny object in the bed, creating a rainbow sparkle. A diamond bracelet, attached to a tiny hand.

The baby, she thought as tears ran down her face.

She reached over and touched the tiny hand. The little girl woke up and moved a bit.

Kim screamed.

The child jumped.

Before she fainted and hit the floor all she could remember thinking was, *thank God my baby is alive.* When Kim came to she called 9-1-1.

"9-1-1 what is your emergency?"

"My fri- is dea-, my fri- is dea-"

"Calm down ma'am and please start over. I am having trouble understanding you."

"My best friend and her husband are dead. They've been shot."

"What leads you to believe that they have expired? Have you checked their pulses and not found them to be present?"

Some people were too damned slow. "Of course I have, lady. Both of them have been shot multiple times you ninny! They are both lying in a pool of blood!" Kim yelled angrily.

"Calm down ma'am so I can better assist you. Where are you calling from?"

"I'm in their bedroom."

"No, I mean what is the address to your location? You're calling from a cell phone. I'm not picking up an address here."

"Oh, I'm sorry. Yes, I'm on my cell phone. The address here is one-four-nine-two-nine Deer Crossing Way."

"Thank you ma'am. Emergency units have been dispatched to that address."

The operator kept her on the line trying to calm her down. She instructed Kim, through her tirades and anger outbursts, not to touch or disturb anything in the house. A stressed out Kim forgot to tell the operator that she had found the little girl, too. In the end, that would be best. Homicide detectives, firemen, emergency crews, and crime scene investigators swarmed the place. It was a madhouse. The head detective on the case, Detective George Dunleevy, instructed everyone not to mention that a child was found alive. He was afraid that whoever did this, would come back to finish the job if they knew they had left a witness.

The police kept the media at bay. Word got out that there had been a double homicide in Gaylord Estates, a multi-million dollar gated community in Oklahoma City. That was unheard of before. It became a circus for the media and nosey onlookers trying to see the action. Forensics continued to gather evidence pertinent to the case while Kim sat in the dining room where she was interrogated relentlessly.

"Did the Mitchell's have any enemies?"

"Was the child a target?"

"How did you come to find them?"

Questions flew at her. She was becoming overwhelmed until Detective Dunleevy stepped in.

"I'll take it from here," he said powerfully, asserting his authority. "Clear the room please."

Everyone scattered like roaches at night when the light was turned on.

"Ms. Curry, I need to ask you a few questions," he directed at Kim. "Come take a walk with me please. We can go outside. Give you a chance to get some fresh air."

"Look, Sir. I told your officers all that I can remember. I'm exhausted." But she got up and walked out with him anyway.

He was right. The fresh air was wonderful and the walk did her good.

"I know you are tired and gave *them* what *they* asked for, pointing to the cops inside the house, but you and I both know that Goldie had some enemies out there due to the nature of his business."

"Excuse me?" Kim said with a major attitude. "And you *think* you know this how?"

"Let's not play games here. I know more than you think I do, even about you, Ms. Kimberly Nicole Curry. I *knew* Goldie. Probably, I'm sure, better than you. He was like a son to me. I know a lot because he told me. I know all about you because that's my job."

"Wh-, wha-, what?"

"Don't trip, 'G' had everyone checked out who came around him and his family. He asked me to look after things like that and I did."

"Yeah, that sounds like some shit he'd do," she said, smiling for the first time at the memory of her friend. "I knew he had friends all over, but a cop? How y'all meet?"

"Hmm. You really wanna know?"

"Yes."

"There was a cop on the force that was jacking dope dealers. He'd go to all the hoods and projects and take people's money. Prince Hall,

Kerr Village, all of them. Of course, he'd leave them their dope. They had to make money, right? Well anyway, that man was my partner. He was crooked as a pretzel. At first, I didn't know what he was doing. I was doing a lot of paperwork and desk work and he would go out on patrol alone. But when discovered the truth, I didn't turn him in, and that made me as guilty as he was. I didn't do anything to stop it either.

My wife got breast cancer. Even with our insurance coverage the bills kicked our asses. When he told me I could use some of the money I got from the dealers, I was all in. Hell, I figured it was only dope money, right? We didn't take them to jail and we left them with a way to come up again. Who was going to tell on us, them?"

"Damn, I had heard about that shit going on a few years ago. So that was you, huh?"

"Unfortunately, yes. One day we were at Will Rogers Courts. It was the third of the month so we knew there was plenty of money. Welfare checks, child support, and social security money was ours for the taking. We counted on the smokers spending big bucks. But we didn't count on a dude named Big Rock being there. This man was prepared to defend his money. Raleigh, my partner, was pissed off. When Rock didn't hand over the money easily, Raleigh threatened to shoot. That didn't faze Rock.

He wasn't intimidated. They both drew down on one another at the same time. It was a stand-off. Our problem was that we were in Big Rock's neighborhood and had no back up. We couldn't call them because technically we were in the wrong. My partner fired his gun, hitting Rock in the shoulder but he didn't budge. Big Rock returned fire and hit Raleigh square in the chest. The bullet exploded upon impact. He was dead before he hit the ground."

"Whoa, that's some deep shit. But I still don't understand how Goldie ties into this."

"Well, Rock worked for Goldie. When we pulled up, G recognized us. He got out his camcorder and started taping the whole scene. They'd been waiting on us to show up. The tape was going to be sent to headquarters and used as evidence against us. G knew that I wasn't the one putting the squeeze on folks and offered me a way out. I took it.

My partners dying gave me and my wife a chance to live. He came up with a plan to save our reps and my job even though neither of us deserved it"

"What did he do?"

"He put some things into play. Had a few of his soldiers stage the crime scene and knock me out. When I came to, the area was crawling with cops but it looked like Raleigh died in the line of duty. I came out smelling like roses. The rest as they say is history. So now, with that out of the way, I need to know who was at the party that you and Leo threw the other day. The killer was probably there."

Kim told him everything about the party she could remember. They'd been having a great time. However, Goldie had exchanged words with a guy, who worked for him, D-Snake, about some money, but it didn't sound all that serious. She told him how D-Snake had met Leo, her man, almost a year ago and was trying to cut a side deal with him. Leo found out that D-Snake worked for someone else and met with Goldie on his own. This cut D-Snake out of the deal completely.

"And you don't think that's serious?" The detective questioned. "Leo was pushing more weight than a freight train. The Jamaicans have the purest, hardest, dope in the city and the surrounding states. If I know anything about D-Snake, I know he was pissed off. G told me about this. I'm gonna question him and see what he has to say. I'm sure that he had plans to take that money and start his own operation."

"Yeah, I'm sure you're right. If he hadn't met with Leo though, Goldie and Leo wouldn't have ever reunited. They were friends from way back. I think D-Snake felt like he was entitled to more than he's been paid. I know G gave him a nice sum for finding that connect even though he did it on a scandalous tip."

"Funny how that worked out. Who knew that Leo and Goldie had been in the same foster care in New York? What are the odds that the two of them would meet again in Oklahoma of all places?"

"It's a small world indeed."

Kim and the detective spoke for another ten minutes before they returned to the crime scene and Kim was free to go home. Her husband came to pick her up. Honesty was examined at the nearest hospital and released to Kim and Leo who were listed as her next of kin. Detective Dunleevy was determined to find his friends' killers. That and keeping Honesty safe was now his personal mission. His life for the past few years had been about Goldie and Silver. Now, it was all about Honesty.

CHAPTER TWO

Something wicked was in the air. That was the feeling Kim got as she and the detective spoke the next day. He continued to gather information from Kim so that he would have something solid to use in his case. Not sure if Honesty was also a target, the detective decided he would put security on her around the clock. While the two of them spoke, Honesty sat, wrapped in a Hello Kitty blanket, on the patio of Kim and Leo's home. Her innocent face did not reveal the hatred and anger that was building up inside. She was alone. Without her parents and no apparent family to call her own, ideologies and mind sets were being formed within. It was not all good.

Honesty heard Kim tell the detective about the relationship between Goldie and D-Snake. She said that it was rumored that D-Snake was trying to get his own hustle. Just days ago, Gina, D-Snake's girl, called Kim and Silver and told them that he was bragging about how he was the next big shit in the city. D-Snake had illusions of grandeur.

The little girl listened to the two adults talk. No one paid much attention to the things that they said around her because they thought that she was too young to comprehend. Everything that people said was stored in a memory bank that she would recall later. She knew everyone's business. Knew who was fucking whom and who got 'burned'. She didn't even know what that meant but she knew it was bad. This was the beginning of the miseducation of Honesty.

"Did Leo know about this 'takeover'?" She heard the detective ask.

"Yeah. We told him everything that Gina told us."

"I put out an APB on D-Snake. He has some explaining to do."

Kim told Dunleevy about the party that night. What she knew anyway.

≈

That night at the party….

Goldie was popping bottles and living it up. He went on stage and grabbed the mic.

"Yo, I just wanna thank my lil bro, D-Snake for holding me down. Cuz I know if it wasn't for you, the Goldie Effect wouldn't be possible. And to my main man, Leo, there's about to be some changes real soon. We going to the next level. Salute."

Everyone lifted their glasses in the toast. Everyone except a guy named D-Snake. He was fuming. After all he helped Goldie do, he got no recognition and this little toast did very little to appease him. It wasn't G who put in the work; it was him and others like him. Anger engulfed him and the more he looked at Goldie the more he wanted him dead. But he couldn't do it alone. That night D-Snake found the flunkies he was looking for from ear hustling.

"Man cuz; look at that nigga right there. He thinks he really doing some shit. Hell, if it wasn't for cats like you and me, there'd be no empire for him or his hoe to have."

D-Snake moved closer so he could hear better without being noticed. The angry man continued to speak.

"Wrecka, if I hadn't pushed all that ya-yo the fool wouldn't have had any money to recoup his loss after he was boo-yawed. Me and D-Snake worked our asses off for him and this is all the thanks that we get? A party at the Key, free pussy, and some cheap ass drinks? Shit!"

Hearing his praises sang was all it took for D-Snake to make his move. Cunningly he slid next to the speaker, a Hoover Crip gang member who called himself, Seven. He began to weave his web of deceit.

"Hey, Seven, Wrecka. How ya'll doing? Enjoying this whack ass entertainment?" Referencing the dancers who performed at the strip club.

He wanted to down play the party to put them at ease. At first they were scared to say anything but once the diss about the party sank in they felt comfortable enough to speak freely just as their big homie had.

"Nah, cuz. This shit here's for amateurs. We on a whole 'nother level. *I* like my bitches to be the total package. Pretty face, little waist, big ass, the whole nine. Some of these hoe's a'ight but they don't get shit from me," Seven said.

"Right, right. Now if Silver got her fine ass up there, then we'd be working with something. That bitch so fine and sexy she make my dick hard just looking at her," Wrecka added.

D-Snake didn't like anyone talking about Silver. Secretly he was in love with her but he couldn't let on, so he just nodded his head "yes" in agreement. Silver was the only person he knew who really treated him with respect. Treated him like a man. Even better than that dumb ass girlfriend of his, Gina, ever did. He was obsessed with her and loved hearing her voice. Sometimes he would call her cell phone just to hear her say "hello".

Seven and Wrecka slapped each other high five while D-Snake just sat there nodding in agreement to the things that they said. He wanted to gain their trust. And he did. After sitting there for a while D-Snake eased his plans into the conversation. He told them that what they needed to do was to strike out on their own and get their own shit established. Their own work, their own hoods, and their own runners. The fellas were cool with that but wanted to know how they could go about doing that. It was common knowledge that what Goldie did not have sewn up, the Jamaican cat, Leo, did. The whole state was damned near theirs.

Wrecka, thinking out loud said, "Shit, niggas, the only way we can pull some shit off like that is if Goldie was out of the picture all together."

Bingo.

"Well, that's what we'll make happen," D-Snake said cryptically.

"What?" Seven said looking puzzled. He was a blonde in his former life.

"We'll kill him."D-Snake was serious. His plan would soon be carried out.

A little later, D-Snake and his friends decided to leave the party. It was execution time. Before he left, he overheard Silver talking to Kim. He was becoming the king of ear hustling.

"So Leo says it is cool for Honesty to crash with you all tonight? You know me and baby ain't been alone in a hot minute. We need some Q-T if you know what I mean?"

"Girl, you know how Leo feels about that bad ass little girl of y'alls. He keeps telling me that we need to have one of our own. The devil is a liar. I am not ready to be nobody's mama."

"Nope because your ass is still spoiled and selfish."

"You get no argument from me on that one. So what you gon' do about a change of clothes for her? You have something in the car with you?"

"No. I forgot to pack her an overnight bag. Just run by the house and pick it up since it's on your way home. Or, you can wait until tomorrow," Silver suggested.

"I'll come tonight. I may wanna keep her for a few days. I'm gonna have my sister Karen's little girl, Cheyenne. 'Member her? Anyway, Leo wants us all to go out and do some family things together. By the way, is the security code still the same? I don't wanna set off any alarms trying to get into the fortress."

"No, its pound, three-seven-four-two. "Sylvia finished.

"Cool."

The two women spoke for a few minutes more before parting. D-Snake, who had been listening intently around the corner, had gathered more information in those few minutes than he ever thought he could have in a lifetime. He had the new security code. Entrance to the house was guaranteed. He walked up to Silver and told her he was leaving the party.

"So soon? But we haven't begun to kick it yet. Are you sure you have to go?"

"Yeah, Sil. A bruh like me got to get some rest because I have to get up early. You know what they say, it's the early bird who catches the worm."

"Dang, well if you must go then you must. Never let it be said that Silver stopped any man from getting his hustle on and handling his business."

"Nah, you good. Hey, I see G and Leo deep in conversation and I don't want to disturb them. Can you let him know I had a good time and I'll get at him tomorrow?"

"Sure thing. Be safe. See ya' later gator."

"Yeah, see you *real* soon," he mumbled under his breath and walked out the building.

D-Snake did not care about Goldie and Leo's conversation. In truth, he was angry with both of them. Even though the party was messed up, he got some valuable information. Not only had he gotten the security code, he had also learned that the baby wasn't going to be at home to get in his way. He wouldn't have to bear the burden of taking out a kid. But he would if he had to. And he learned his girl Gina had been running her mouth to that bitch Kim. He couldn't wait to get home and teach her a lesson. She was a fuck up. Every time he turned around she was messing up one of his plans.

Well tonight he was going to show her who was running things in that relationship. Then he was going to leave her ass alone. Yeah, tonight she was going to learn once and for all who she was fucking with. Had D-Snake chosen to find out what Goldie and Leo were talking about, He would have discovered that Goldie was planning to set him up in Tulsa, Oklahoma. D-Snake would finally have his own territory. Later D-Snake would find out the truth, but by then, it would be too late.

≈

"Kim, never mind about watching the baby. Her daddy wants us all at home."

"Are you sure? It's not a problem."

"Nah, you cool. But thanks anyway. Good looking out."

"No, prob. Call me if you change your mind."

"I will. Love you."

"Love you, too."

They hugged one another and Golden and Silvia Mitchell walked out the Key for the last time.

≈

D-Snake was fuming when he pulled into the driveway. All the lights were on inside his house as usual. Gina was scared of the dark. He bought her all these night lights but she claimed they didn't give off enough light. *For the bitch to be so scary she certainly don't mind running her mouth to the wrong people*, he thought.

Inside, he spotted her sleeping on the sofa. He walked over to her and looked down at her with a long, hard, penetrating glare. He loved this girl. Too much. Yet not enough to sacrifice his dreams for. No, not that much. D-Snake took a long drag of the blunt he was smoking on and sat down. Then he reached into his pocket and pulled out a small brown vile that contained PCP, or wet, as it was called on the street. The wet was three parts embalming fluid and one-part various chemicals. It gave everyone a super charged high. A high so euphoric it often cause delusions within minutes of smoking

D-Snake dipped his blunt in the bottle and turned the marijuana cigarette up so that the toxic liquid could drain and get the whole stick wet and soak its contents. The last time he smoked this shit, his homies had caught him on tape running down Kelley Avenue butt naked. He relit the blunt and began smoking. It did not take long for him to get to La-la Land. D-Snake told himself that there was only one thing left for him to do. Being as quiet as he could, he walked past a still sleeping Gina, to the hall closet and got out her son's metal baseball bat. There was a pillow that had fallen on the floor off the sofa that he picked up and placed softly on Gina's head. He was careful not to wake her.

He raised the bat over his head and with all the strength he could muster, he brought the bat down swiftly, crushing Gina's skull and smashing her face in. He heard her bones crack when the bat hit her head and she died instantly. He watched in a drunken like stupor as her body convulsed one final time and lay still. She never knew what hit her. D-Snake sat in the chair by the sofa and let his mind wander to his happy place. In this place, Gina was still alive and he began to talk to her.

"Why you have to go and tell my business girl? Shit, you know a nigga trying to come up so a bitch like you can live in the lap of luxury. I ain't just doing this for me. I'm doing this for us, Gina. For us! You hear me? Answer me girl!"

He got up and slapped her thigh. It was soft to the touch.

"Damn, girl. You sure are soft. You know exactly what to do to make me forgive you, huh? Don't you girl?"

D-Snakes dick got hard. He took the pillow off her battered head and despite the disfigurement, blood and gore, that was now displayed, the only thing he saw was her mouth agape. He pulled his pants and boxer shorts down and slid his hard member completely into her mouth and started moving slowly back and forth, then in a circular gyrating motion, still talking to her lifeless body.

"You ain't never had it this deep, have you Gina? What you trying to do? Get a bruh like me to marry you or something? Shit, you keep sucking me like this and I will. Yeah, that's it baby. Take this sweet meat like the pro you are. Damn, I am about to shoot this load. You ready? You ready for me, Gina? Awe shit, here it comes, swallow it all."

After releasing his semen in her mouth and covering her face again, he took a few steps down to the end of the sofa and pulled Gina's pants down. Once he got them off, he leaned over and sniffed her warm center. He let his tongue travel until it reached her core and he licked and sucked on her until he got hard again. He got up, pulled her body down on the sofa, giving him easier access so he could have sex with her. D-Snaked pummeled her pussy until he came again. And again.

"Baby that was the best you ever gave me. I love you girl."

With that, he redressed, covered her, and left. He called Wrecka and Seven and told them that he was on his way. High or not, he remembered his mission. The fella's were hyped about what was getting ready to come. This was the lick they'd been waiting on. Wrecka said that they could meet at his house because he was the only one who lived alone. They needed a private, secluded meeting place. Seven was already there when D-Snake pulled up. The temperature dropped on the ride over so when he got out the car, the strong gust of wind slapped him in the face, bringing D-Snake's high all the way down.

Reality set in for him and he recalled what had happened earlier in the evening with Gina. That sobered him even more. It was too much to digest at once. *I need to be fucking high again*, he thought walking towards the house. Inside, the three of them plotted, planned, and perfected the caper that would go down that night. It was important for them to get in and get out quickly because Goldie lived in an exclusive neighborhood and D-Snake did not want the neighbors to get suspicious, seeing a strange car in the area that time of night. Wrecka had gotten gun silencers from the Iranian who owned the Chinese restaurant in the hood and Seven had stolen a black Volvo station wagon that had belonged to some yuppie couple. D-Snake had the code to the house. By morning, the three of them would be millionaires.

"So D-Snake, we takin' the baby girl out, too?"

"Nah, dude. I don't kill kids. Besides, she ain't even gon' be there. I overheard Kim saying she was going to keep her tonight."

"I can't believe you gon' kill Silver though. I thought you were in love with her by the way you be eyeballing her and shit."

"I'll give her the chance to choose and depending on her choice depends on whether she lives or dies. Shit, I'll be ballin' by then and can have my pick of any honey."

"You ain't worrying about your girl running off at the mouth about this like she did your other shit?"

Seven was going to drive D-Snake crazy with the twenty questions.

"Yeah, ain't she the reason G found out about the side deal you was tryna cut?"

Now Wrecka was starting in.

"I'm not worried one bit. Gina won't say shit," he said taking a long drag of another wet blunt. "How can you be so sure?"

"Yeah, how can you?"

"Because."

"Because what cuz?" They asked at the same time.

He took a drag, blew out the smoke slowly, and smiled. "I killed her."

CHAPTER THREE

In her dreams Honesty could see and hear everything that happened. She replayed each of the night's events over and over. It was as if she was watching a bad horror movie. Only with this one, she could not stop the tape or turn off the television.

The house was quiet and very dark she remembered. Through her window she watched the trees' arm like branches wave at her. The tree was her friend. She waved back. After the exchange she climbed out of bed and went to get her baby doll out of the plastic baby bed that sat next to her own. The two of them were going to have a tea party.

The small, pink wooden table was already set up. The only thing the pretty little girl was missing was water. She had to be very quiet because her door squeaked every time she opened it. Her father would assure her every day that he was going to fix it and every day he did not. Honesty remembered rolling on the floor with laughter when she thought he said that he was going to fix the squeak with some bumble bee forty. She pictured forty bumble bees helping her dad fix her door. One held the hammer, one had nails, and the others held the door up. When she questioned her daddy about it, he told her that it was *WD-40* that he was going to use. Regardless of what he was supposed to use, the door was never fixed.

With her water in hand, she made her way back to her room for the party. Her doll, April Showers, a hand me down Cabbage Patch Doll, given to her by her mother, was sitting in the chair she had placed her in before leaving the room. She was her best friend. Honesty broke into an imaginary conversation with her.

"You wanna hear a joke?" The doll asked.

"Sure do."

"A joke."

Honesty cracked up laughing. So loud, that her mother heard the commotion and came into her room.

"What is going on in here young lady?"

"We are having a tea party, Mommy."

"It is late and you are supposed to be sleep. It's almost two in the morning."

"But April was thirsty and I promised her some tea."

"I'm going to promise you an ass whooping if you don't go to bed. Matter-of-fact, tuck your doll into her bed and come with me. You're going to sleep with me and daddy tonight."

"Yes, Ma'am." Honesty knew better than to talk back so she just did what she was told.

"Come on baby, come to Mama," Sylvia said, holding her arms out to her little girl.

She ran and jumped in her arms and laid her head on her shoulder. Her mother smelled so good. So fresh. Chamomile and Lavender. It was a scent she created herself, mixing one lotion with another and adding a touch of perfume to it. It was her smell. Her scent. The one when Honesty was older, and she smelled those aromas, would cause her to think of her mother. She nestled her head between her mom's shoulder and neck and inhaled deeply, creating a memory.

"Mommy, when we get to your room can I please brush your hair?"

"Yes honey but not for long. We need to sleep. Daddy has big plans for us tomorrow."

"What kind of plans?"

"It's a surprise," she answered as she opened the door to the master suite that she shared with Honesty's father, Goldie.

"Well, well, well, look who has come to join us. What happened, your mother caught you having another late night tea party?"

"Yes, Sir." She loved her dad's voice. It was deep and soothing. Something about it made her feel safe.

Depending on the tone, that same voice could also evoke fear in her. Not that he ever screamed and yelled at her, but she had heard him reprimand people before and she vowed to never be on the receiving end of that kind of wrath. Her daddy didn't play that.

The lamp on his side of the bed was on and he looked so majestic sitting up reading his newspaper. His chest was bare when he got out of bed and walked across the room and lifted his daughter out of her mother's arms. He put her on his shoulders and ran around the room making airplane noises. Before the plane came crashing down on the massive king sized bed, she told her daddy that she was going to brush her mom's hair before they went to sleep.

"Is it okay with you, daddy?"

"Yes, but only a few strokes baby. You need your beauty sleep so you can stay beautiful."

Remembering that her mom had told her boys were opposite of girls, Honesty asked, "Daddy, if girl's need beauty sleep then what do boys need? Ugly sleep?"

Goldie laughed. "No, we need handsome sleep. That is why girls are beautiful and boys are handsome."

"Oh, ok. Mommy your hair is breautiful. I want my hair to look just like it."

"The word is *beautiful* baby and you don't have to worry, your hair is going to be prettier than mine."

"Mommy you look just like Pocahontas from my movie."

"Thank you, darling. You look just like me so I guess that means you look like her too."

"I do mommy?"

"Yes, baby, you do."

"Ok, now it is time for both my beautiful ladies to get some sleep. Time to catch some Z's."

"Who's throwing Z's?" She wanted to know. "Will one of them hit us?"

"Huh?" He looked puzzled. Her mother understood her though.

"No one is throwing Z's baby. That is just something grownups say when they want to go to sleep."

"Well why you didn't just say that daddy? Good night Daddy. Goodnight Mommy?"

"G'night Pumpkin."

Her parents tucked her in between the two of them and leaned over her and kissed one another good night. She giggled at the exchange. If she never saw what real love was again, she would always remember what she experienced with them. Goldie set the automatic timer on the television to cut off in half an hour when his program went off, and leaned back into his pillows. Her mother stroked her daughter's hair gently and hummed until the little girl fell asleep. She woke up a short time later because she had caught a chill and tried to pull the blanket up over her. Her dad made it impossible to pull because he was lying on it. He was half on his stomach and half on his side, giving Honesty just enough room to burrow into the space for warmth.

≈

In your own house, even in the dark, you can see. In your mind's eye, you know exactly where everything is. Only visitors and those who were not supposed to be there have issues in a strange house at night. She could not hear them. She could not see them. But she could feel them. Someone was in the house. Downstairs, intruders searched the house, looking for stashed money and dope. Seven bumped into the corner of a table and let out a yelp.

"Mother fucka be quiet. What you trying to do, wake the dead?" D-Snake snapped angrily.

"Nah, cuz. I'm trying to *make* the dead," Seven snickered.

D-Snake laughed under his breath. He was in total agreement. Through the darkness the two men crept silently, careful not to bump into anything else and disturb their marks. Because he had been there before, D-Snake was familiar with the home's layout. Goldie trusted him. Many times before he had gotten drunk and had to stay the night. Often times he would awaken to find that someone had removed his shoes, propped his head on a pillow, and covered him with a blanket. A hot cup of coffee and breakfast would be sitting on the table, hot and ready for him. Silver.

She never left him out in the cold. Neither did G. He made him feel like part of the family. At 17, D-Snake had never really had a stable family life. Having had a crack head for a mother and a dad who spent more time in prison than on the streets, he was pretty much bounced around from one family member to the next. No one ever physically abused him but he did suffer severe mental and verbal abuse. Relatives told him repeatedly that he would never amount to anything.

The last family member he lived with, Aunt Thelma was too old to notice or care what he did or who he did it with. One day he got up and left the house and started hanging out in Prince Hall. A ghetto fabulous apartment complex located in the center of the city's east side. It was a hot spot for drugs, gangs, and prostitution. That is how he met Goldie. He had started kicking it tough over there and the Crips who hung out there saw that he had heart.

One dude named Big Mane gave him a dope sack to slang. He told him to come back the next day with all his money. A thousand dollars. He was shocked to see that the youngster was back within a few hours with all his money and the entire product sold. Mane liked the way D-Snake hustled and from that day he kept him close to him. D-Snake had found in Mane something he had always coveted…a big brother.

Mane and Goldie were close. When Mane got killed at a car wash on 36th and Kelly, Goldie took up where his friend left off and took D-Snake in. He got the little kid a place to stay and kept him supplied with work. Goldie was like the father D-Snake never had. G would tell D-Snake about the ins and outs of the dope game all the time. He kept telling him that one day he would be able to run his own operation but D-Snake was tired of waiting for that day to come. Ever since that damned Jamaican came into the picture G had started to treat D-Snake differently. Like a flunky.

D-Snake knew G loved him like family but something just kept eating at him inside that would not let him fully grasp that love. He loved G, too but as much as he did, he felt that G didn't respect him the way he did him. The way he should. It was fucked up that he would choose the Jamaican cat over him. Especially after all he had done for him.

D-Snake rationalized what he was about to do. Yeah, he loved that cat Goldie but that love was personal. The thing he was about to do right now, was not. This was business. Strictly. He snapped out of his revelry just in time to see Seven approach the steps. They had already searched the downstairs and didn't find anything. Goldie's office, which was on the first level of the house, usually held loads of money and dope in a safe that was well hidden under his bookshelf. Tonight, that safe was empty. Not even a grain of dust could be found inside. That was odd to D-Snake because whenever the money was going to be in a different spot, G would let him know where. D-Snake used to bring large sums of cash and put it away for G. He had the safe's combination. But that is when things between them were good. When they were still tight.

Trust was a non- issue with the two of them for the longest time. Goldie must have believed that they were better than that. *But if a man trusted you with his family, then his money wasn't shit,* D-Snake thought. But the empty safe was an indication that Goldie didn't trust D-Snake as much as he thought.

When they made it to the top of the steps, D-Snake decided the two of them should stick together. They were not in a rush. They had a get-a-way driver outside.

Wrecka *was* in the car waiting for them but he really didn't want to be there. To keep his mind off of what was going down in the house, he smoked his blunt dipped in wet and got high. D-Snake knew Wrecka didn't have any self control when it came to the liquid dope. The man got high off his own supply. A dope man's worst customer was himself.

Seven went down the hall away from the master suite. He reached out to open Honesty's door but his hand was snatched away quickly by D-Snake.

"Cuz, do not touch this door. This is his little girl's room."

"So, she ain't in there right? You said she was staying all night at someone else's crib didn't you?"

"Yeah, I did and yeah she is, but this door squeaks and makes noise like it's a hundred years old. G said that he was going to fix it but if I know him, he hasn't. If you touch this door you will not only wake up everyone in this house but the entire neighborhood."

"It's like that?"

"Straight like that."

"But what if the stash is in there, cuz? We been in this place for almost an hour and I ain't got shit but a fucking bruise on my knee from bumping into that table downstairs."

"Man listen here, Goldie ain't gon' put no safe in his baby's room because he tries to keep that part of him as far away from her as possible. Trust me on this. I know this cat almost better than he knows his damned self. If anything, he moved it into his room. After we handle him, we will get the loot and bounce."

"Sounds like a plan to me."

They searched the hall closets and spare rooms on that floor before making their way to the end of the hall to the bedroom where the Mitchell family slept. D-Snake put his hand on the door knob and turned his face to look at Seven.

"Goldie sleeps on the left side of the bed. You go to that side. Take his ass out immediately. Don't blink or bat an eye. G is quick. If he moves it's all over for both of us. Go for the head. We need him dead like yesterday. I'll take care of Silver. I'm going to give her a chance to choose me or G once and for all. If she don't choose right, tho', then she history, too."

"A'ight. Bet."

He twisted the door knob slowly and they both entered the room. Seven walked quietly to Goldie's side of the bed. He was nervous with fear. This would be his first 1-8-7. Most of the Hoover Crip gang members he hung with had at least one murder under his belt. Those who did had a blue tear drop tattooed under their left eye. More, depending on the number of bodies they had attached to them. He had none. And this one wouldn't count either.

He couldn't go bragging that he was the one who killed the big homie. They would lynch his ass. His homies loved G because he always served them love when it came to the dope they bought from him. Also, when he would have bar-b-que's and special events he made sure all of them were given V-I-P treatment. He would be quoted off the set if they knew. Nah, he would have to keep this to himself. Get the loot and get the hell out of dodge because he wasn't going to be taken out like a punk. He walked up and frowned as he watched Goldie sleep. He was lying on his stomach, hugging his pillow like it was his bitch. *Pussy!* Seven thought. But he was scared to pull the trigger.

He checked his silencer making sure it was on securely, aimed his gun a half inch away from his OG's head, raised the gun, and then lowered it again. Seven couldn't do it. But three rapidly fired gun shots ended, G's life anyway. D-Snake was standing next to Seven with his gun cocked and the barrel smoking.

Silver sat up abruptly to see what the commotion was. Her eyes locked with D-Snakes, who had run quickly to her side of the bed after killing Goldie.

She didn't speak.

He didn't move.

Instead, he stood amazed at the sight of this beautiful woman. Her long hair fell softly across her forehead and cascaded over her pillow. Gorgeous. He had never seen anything so beautiful. She turned her head to look at her husband and a lone tear slid down the side of her face. D-Snake saw a look of hatred and rage in her eyes that he had never seen in his life when she looked back at him

Silver's eyes softened as she whispered, "my baby."

D-Snake felt anger rising up inside him because he thought that Silver was talking about Goldie. She had chosen him. D-Snake loved Silvia and wanted her to be with him. He had hoped by him gaining G's wealth and status that would cause her to want to join forces with him. In D-Snake's twisted world, he found it hard to believe that a woman was with any man out of love. He thought it was all about the money. He was mistaken. Silver loved Goldie.

D-Snake fired one gunshot to the center of her head. She was dead by the time her head hit the pillow. Rage wouldn't allow him to be satisfied with just the one shot. He shook his head, exhaled, and fired five more shots into Silver's head, face, and chest. *Now* he was satisfied.

"What the fuck you do that for D-Snake? I was going to handle G," Seven raged.

"Yo' ass looked like you 'bout to cry or some shit and it was taking you way too long to do the shit. I had to do it. Plus, it made my dick hard thinking about killing that buster."

"Damn. I thought you were going to let Silver live. Give her a chance to choose."

"She made her choice."

"When?"

"When she looked at cuz and then looked back at me. I saw something that said I could never replace him."

Seven did not understand what he was talking about but asked anyway.

"What did you see?"

"Love. I saw her love for him. Her eyes said that she would kill me over him if she ever got the chance. She loved him just that much."

"Cuz, I hope I find me a down ass bitch like that one day."

"Nah man. I think she was the last one. They don't come like her no more. They extinct."

"Oh-kay. Let's sweep this place and find the money. We only done half of what we came here to do.""Bet. Let's get it."

D-Snake and Seven searched everywhere they could think of and even places they could not. No area went untouched. They policed the entire house and yet found nothing. Tempers were flaring and they were beginning to curse each other out in frustration. Their search intensified but they still came up short. Before either man realized, dawn was upon them. It was past time for them to leave. Exhausted, they reluctantly left out the house.

Angry.

Empty-handed.

Murderers.

Once in the car, another argument ensued. Wrecka had smoked *all* the weed and *all* the water. And neither of them had shit to show for killing the one person who kept money in their pockets and food in their bellies for the past three years. They were fucked in the game. This was a mission impossible.

Their fates were sealed. With this town being as small as it was, word would get out who killed G and his girl and when it did, they would be marked for death.

Honesty had seen their faces but they hadn't seen hers. Their eyes would continue to haunt her dreams until she learned how to release the hate and rage that now filled her heart. It was time for Honesty to let someone know what she had seen. Her daddy used to call her his little "G". It was time for her to step up and be Goldie and Silver's diamond baby. She knew that Kim and Leo were both nearby. Hot tears ran down her face. Her pillow soaked quickly.

She sat up in bed and yelled "Daddy" at the top of her lungs. Everyone outside her room came rushing in. Leo picked her up and cradled her in his lap. Rocking her until the crying slowed and she was able to speak audibly. She wiped her tears, turned to face her new guardians and with the strong , clear voice of a grown ass woman, she spoke.

"I know who killed Mommy and Daddy."

CHAPTER FOUR

Gina *was* going to have D-Snakes baby. Was being the operative word. After Honesty told what she saw that night, Detective Dunleevy put out an all points bulletin for the bastards who destroyed her family. The first place the cops looked was Gina's house. Kim told the detective that Gina had helped her in the past and was sure she could count on her again to help locate her boyfriend. However, Kim was not counting on Gina being dead. Another friend, gone. The medical examiner couldn't tell how far along she was without doing an autopsy but just by the looks of things, she was at least five months pregnant.

Word spread quickly on the streets regarding who killed Goldie and Silver. Everyone had questions about Honesty but no one had any answers. Leo offered a reward to anyone who could tell him anything about the men who took his brother's life.

A few days later, Kim reluctantly picked up the phone to call Silvia's only known relatives in Philadelphia to tell them what had happened and when the funeral was scheduled to take place.

"Hello, may I speak to Janet" Kim asked.

"Janet who? Who dis?" Someone snapped on the other end.

"Um, my name is Kim. I'm a friend of Janet's niece, Silvia. I was cal-"

"This Janet," the woman interrupted. "Why you calling me, Silvia ass in jail or some shit? I ain't got no money for the bitches bail either so don't bother fixing yo' mouth to ask."

Janet's attitude was expected. Silvia had long told Kim of the animosity the aunt had for her niece. It was bitterness laced with jealousy. All because Sylvia and her mother, Venetta, were pretty and light skinned with naturally straight hair.

"I'm not calling for money Ms. Janet, I was calling to tell you that sadly, Sylvia and her husband Golden were killed a few days ago."

"Sylvia's dead you say?"

If she wasn't mistaken, Kim could have sworn she heard snickering in the background and it infuriated her.

"Yes, Ma'am," she said through gritted teeth. "I was just calling to give you guys the funeral information."

"I'on know what fo'. Ain't nobody got no money to be spending to travel to see a hoe and her pimp buried. Shit, bitch ain't so much as sent me a birthday card. I wish I would."

Exhaling and counting silently to ten Kim continued, "We didn't expect you all to come out of pocket for anything, Ms. Janet." Showing the mean woman respect was taking its toll on Kim.

Not long after Silvia and Kim met, Sylvia shared with Kim the details of the relationship she had with her family which was none. Her aunt Janet was jealous because Sylvia and her mom Venetta had "good hair" and lighter skinned while she and her daughters had nappy hair and dark skin. It didn't do Silver any good trying to make peace with her family and Kim knew it wouldn't do her any good either. She ended the call by telling her that travel arrangements had been made for her and her family and she could expect another call from her the next day with the specifics. Before they hung up, Kim told Janet that she and her family would also be staying for the reading of Sylvia and Goldie's will. Kim could hear Janet salivating. Like she was expecting to receive something.

Janet, along with her girls, arrived in Oklahoma City the day before the funeral. Kim sent a chauffeured car to pick them up. When Janet landed at the Will Rogers World Airport, she had preconceived ideas about what the country bama black people were going to be like. So when she was escorted to the sleek, black Lincoln Town Car, by a handsome driver, she was speechless. On the way to the house, Janet and four of her daughters reminisced about Silvia. But not in a good way. Siobahn, Janet's youngest daughter and Sylvia's favorite cousin, just sat in the corner like a shrinking violet and listened.

"I always knew that child was going to end up in some mess. She was just like her hoe ass mama. Walking around thinking that they pretty and shit. Thinking that they were better than us. It's a damned shame."

"Mm, hmm," the four girls agreed in unison.

"Mother, Silvia was your niece. The least you could do is pretend that you are sad that your only sister's daughter is now gone."

"Ain't nobody studying that bitch. Hell, she gon' burn in hell just like her slut ass mama."

"She never did anything to any of you. All she ever did was have the audacity to be born beautiful and you all have hated her since she was a baby. I'm going to miss my cousin so much, but I'm glad that even for a little while she was able to get away from the likes of you all. Lord knows I am praying for my day to come."

"Fuck you and that bitch, Sha-von. No matter how you spell it, it's still the name I gave your stuck up ass. You can stay your ass in funky ass Oklahoma for all I care. Hmph."

Since Siobahn had never spoken up about anything before, her family was stunned. Even though Janet got the last word in no one said anything after that. The driver smiled at the cousin for defending his boss. He had had the intercom on the whole while. He looked at the vicious women and shook his head in disbelief. Vultures. As tempted as he was to put them out on the highway, he kept his professional wits about him and put the pedal to the metal and dropped them off as soon as he could.

Less than ten minutes later he pulled up in front of Kim and Leo's house. He got out and opened the door for the women and began unloading their luggage. Janet and her girls stood outside the car staring up at the house with mouths agape. Before them stood a gorgeous seven thousand square feet home which sat on two sprawling acres of lush green grass with pristine landscaping. A basketball and tennis court sat on the west side of the house and an Olympic sized pool sat on the east side of the house.

The front of the house boasted two large plate glass picture windows that went uncovered. From where they stood they could see the massive chandelier that hung royally over a marble dining room table. None of them had seen a house this lovely in person. Felisha, the third to the oldest, broke the silence.

"Shit, I wanna see what this place looks like inside. This bitch's house is bad. Let's go."

Inside they found the house came equipped with seven bedrooms, six full bathrooms, two powder rooms, a media room, study, a gourmet Italian kitchen, two dining areas, three living areas, a gym, and a security room.

"Who all live here? All the African's from Leo's tribe?" Janet asked sarcastically.

"He's from Jamaica and only my daughter and my son-in-law live here. But now that they have Honesty she'll be here too, "Mrs. Louella, Kim's mother said walking in the foyer.

"Well I guess. But who say they gon' keep Honesty. That's my great niece and we the only living family she got to her name."

Leo and Kim stepped into the foyer at that time and he was about to say something when Kim put her hand on his chest and stopped him.

"There'll be plenty of time later to discuss this," she said. "Until then, let's get you all settled in. Maria will show you all where you'll be staying while you're here with us."

Janet and family followed the housekeeper mumbling under their breaths. She was jealous with a capital 'J'. It was so sad that even at a time like this, Silvia and Honesty's family could not find love in their hearts to put the past behind them and grasp the present.

≈

The day of the funeral was very hard for everyone. Especially Honesty. Outside the day was beautiful. Seventy degrees with a gentle breeze. The birds sang their love song to God as Silver would have said. Flowers danced in the wind. They were happy and alive. But inside the soul of a six year old little girl, a storm brewed. Rage and anger created dark clouds that would prevent her from trusting for years. She did not cry visible tears. She mourned the devastating loss of her parents without showing any emotion. Kim, however, could hardly talk for crying. But Honesty was determined to be a soldier for her parents.

More and more people were showing up and Kim was beginning to get nervous. It was nine o'clock. The funeral was supposed to start at ten and the funeral directors had not arrived yet. Leo was urging her to calm down but it was no use. Between the constant nagging from Janet and the begging from her own fraternal twin sister, Karen, Kim was about to have a breakdown. Just as she got ready to shout at the top of her lungs, she fainted. Luckily, Leo was right there to catch her before she hit the ground.

He eased her gently to the floor and managed to handle the growing crowd with calmness but inside he panicked. The woman he loved just passed out. He did not know what was going on with her. As much as he willed his mind to think good thoughts, he could not help but to think what he would do if he lost the only woman he loved. Hell, he had just lost his brother and sister and was not ready to lose Kim, too. He waved a make shift paper fan in her face and called out to her softly. Her mother with a boisterous voice yelled out.

"Gimme room, move over. Mrs. Louella is here." She knew what she was doing. "Let me down here so I can get this girl up. The funeral folks are here and we need to be on our way."

"Mama, dang. Don't be so insensitive. Something could be seriously wrong with Kimmy," Karen said. *I wish,* she thought spitefully.

"Girl shut up that nonsense and hand me my smelling salts out my purse. Ain't nothing wrong with my baby." She waved the salts under Kim's nose until her eyes flickered and she came to and they helped her up off the floor.

"Nope, ain't nothing wrong with my baby. Is it, baby? Nothing that time, patience, and a good doctor won't fix."

"Mama Lou, what are you talking about?" Leo asked, concerned.

"Well child, I'm surprised y'all don't know yourselves. As much as the two of you been going at it." "Know what!" The crowd yelled.

"Kim is pregnant. If I'm right, she'll be having the baby in 'bout, hmm, six months."

Leo picked Kim up and twirled her around in the air. This would be the first child for both of them. Joy quickly replaced the sadness that was in the air.

"When someone dies, God always sends a beautiful baby," Mrs. Louella said wisely.

Honesty looked on. She was happy for Kim and Leo. She knew her parents would be also. But as much as she wanted to let the joy penetrate her heart, she held on to the anger. She would allow it to feed her until the men responsible for her parents death were brought to justice. Whoever said a kid would just forgive and forget was a liar. Honesty could hold a grudge longer than Interstate 40.

"It's time for us to go everyone. Let's load up." The funeral directors put an end to the celebration and reminded them all of why they were gathered together in that place.

But after listening to Mrs. Louella tell them about life and death they were no longer going to two funerals but to two home going celebrations. The services were held at Christ Temple Church, which was Mrs. Louella's church, since Goldie and Silver had never joined one. The procession from the house to the church was the longest that some people had ever seen. They had to have police escorts to help with the long procession.

They made it to the church and when they did the mood changed. So many had gone ahead and were at the church already. When the family filed in they heard the wails and moans from the mourners.

All this for Mommy and Daddy? Honesty thought as she looked around at all the people in the church.

Hundreds of people were filling the church to pay respects to the couple. She had no idea how many lives her parents had touched or to what magnitude. When she walked down the aisle with Kim and Leo, people in the pews looked at her and then whispered something to their neighbors. Some started crying all the more.

Mr. Coulter, the owner of Coulter's Funeral Home tried to bring the service to order. It was very hard because so many people were crying and some were inconsolable. It was mayhem.

"People please. I know that you are sad and I know how hard this is for you all but we have to get this service started. Please." He sounded frustrated. Leo gave him a look that gave him the go ahead to begin. When the music began the voices quieted. The service moved along nicely until Silver's friend Denise Tennory got up and sang 'Walk Around Heaven All Day'. That broke the dams of all the mourners who had been holding in tears up until that point. Denise could blow. Honesty did not understand how one song could evoke that much emotion. One day, she would know all kinds of things.

At the end to the services another group got up and sang 'It's So Hard to Say Goodbye to Yesterday'. The Boys II Men version. That was Goldie's favorite song from his favorite movie, Cooley High. Women who used to fuck with Goldie were falling out and crying out his name as they walked around and viewed his body for the last time. Silvia had known that G fucked around on her but she never saw it or heard about it. It was just a feeling she had.

Honesty was one of the last people to view the bodies. The gold casket that held her father and the silver one which held her mother were side by side. The funeral director had them parallel to one another so that when the viewing began, onlookers could walk between the two of them and view them that way. The little girl tugged on the director's suit coat and asked him to pick her up to see her parents.

She did not understand death. Barely understood life. But she knew that the two people whom she loved and who loved her more than life itself were gone. How was she to get past this? Heal? Move on and live? At six, she tried to figure it out. Yet, she had no clue.

At the burial ground, Leo was pulled away by a guy in a black leather trench coat before the graveside service began. Honesty remembered the man was Tristan, Leo's nephew. Whatever he told Leo put a scowl on his face. It remained there for the rest of the service.

"What is it, babe?" Kim reached out to him.

Leo pulled away from her grasp. "No worries, Woman. Me brudda will be avenged soon."

Kim knew he was pissed because the angrier Leo was the thicker his accent got. When the burial was over they all went to Kim's house and had dinner. Everyone was reminiscing and laughing about all the things that the Mitchell's had said or done in their short lives. Maria and others served and picked up after the many guests who swarmed the house as Kim rested. She was going to have a baby. Honesty would not be alone anymore. There was Karen's daughter, Cheyenne, but she was always picking fights with Honesty, none of which she ever won, and breaking her toys.

Honesty walked around the house, familiarizing herself with her new home. There was so much to the house and so much to learn. She was going to have a good time. Having spent so much time there, she had a room of her own, decorated with pretty pastel pinks and purples. Her furniture was off-white French provincial style. Leo had picked out a full-sized bed so that she could grow with it. At that time, he had no idea she would be occupying it on a full time basis.

People started to leave around six that evening. Janet even came around and genuinely mourned her niece. They helped get the house back in order and treated the other guests well. It was a good day despite the circumstances. Everyone was still sad but left with a lot more peace within them than when they first came. The next morning, Frank Wallis, Goldie's attorney, sat the family down for the reading of the will.

"They sure don't waste any time down here in the country, do they?" Janet whispered to her daughters.

Frank cleared his throat and began with a disclaimer. "Please pardon the language in the will, I am only reading it the way it was written.

I, Golden Eric Mitchell, having been found in sound mind and body, do declare the following statements, my last will and testament, to be read to all parties present, by my solicitor, my friend, Frank Wallis.

Frank, you have been the best attorney a man in my position could have asked for. Thank you for keeping with my family at all times. I leave you the building that your office is housed in. Your partner, already has the deed in a lockbox back at the office. That blue key I gave you for safekeeping opens it. You've owned the building and had the deed in that box all along. I knew I could trust you not to go in it. The money you've been paying for your office rental has been held in trust, under your name for your daughter, Leah at the Oklahoma Bank. Now get your shit and move your punk ass to the top floor, nigga!"

The attorney wasn't expecting anything and paused for a brief moment. The building was a prime piece of real estate in the heart of downtown Oklahoma City. It boasted 15 floors, a gym, a terrace level food court and four level parking decks. The property was worth over two million dollars. And only Goldie knew how much money was in the bank but Frank was excited to find out. Frank read on and a few people gasped at Goldie's generosity. He left something to anyone who had ever helped him or his wife.

"To Phil, my driver and bodyguard, since I'm no longer here to be your partner in the car service, you're going to have to go it alone. Frank has all the titles for the cars and the deed to the building where Black Tie, Black Cars is. It's all yours bro. I love you man.

Dunleevy, you've been like a father to me. Here's a little something to hold you over should you decide to retire from law enforcement. Thank you for being there."

That little something was a check for two hundred grand. Detective Dunleevy wiped the tears from his eyes and looked over at Honesty. Whether G left him something or not, he was going to always be there for Honesty.

"On behalf of my wife, Silvia Denise Mitchell, I would like to give her favorite cousin Siobhan, a small token of appreciation for being there for my wife when she needed you the most. Hopefully, this will help you make a fresh start on your own."

Frank walked over to the young lady and handed her an envelope that had a check for five hundred thousand dollars in it. Janet leaned over and saw the amount and started screaming.

"Oh, hallelujah. Thank you Jesus. You're sovereign God."

"I'on know why you're thanking God. This is my money."

Janet gave her youngest daughter a funky look and said "Fuck you, bitch. I'on need shit from you. I'm sure of that!" Rolling her eyes, Janet turned her attention back to the attorney. She just knew that her niece had looked out for her.

"May I continue?" Frank asked rhetorically. "To Janet Lewis, Silver's aunt, you will be able to remain living in the house that Venetta Lewis paid for in Philadelphia. However, you will have to pay rent in the amount of $500 per month beginning next month. Payments are to be placed in an account designated for all rent payments only. All deposits are to be made in cash only!"

"Is that it? Ain't that 'bout a bitch!"

"Additionally, here is something just for you," Frank said, leaning over, handing Janet an envelope that looked like the others which contained fat checks. Janet opened the envelope and seethed with anger when she saw what was written on it. Leo laughed when he saw it. Kim, knowing how Goldie was, covered Honesty's ears.

"My brudda is a fool. I love him long time!" Leo said affectionately.

The check said pay to the order of Your Ugly Ass Auntie in the amount of 'Not a mutherfucking thang'.

"Janet, sorry to spoof you but I know you didn't think that I was going to leave your trout mouth, thousand pound of cow shit smelling breath ass shit. You must be out your rabid ass mind. You can slob on my knob on a good day and swallow a stiff dick while you're out it. Kim you can uncover my baby's ears now."

Janet stood up so fast the chair tipped back and hit the floor. "I ain't gotta sit here and listen to this shit. Let's go, girls." All of her daughters got up except her youngest. "Oh, so you gon' stay here with these shady bastards? Hmph, don't come back to Philly 'cause you ain't got shit coming." The woman made a very hasty, very loud exit.

After the dust settled, Frank continued to read the will until it was done. In the end, Aunt Janet would learn that Kim was given permanent custody of Honesty and that the bulk of her parent's estate was being held in trust for her. Without any money, Janet didn't want the child anyway. Kim got up and hugged Siobhan and told her that Silvia loved her like a sister.

"You were the topic of many conversations, Shay. Be blessed with that money and use it wisely. God and Sil, just gave you a way of escape."

"I know. I'm going to miss her so much," Shay cried. "I've always wanted to leave Philly and all that negativity but I never wanted it to be like this."

"What are your plans?"

"Well, I've been looking for a job in Los Angeles. I've had a few hits but because I was so far away I don't think anyone took me seriously. Now that I have a little money, I'll just head that way and see what I can see."

"I know you're going to do great. You have my number, please use it, okay?"

"I promise. Love you, Kim."

"I love you too."

Janet and her girls were packed and ready for their flight. When they left they were driven back in a taxi mini-van, instead of the cool comfort of the chauffeured Lincoln they arrived in. Siobahn booked a flight California and took the first thing smoking. When Kim waved the last guest goodbye, she leaned on the back of the front door in exhaustion. Leo pulled Kim into the study and told her what was going on. Tristan had found one of the dudes involved in the murders and was holding him in an abandoned building downtown.

"I know you don't want me to go but I have to handle this myself. That was my family they took out."

"But baby, you have dudes who will gladly take care of that. Why do you have to go?"

"Do you think that I would leave something this important to just anyone?"

"I know this is big for you. For us. But baby if what Mama says is true and I am pregnant, *we* need you to be here for us. Please don't go," Kim pleaded.

"Don't worry about me Kimmy. You know I got this under control. Let me handle this. I have to. For Honesty."

"So which one do you all have?"

"Wrecka. He was the lookout. From what I been told he didn't pull the trigger or even go into the house but maybe he can tell me who did what and why?"

"Okay. I know it's futile for me to try to stop you so promise me if things get too hot and heavy, you will leave. I want you back in one piece."

"I promise you my love. Now go and lie down and take care of my son."

"How do you know it's a boy? We don't even know for sure if I am pregnant or not."

"Girl you know your mother knows and my spirit tells me it's my heir."

"Oh, Lord now here you go. Let's get out of here and go put our little girl to bed."

"Me like da way dat sounds, ma. You are going to be a great mother."

"Thank you."

Honesty heard the entire exchange. She was hiding under the desk.

≈

Hours later on the other side of town, Leo and Tristan got their minds right for the job at hand. Wrecka was being babysat by an associate of the two men. When they got there, they were disappointed that he had little information to give them regarding the actual whereabouts of D-Snake. Knowing how much he liked PCP, Leo believed Wrecka when he said that he was higher than a kite on that fateful night.

"Big Homie, D-Snake was so mad, he kicked my ass for smoking all the dope. He didn't get shit out that house that night. He was mad at me and Seven, too."

"Why?"

"Because Seven told him he was making a mistake and that we should leave. He wouldn't shoot either one of them and he didn't either."

Leo had planned on using a series of torturing techniques he had learned in Manila but didn't have to because Wrecka was singing like a canary. He ran the whole story down from how they all met to the actual plot. He told Leo that D-Snake overheard Kim talking to Silvia and that is how he got the security code. Leo was up in arms at the things he was hearing. He would never tell his wife what he learned. She would be devastated. Wrecka, whose real name was Greg, told Leo how D-Snake was infatuated with Silver and how he had planned to give her a choice to live or die.

"How in the hell was he supposed to do that?" Leo asked, pissed off.

"After he killed G, he was supposed to ask her if she wanted to roll with him or not. If she did, he was going to let her live. If not, then she was good as smoked."

"I guess it is clear who she chose then."

"Nah, it didn't even go down like that according to Seven. He said she looked at D-Snake funky or some shit and he shot her in the head a few times. The boy was ruthless."

He let them know the other two were headed for the Mexican border. The interrogation was over. Leo shook his head and looked at the man before him, tied to the wooden office chair. Wrecka knew that his time was up. He closed his eyes.

"I'm sorry, Cuz. Please don't do this. I swear man, I didn't wanna do it, please." Wrecka begged.

Tristan walked up to the man and injected a series of lethal poisons into his right arm. In less than ten minutes he was dead. The young assassin and his uncle walked out into the night's cool breeze. Neither of them felt avenged. Leo would not rest until he brought the true killer to justice. His kind of justice.

No one had any information to give to Leo. It would be ten years before he had his next lead. During that time so much would happen for him and his family. Kim would give birth to his son, Kalif. Complications from the delivery would prevent her from having any more children but they were blessed regardless and knew it. Leo would also mainstream his illegal tender to honest cash flow by opening businesses in and around the Oklahoma City area. He was proud of his family and loved them dearly but he was concerned about his daughter. Honesty would grow, learning defense techniques and perfecting the game that her parents began so long ago. She was doing things on her own terms.

On the night of her sixteenth birthday, she read all the articles and newspaper clippings that she had saved regarding her parents murders. She would not forget. When she laid down that night, she heard the only Bible scripture her daddy ever quoted to her.

"Be not deceived, God is not mocked,
for whatsoever a man soweth, that shall he also reap."

CHAPTER FIVE

What's done in the dark comes to the light. After ten years of searching Leo had finally gotten the tip he was waiting for. He knew where D-Snake and Seven were. So did Honesty. It was rumored that they were on their way back to Oklahoma City. When they got there they would have a few surprises waiting.

Honesty never forgot the promise she made to her parents. At the anniversary of their deaths each year, she renewed her vow silently to avenge them. On the outside she seemed like a happy person but on the inside she fumed. She was far from a normal teenager.

She had not one but two sets of dope dealing parents. The first set taught her that there was a game and how to play it. But the second set was teaching her the rules and guidelines. One thing she noticed was that the game was changing and not for the better. Gone were the days that niggas got out there and hustled for what they wanted. Now it was a bunch of disrespectful cats out there that jacked for a living. For that reason, Leo had said that he was going to get out the game. The game was for youngsters.

When jacking became the norm, Honesty, put her ear to the ground to see who was doing what. That is how she found out where D-Snake and Seven were. When they failed to get the money from her dad, they were left broke and busted. Staying in the 'O' was no longer an option. They were hot. D-Snake saw to that the moment he killed Gina. He created a long list of cats who were out for his blood.

Together D-Snake and Seven took what little money they had and hit the road. Presently, Honesty knew that they were living in some Mexican city. She was waiting on further word from her contact to let her know the exact location. She knew that one day they would come back and when they did, she would be waiting for them. No matter how long it took, she was going to do what she set out to do before she was old enough or big enough to ride a bicycle. Kill D-Snake.

≈

In Juarez, Mexico D-Snake and Seven sat in a dimly lit Cantina, drinking shots of Tequila with their Mexican Ese', Miguel, who they called Mike. The three of them celebrated a jack move put down on some young ballers in Colorado that made their pockets fat. D-Snake wanted to take his loot and get his own work and find a city that he could put on the map as his own. Seven, not willing to say aloud that he was homesick, said he was going to buy him some wheels. He had to say something to take the heat off him. Mike was making a little extra dough now and could now invest in his cousin's operation. They all had plans.

Seven and D-Snake had been in Mexico for a few years now. They had met Miguel when they were pulling a heist in Texas. D-Snake kept in touch with him and when things went bad for him in Tennessee he called Mike and asked him if he and Seven could head that way. Dude said "yes".

Miguel was fair and really didn't ask for much. Truth be told, he was happy that the two low-life's came down his way. They acted as muscle for Mike and people in his town started to believe that he had more dope than he really did. Now more people wanted to do business with him.

Things were cool with the three of them. That is until Mike's cousin Jessie came into town. She had her own big time operation in play and wanted to expand. She was pushing more weight than Jenny Craig. It was her intention to help her cousin come up like she did. She was thick and beautiful. A power house. So lovely she made J-Lo look like a dog.

When D-Snake saw her, he wanted her immediately. Mike told him to keep it moving because she was out of his league. He didn't listen. He was out of his league. Jess was not interested in him. She did not do sidekicks. The fact that he didn't have his own set up had nothing to do with it either. She said she needed a real man. One who was capable of making and keeping his own money. All D-Snake did was jack people. Jessie said she could deal with a liar but she could not deal with a thief. He was a punk. A coward. A hustler who had lost his hustle. A flunkie.

D-Snake was tired of being put down. Most of the niggas he knew who did have a decent operation had some help getting there. Hell, he had helped some of them move dope from state to state with little effort. All he needed, he thought, was someone to give him a hand up.

I could always ask Goldie to front me some work, he thought. D-Snake had been wet so much he forgot just that quickly that G was gone and he was the reason.

D-Snake did not just bite the hand that fed him, he cut it off. He would have to look for help elsewhere. While he was pondering where he was going to get his big break from, Jessie was putting Mike up on game. The more money he made the more he wanted to make. He was also becoming more distant from Seven and D-Snake. It was like a love lost marriage. Good for the first few years and then just nothing. One day they all woke up and noticed that they were headed in different directions. Mike still liked the fellas the same but this was business. When Mike's cousin came over, D-Snake made sure he was close enough to hear the conversation.

"Money associates with money, Mike and in order for you to get the clout you want, you have to change who you hang with."

D-Snake also heard her tell him that he needed to drop the two of them like a bad habit.

"Mickey, look. You are my my cousin..my best friend. More like a brother. You know I would never steer you wrong. But those two jokers you have hanging around are bad business. I mean, what have they done in all this time that they have been here? What have they accomplished?"

Miguel was silent. She continued.

"See, you can't even answer because you *know* they haven't done shit. Yeah, they helping you with light weight shit, but you bigger than that now. Oh wait, they have managed to make a couple of trips to El Paso, and Laredo to jack some youngsters up there."

"How you know about that?"

"What you mean? Are you serious? Who doesn't know about that? Word is out on the street about them, kinfolk. They have jacked too many of the wrong people. They have death written all over them. You know they took out G-Money all those years ago, don't you? Why you think they can't be in one place too long? Come on man, wise up. You need to cut them loose now before they bring you down."

Not waiting for Miguel to respond, Jess walked off and left him to think about what she just said. D-Snake took Mike's silence to mean that he was still down with his crew regardless of what his bitch ass cousin said. Until Miguel came to the two of them the next day and told them that they had to clear out.

D-Snake was pissed off. He didn't say anything to anybody but inside he was fuming. Seven didn't care one way or the other. He was tired of being there anyway. His girlfriend, Lettie, had just told him that she was pregnant. Things were not supposed to be this way. He was supposed to be enjoying this time with his woman and his unborn child and he couldn't. Unfinished business had to be settled first and D-Snake was not a part of that.

Seven thanked Miguel for his hospitality and told him he would look him up when he got his shit together.

"You stay up homes. I see you doing good things. Just change who you do it with," Mike told him.

"I already know man. Well my shit is packed and I am heading north. Get atcha boy."

"Yo, you not waiting on your homeboy?"

"Nah, Cuz. I got to go my own way. It's partly because of that nigga that my ass is down and out anyway. Listening to his boo-boo ass ideas. Shit, I ain't seen my mother in years. I need to go check on her and see her pretty face at least once before I get to my new spot." *If I live that long*, he thought after he finished speaking.

'A'ight homes be careful. I hear they got your death certificate signed and the plot ready."

"Shit a nigga been knowing that. But I ain't scared. Seven minutes, Mike."

"Later."

Seven threw his last bag into the back of the Lincoln Navigator that he had won last week in a dice game and headed to Oklahoma. He did not see D-Snake before he left or else he would have told him goodbye. It didn't matter though. The time had long past since the two of them should have parted ways. He was angry at himself because he had been following around behind a man who didn't even have a clue.

His life was so messed up because he did not have the courage to say "no" so many years ago. On that fateful night he wanted to turn around and run as fast as he could away from that house. Something inside told him to leave. A loud voice screamed for him to get out, and yet, he didn't listen. If he knew back then what he knew now. Hindsight is a muthafucker.

Seven was tired of making up fake names and lying about who he was. He was just as tired of being called 'Seven', the name his big homie, Thuggy, from 107 Hoover Crip had given him the day he was quoted onto the set. For a little while, he just wanted to be Marcus Jefferson, his mother's son. Deep inside he knew that going to see her was risky and he probably wouldn't live that long once he got back into the city but that was a chance he had to take. He had to see his mama.

There was money he had stashed that he got from all those heists he and D-Snake had pulled over the years that he wanted to give to her. She may need it for his funeral. Also, he wanted to tell her about Lettie and give her information so she could keep up with her grandchild. Marcus loved her. Would have married her if he could, but the life he was leading prevented him from getting too close to her.

She knew the truth about him. All that he had done. And yet loved him anyway.

Lettie was a virgin when she got with him. Had told him that she wanted him to be her first, her last, her only. With Seven, it had just been about sex before when it came to chicks he fucked with. But she commanded something different from him. Made him want to take his time and move slowly. He savored her and looked forward to every moment that they would be together.

Seven, *Marcus*, was tired of running. Tired of pretending to be okay when he really wasn't. Tired of lying and living a lie. His girl knew that he was leaving. Had felt it in her heart. She was afraid that she would never see him again alive. Only in the face of the son or daughter that they would have, would she be able to look upon his likeness. He had given her his mom's information and said that he would do the same for her. Before he left, he repented of his sins and asked God to forgive and save him. He wanted to change. If he had a chance to talk to Leo before he died, he wanted to ask him for forgiveness too. It was time to face the music. He was going home.

≈

D-Snake sat in the cantina drinking. A violent storm brewed inside him. Ten years of pent up anger over failed come up attempts were eating at him. He was 27 years old and didn't have shit to show for hustling. Not a damned thing. At least Seven had managed to come up with a fly ass ride. *In a dice game though?* He still couldn't believe it. Some niggas had all the luck. Hell, he didn't even have enough money to pay for these drinks.

Paco, the bartender, just kept the drinks coming because he knew D-Snake was down with Mike's crew. No one knew that he was out yet and he certainly wasn't going to tell them. The bar tab would be settled at the end of the month like it always was. After inhaling one more drink, D-Snake got up and went back to Mike's villa. The place was like a ghost town.

As he walked down the long driveway, he noted that Seven's truck was gone along with every one else's. *That pussy must have left me*, he fumed. He figured he would though. His once down home boy had changed over the past few weeks. Started talking mumbo jumbo about God and repentance and other things he wasn't trying to hear.

D-Snake went inside to look around the house and spotted a set of car keys on the table. The 'H' on the ring told him that those were the Honda keys. Miguel used to let his flavor of the month drive it. He used to tell the new girl "I bought it just for you, baby." and she would believe him. They all did. Stupid bitches.

It was a nice Honda Accord that was equipped with a candy red paint job, ground effects, a Bose system, with four twelve inch woofers, a sunroof, navigation system, and a theater package. This month's flavor, Laura, never drove the car because it was a standard. She couldn't drive a stick.

I will just take this off her hands, he thought.

With keys in hand, he searched all the spots he knew Miguel stashed money. The last placed he look was behind the wet bar in the mini fridge.

"Boo-yah!" He said excitedly when he spotted the foil package.

He opened it up and from the looks of things figured there must be at least twenty G's there. D-Snake took it all. He was in heaven. Now that he had money and a ride there was no time to waste. He wanted to shake the spot before anyone from the crew came back or Mike himself. He hurried out of the house, jumped in the car, and hit the road with a kool-aid smile on his face. He was back in business.

CHAPTER SIX

Martha Jefferson was kneeled down on the side of her bed praying. Her heart was troubled. There was an uneasy feeling that plagued her soul ;she could not shake it. None of her friends understood what she was going through. She was the only one of her girl friends who had a son. The only one who had to be a mother and a father to a male child. That was not an easy feat. The only person she could turn to was God. She prayed and asked for guidance.

"Lord, I am so lost right now. I need you Savior. My son, the little boy You gave me to watch over is out in the streets leading a life that is not pleasing to You. Please deliver him from the life of crime that he has chosen to live. They say that he killed someone, God. I don't know if that's true or not but You sit high and look low and know all things.

I hope that he knows enough to ask You to forgive him. If he ain't done it, I ask You now on his behalf. I stand in the gap for my son Marcus. Bring him back to me safely, Father. I need to see my baby. Help this family, Savior. We need You. Move in a mighty way and keep your hedge of protection around us. Jesus, be a fence all around me and the people I love. Lord please watch over my baby wherever he is. I plead the blood of Jesus over him and my girls. Have your way, Lord. In Jesus' Holy Name I pray. Amen."

She got up from the floor and prepared to start her day which did not begin if she didn't pray first. Mrs. Jefferson went into the kitchen to put on a pot of coffee. For years she had the same routine. Wake up, pray, start coffee, get the kids up and out for school, pray again, then watch her stories. This morning would not be any different as far as she was concerned.

Mrs. Jefferson's house was the house that all the neighborhood kids went to when and if they needed anything. Food, clothes, a place to sleep, a hot bath. Nothing was out of reach for a person in need. It wasn't unusual for a person to come to her house early in the morning either. Some kids who didn't eat breakfast at home would come over before school. There was also Winifred, her nosey next door neighbor, who came over to watch the Price is Right and then the stories with her. When she heard the knock at the side door, she assumed it was one of them.

"The door is open, baby," she said as she leaned into the oven to take out her muffins. "Just make yourself right at home at the table. I will be out to serve you in a minute."

She placed two hot muffins on a saucer and poured a cup of coffee for her guest and set them on a tray. She didn't even know who was in her house, but Mrs. Jefferson was talking to them anyway.

"How you doing this morning?" She asked walking towards the dining area. "I tell you my arthritis has really been acting up since the weather changed. I have to go and get some med-." She lost her voice.

Standing under the threshold of her dining room was her son, Marcus. Joy bubbled over in her heart as she praised the Lord for answering her prayers so quickly. Tears streamed down her face as she dropped the tray, ran and hugged her son with all her might.

"Mama, I know you're surprised to see me and all, but… I had to see you. Had to come hold you in my arms again like I used to. Love on you a little. I love you, Mama. Please forgive me for all the mess that I took you through," he cried, leaning down to rest his head on her shoulder.

Mother and son stood for what seemed like hours, hugging and crying. Seven had no idea how much his mother had prayed for him. Mrs. Jefferson had no idea how her son had prayed to see her again. This was a long overdue reunion. He sat his mother down. There were things that he needed to get off his chest. And he knew that he had to do it quickly.

He started by telling her about the night of the murders. Although he did not actually pull the trigger, he felt responsible for the deaths. If he had not been a follower, maybe a man and his wife would still be alive today. The story continued with him telling his mom how he and D-Snake went from city to city jacking dope dealers and robbing people to get money. They had to be on the go constantly because so many dudes were looking for them.

His mother sat and listened. Some of the things her son told her were so graphic and ugly. She could not believe that her baby, her flesh and blood, could have done such things. But then again, he was in a world where such things were common. Murder, prostitution, drugs, fast money.

She just shook her head and sighed. *Help us Lord*, she said within. It hurt to hear how her son had endured such needless hardships but she noticed that the more he spoke the less weighed down he looked. For that, she was grateful.

"For the Mitchell's deaths, I have to answer for that. For all that I have done in my life; I have to answer for that. There are people who want to see me dead because of that couple. Even after all these years. That's why I came home. To see you and settle that debt. I have money here that I want you to use to pay for my funeral. Tell them to make me look good, Mama.

Also, I have a baby on the way by a beautiful young woman named, LeTalia Calderon, but I call her Lettie. She is so amazing, Ma. Reminds me so much of you with her feisty ways. I gave her your number and here is hers so you can keep in touch should things go bad for me. I want you to like her, Ma. She means a lot to me."

"Do you love her, son?"

"Yes, Ma'am. Very much."

"Then that's all that matters."

"While I was in Mexico, I got saved. You don't have to worry about where I'm going when I die now. I will be with God."

"What's with all this death talk, boy? You gon' live. I decree and declare it, and call it in the Spirit. You will become what God designed you to be. A man. God did not bring you all this way to die. Satan is a lie. Let's pray."

Together mother and son asked God to spare his life. His mom had said that he needed to call his girl and get her down there as soon as she could. They needed to be together. Marcus was happy. And for the first time in a long time, he wanted to live.

≈

Leo, Kim and their family sat on the third row of the Lion of Judah Church. The message this Sunday was about forgiveness. This was not what Leo wanted to hear. He did not want to have to forgive the people who killed his best friends. He wanted to hold on to the anger and rage but he could not. How could he be a good example to his son with all this animosity inside him? Sometimes he would find himself snapping at Kalif, his and Kim's son for no apparent reason. He had to let it go.

He looked at Kim. Saw that she was crying. Looking at the tears run down his wife's face made his heart heavy. He realized that in order for them to live the life that they had talked about, he was going to have get free from the bondage of revenge. At the end of the service when the Pastor gave the call to salvation, Leo was the first one up and at the altar. Mrs. Louella started running around the church like she was on fire when he did that. This was her prayer for him. To be saved.

Honesty looked at him. She understood what he was doing. The two of them had talked about this many times. Leo wanted her to let the grudge go as well. She could not. *Would* not. She wasn't angry at Leo for doing it, but those were her parents, not his, and she owed it to them to settle this.

"Not today God," she whispered.

Leo was a different man when he walked out the church. But there was something he still needed to take care of. His lookouts had told him almost a week ago that Seven was at his mother's house. It was time for him to be paid a visit. They had unfinished business.

≈

Friday night was the time to kick it at Club Karma in North Dallas. D-Snake was living it up and getting dressed to go. He had arrived in the Lone Star State a new man. Having been there before on drug runs for G long ago, he knew where to go. With plenty of loot and a fresh whip, it was easy for him to weave tall tales of how he had major dope connections. Texas was going to be good for him. The people there were so easy to fool. And because of his larger than life tales, D-Snake had finally gotten something he had always wanted; his own crew.

One of his closest homies in Texas, June, was down for whatever. He had served six years in a federal prison for bank robbery. That's what D-Snake wanted on his team, risk takers. Now was not the time to kick it with a bunch of pansies. June, having lived and hustled in Dallas all his life knew who the key players of the city were and had begun introducing D-Snake to them. His business was doing well. But all work and no play makes D-Snake a very dull boy so he and his crew stepped into Club Karma suited and booted. D-Snake's head was turning every which way but loose checking out all the fine ass honeys in that place. One light skinned, leggy chick caught his attention above all the others.

"Hey June, don't that chick right there look like Beyonce?" He was getting excited. The girl did look just like her and he was in Texas after all, where the beautiful megastar is from. She could have been her close relative or something.

"She sho' do my nig. You gon' go over der and holla at her? 'Cause if you not, I sho' will," June snickered.

Nah, dude. You sit that there down. I got this." And strolled over to the singers-look-alike.

"Shawty, what yo' name is?" Giving himself a drawl like a southern rapper. He was not prepared for her answer.

"Giana."

He stumbled. Did she just say her name was *Gina*? With the loud music blaring in the club it was hard to hear. Had he heard correctly? In all the years since he had killed Gina he had not met anyone or come across another woman named Gina and he was grateful. He felt that she would come back to haunt him in one of her namesakes.

"I'm sorry, what did you say?"

"Giana. Gee-on-a." *Stupid ass mark*, she thought. She was going to take this nigga fast if she could. He looked ripe for the picking.

"Oh, ok," he recovered. "It's lovely just like you. So, uh, can I buy you a drink luscious?"

"Yep, you sure can," she said and the two of them walked over to the bar.

"You can have whatever you like."

Giana's eyes got round like saucers when she the wad of cash D-Snake pulled out of his pocket. *Yeah, he gone be mine tonight*, she thought maliciously. Giana was used to rolling cats from out of town. All of them were easy marks. They were so caught up in her looks and her body that they lost all reasoning. Once she got the dude alone and did a striptease he was turned to mush after that. Taking his money was the easiest thing she ever did. This one here would be no different.

The two of them talked, drank, and danced for a while. D-Snake was happy that he made June drive himself to the club. He did not want to have to leave this honey to take anyone home. They made plans to have a night cap together. Trying to impress her, D-Snake told her they would end their evening at the W hotel. Giana was all in.

"Can you excuse me for a moment? I want to let my friends know that I will not be going home with them tonight. Be right back."

He watched her sashay her thick hips across the club to a group of pretty girls. This was definitely his new place. He had found some young flunkies in Irving, Texas and jacked them real quick. They didn't even know it was him who had taken them fast like that. They never saw it coming. From them, he had taken another fifteen g's and that made his stash increase considerably. D-Snake raised his glass to Giana and her friends when they looked his way. All of them were dime pieces. They smiled at him when they noticed him looking their way.

"Girl he is so cute. Do your thang." Tiffany, Giana's cousin and best friend said.

She had spotted D-Snake when he came into the club and had initially wanted him for herself. But when she saw him approaching her cousin she knew she could hang it up. *Another one bites the dust,* she had thought. Although Tiffany was just as pretty as her cousin, she was a lot more reserved and conservative when it came to her mode of dressing and the amount of makeup she used.

Where Giana was fire, Tiffany was ice. She wasn't showing too much of anything to anybody unless they were a couple She knew it was time to step up her game though. She didn't want to be alone forever. But she didn't want to be with a D- boy, anyway. The minute he got caught selling dope she would be back in the same boat as she began. Alone. Or worst yet, he could get killed. And that would be unbearable for her. Nah, she needed a real man. One who held down a 9 to 5.

"Tif, I'm gonna roll this fool. Take him for every penny he got. Gigi needs a new pair of Prada's."

"You be careful. He doesn't look like the dudes around here who you're used to fucking with. He looks like he's crazy."

"Girl I'm not worried about him. He's a big ol' teddy bear in my hands. Just cover me when you get back. Tell mama something so that she doesn't worry about me. Like I ran into some old friends from school or something. She likes to hear shit like that."

Reluctantly, Tiffany agreed and the girls parted ways. D-Snake escorted Giana to his car and held the door open for her. That impressed her because she never had a man do that before. He was reeling her in. Chivalry shown to a hood chick was a sure fire way to get him some pussy the same day he met her.

On the way to the hotel, Giana turned in her seat a bit and spread her thighs, giving D-Snake a nice view of what he would be getting later. The car swerved.

It blew his mind when she licked one of her fingers and slid it inside her pussy. When she took it out, she licked it and made a slurping noise. D-Snake was rock hard. The car couldn't move fast enough for him. Gigi continued to tease him by masturbating in the front seat. She rubbed on her clit and fingered herself, bringing herself to multiple orgasms in a short time.

"Watch this baby," she said, as she made her vaginal muscles contract and squirt her juices across the front seat of the car.

Some landed on the steering wheel. D-Snake took a finger and wiped it off, tasting it in the process. His mind was gone. This man was sprung. Never in his life had he seen any woman do that shit.

They arrived at the W hotel and checked into their sixteenth floor suite. It overlooked downtown Dallas. Giana had driven down Victory Park Lane so many times and fantasized about being at this hotel. Not that she fucked with low rent dudes but they never brought her to a place like this. The best they did was the Hyatt Regency. This man was different. She revamped her plans and decided not to rob him after all. He was a keeper.

They sat and talked for a while and swapped lies. D-Snake told her that his real name was Tre'on Matthews but for her not to tell anyone. That was an old trick he used to get girls to trust him. They thought he was giving up some valuable information to them. He used that trust to get them to do things for him that they normally wouldn't do. It worked every time. He poured her another drink and sat down in the oversized arm chair. She got on her knees in front of him, unzipped his pants, pulled his dick out, and began sucking him like a Hoover vacuum cleaner. His dick felt raw.

"I don't normally do this kind of thing," she lied.

This bitch was a pro and he didn't fall for that bull. He came on her face and again in her mouth as she brought him back to full erection over and over again. They fucked and sucked on one another for hours before finally falling asleep. The maids knock at the door brought them out of their slumber. He mumbled something about staying another day and for her to just leave them some fresh towels and she was on her way, smiling as she pushed her cart down the hallway because she had one less room to clean.

D-Snake went to the front desk and paid for three additional days. This girl was on her way to having him sprung. Had him spending money that he couldn't afford to spend. She showed him all the hot spots and trendy shops in Dallas and the surrounding areas. He bought her fine perfumes, clothes, shoes, and even small pieces of jewelry. Diamonds. Shit, this was her type of man. She knew she had made the right choice to keep him around.

Gigi also took him to South Dallas where all the street action played out like a movie. Drug deals, murders, gang fights, and prostitution were common place in her hood. He loved it. This was where he belonged. Shit, he had just unloaded six large on this bitch and he needed a way to recoup his loss. He found that when Giana introduced him to a young buck named Cash.

It didn't take long for D-Snake to see why they called him that. The dudes' money was long. D-Snake needed to get in good with this cat so that he could find out where he kept his money. His motto was "show me the money" just like the man in the movie. After three days of kicking it together and hustling, D-Snake learned where he kept his money and dope. *Texans were slow*, he thought, because they trusted people way too easily. This youngster would not know what hit him. They were now best friends.

Cash reminded D-Snake a lot of himself. Or at least the hustler he could have been had he not killed Goldie. But oh well. One night they all made plans to go to the beach in Galveston. They had all hit the road at the same time. But D-Snake doubled back before getting too far out of town and relieved Cash of what he thought was all his money and dope. With friends like D-Snake, who needed enemies?

They all kicked it at the beach for the weekend getting high, drunk, and having raunchy sex parties in the hotel. D-Snake wanted Giana to join in with him and Cash but she was not having it. She said that she would not take her clothes off in front of another man. D-Snake felt that there was more to it than that but let it go. They left their den of ill repute and made their way back to big "D". It took less than thirty minutes for Cash to realize that his shit was gone after he got home.

D-Snake and Giana had returned to the W hotel and chilled out like nothing had changed. Giana, who was asleep in the car when D-Snake stole from Cash, was being quieter than normal. She usually talked a mile a minute. D-Snake's cell phone rang. He looked at the caller I.D. It was Cash. He didn't want to answer it but did any way to keep any suspicion off himself if this was about the missing dope and money.

"What up my nig?" Cash asked. D-Snake could hear him blowing smoke. He must be blazing.

"Not shit. Just sitting here chilling with my woman. What you got going on?"

"Not a damned thang. Just wanted to know when I could expect you to bring me my shit back?"

D-Snake played dumb. "Oh, yeah, that bag I borrowed from you? Shit, I'll have Giana bring that by whenever you want it."

"Nah, my nig. I'm talking about my money and my dope, bitch ass nigga. I know you got my shit. Don't try to play me like a fool. I have a witness and she ain't gon' lie to me. I thought you and me was cool? Guess not. I'll give you one hour to return my shit and after that, I'm coming after you with my guns cocked and blazing. I put that on my mama." The line went dead.

D-Snake was not used to dealing with cats like this one. Not once during the whole conversation, if you could call it that, did Cash raise his voice. He was calm. Too calm. His mind started to ponder who could have told on him. Giana. Fucking broads. They talk too damned much.

Damn Gina, he thought. *Not again.*

He would show her who she was talking too as soon as she came back into the room from the ice machine. When she walked in, he was standing in the middle of the room, naked. She placed the ice bucket on the table and walked towards him. He tore her clothes off her, making empty promises to buy her new ones. Not waiting for her consent he shoved her to the floor in front of him and shoved his dick into her mouth. She was gagging and trying to back up.

"I thought we had something, Gina? Why you keep betraying me girl? Huh?"

His anger was clouding his judgment. He didn't see Giana's face anymore. Instead he saw Gina's. The one woman he really loved. He was reliving that night all over again. Minus the bat. He continued to shove his meat in her mouth, laughing at her when he saw tears streaming down her face. When he spilled his seed in her mouth and on her face, she pulled away, coughing and sputtering.

"What's the matter with you? I did not betray you. And why the fuck you keep calling me Gina? Who the fuck is she? You know my name, now use it bastard. You not gon' treat me like shit. I love you Tre'."

"What the fuck ever bitch you don't love me. I know you told that nigga Cash about what I did. Why you do that shit? I loved you girl. Thought you and I was gon' build some shit together."

Regardless of how hard she pleaded, Giana could not get through to him. He was so angry and talking to him was futile as he used and abused her body for his own sadistic purposes. Her final humiliation was when he bent her over and shoved his dick in her behind, taking it out, and replacing it with the neck of a champagne bottle. It was painful for her. He was not gentle in his ministrations at all. He rammed the object in and out and fingered her at the same time.

Giana did not plan on getting turned on but she did. Her pain turned to pleasure and before she knew it she was wetter than Niagara Falls. She was angry however that her body would betray her in such a way. As her body convulsed, she lay confused as to why this man would think that she would rat him out like that. She was not a snitch. Any money that he had, she knew she stood to receive a large cut of. Why would she mess up her own money?

D-Snake finished the job, pulled on his pants and beat Giana with the metal end of his belt. Each swing left a huge red welt on her body and she began bleeding from many of the lashes. All the while he beat her, she screamed that she did not snitch on him but all he could see was Gina's face. All he could hear was Gina's voice. She had become Gina. It was time to kill this bitch. He was about to kick her in the head when his cell phone rang. It was Cash again. He answered it.

"Look, I don't know why Giana told you I took your shit but she lying. I would never do anything like that to you." He said lying through his teeth.

"Giana? Man, she ain't told me shit but I know for a fact you did it. Your hour is up. I'm on my way. And Giana better be alright cuz. I know she didn't tell you but that's my sister muthafucker and she bet' not be hurt. Nah, she ain't told me shit bruh. I got a nanny cam in that China doll that sits on top of my fireplace. I got your bitch ass on tape." Click.

D-Snake looked at Giana. She was still alive but unconscious. He had fucked up again. It was time to relocate.

CHAPTER SEVEN

Leo stood alone on the front porch of Mrs. Jefferson's house. The time had come for him to confront Seven. No one could do this but him. No longer business, this was personal. He took a deep breathe, exhaled, and knocked on the door.

Seven answered, "I have been waiting for you." Nervousness shook his voice. Something told him to expect a visit this morning so he had sent his mother and Lettie to a day spa to get them out of the house. Lettie's being here was his mother's idea. She decided that it would be best for them all to have her close. Mrs. Jefferson was a praying woman, but after listening to all her son's escapades over the years, she felt like he was living on borrowed time. Just as soon as Lettie got into town, Mrs. Jefferson escorted the young couple to the court house to get married. That was another one of her ideas.

"We not gon' have no more babies born into our family out of wedlock. You need to do right by this girl and make her your wife no matter what. Before God and man. You done already exercised your husbandly privileges. May as well go all the way," she said shortly after meeting her son's girlfriend.

Seven loved Lettie with all his heart and really wanted to marry her long ago. However, because of his lifestyle he was reluctant to make her a single mother and a widow in the same breathe. But now, staring in the face of the man he knew came here to kill him, he was glad that he had married her. That way his son or daughter would carry on with his name.

"I'm ready to go. Let's get this over with," Seven said trying to muster up courage. There was nowhere for him to run. Nowhere to hide.

"Hold up. I need to talk to you. Can I come in?" The request shocked Seven. All he could do was nod his head "yes." This was awkward to him. The Leo he knew before did not ask for anything, he just took it.

"Uh, yeah. Come, come on in." Seven stammered.

He escorted Leo into the living room where they took a seat and sat quietly. Seven had no clue what was about to go down. He was sad. He knew that his final moments were at hand. Leo was antsy. He was moving around in the seat like he had to go the bathroom. He was just as uncomfortable as Seven. His thoughts were muddled and he had a lot to say but did not know where to begin.

"Right now, I am so fucking angry dude," he said pounding his fist in his hand. "My brother is dead. And you may not have been the one to pull the trigger but I still hold you responsible. For my sister, too. I can't believe you just stood there and watched your maggot ass friend blow a hole in her head. Why man? Why?" Pain ripped through his chest as he spoke.

"I don't know. I was fifteen years old. Young. Stupid. Trying to make a name for myself, following after my homie. I was down for whatever he suggested. When I saw him lying there asleep, I couldn't do it. Murdering somebody, especially him, wasn't in me. When I was on the run, I used to get high just so I wouldn't remember. I tried so hard to block out the look in Silver's eyes. I know that's not gonna bring them back but, I'm truly sorry. I hope one day you can forgive me. I'm a changed man now." He was referring to his new found salvation.

Leo looked at him with a serene face, throwing him off. He said calmly, "It wasn't in you to kill them, huh? Well, guess what? It's in me to kill you."

With that said, he pulled a 9mm gun from out the back of his waistband and set it on the coffee table that separated the two men. "I want to kill you so bad my nuts ache!"

Seven's heart rate increased and beads of sweat formed on his forehead. Hot tears ran down his face.

Leo continued, "but like you, I'm a different man. A lot has happened over the last ten years. The game has changed. There is no longer honor among thieves. It's cut throat."

Seven nodded in agreement.

"I'm not going to kill you," he said putting the gun away. "I forgive you. Now forgiveness is one thing and forgetting is another. I'm not perfect. Seeing you on the daily might cause that hurt and anger to return. Being honest, I can't be around here seeing you live your life with your new wife and child, knowing that my friends never had a chance to raise and live with their own baby."

Seven looked surprised at the mention of them.

"Yeah I know 'bout them. So this is what *is* going to happen. I won't kill you. Won't allow anyone else to kill you. You have two days, 48 hours only, beginning right now, to get out of town. If you're still here by the end of that time, I will come back and kill you myself. And since you seem to love your mother so much, you might wanna take her with you because if you cross into this state again, you'll surely die. You understand what I am telling you?" Leo was serious.

"Yes."

Seven understood. Perfectly. God had given him another chance. Leo was one of the hardest dudes Seven had ever met. If God could change him, what else could He do? Seven wanted to know God even better now. He thanked Leo as he walked out the door and began to praise God once he was alone.

Leo had some explaining to do to his wife. When he left home that morning, he had left her with the impression that he was going to come back home with another body tied to his soul. It was time for him to come clean with her.

Seven vowed the moment Leo had walked out the door to drop anything negative associated with his past. That included his street name. He called his mother and new wife and urged them to get home quickly. Both women cried and prayed as they drove. It was Mrs. Jefferson's morbid speculations that caused Lettie to almost hurl. They hadn't been in the driveway ten seconds when Marcus came running out the house.

"Oh, Jesus! Son you're alright." His mother screamed, hugging her son.

He gripped her tightly hugging her back. Lifting her body off the ground. It took only a moment for him to tell them all that went down after they went into the house. When he got to the part about having only 48 hours to move, Mrs. Jefferson jumped up and began opening cabinets and closet doors.

"Mama, what are you doing?" He asked. Three lines appeared as he creased his forehead in confusion.

"Boy you ain't gotsta tell me twice. I'm packing. Get your sister's on the phone for me, will you? I need to tell them this house is theirs. They was just 'bout to get evicted from their apartment, too. Just look at God and see how He works."

The young couple continued to sit and look at the older woman in bewilderment.

"I dunno what y'all waiting on! Get up off your rear ends and get moving. It's time to shake the spot!"

"Mama, where you learn that at?" Marcus had never heard his mother speak that way before.

"Boy, you can't be around all these young folks and not pick up a thing or two from them. We used to talk all the time and they'd teach me their language. I'd like to think they learned a few things from me as well."

Since Mrs. Jefferson was leaving her house to the girls, they didn't have to worry about moving any furniture. Whatever they needed as far as that was concerned, they could buy when they got where they were going. With the help of his sisters and a few of his mother's friends, the group packed everything they wanted to take. This took less than nine hours. Marcus' mom had lived in that house over 41 years. Marriages, births, even deaths were recorded in the history of that home. It was a sad good-bye for him. He looked at his mother.

"I'm sorry, Mama. Making you leave your home and all. I know you gon' miss it."

"Son, now you look here. I *choose* to leave with you. I love you. Your old mother don't have one regret. Plus, *I* can always come back to visit, you're the one who can't," she said giving her sons hand a squeeze for reassurance.

Tears flowed down the faces of friends and family when they were all loaded up and ready to go. Many of them could not understand why God was taking their friend away from them.

"Don't look at it as God taking me *away*, but look at it as Him taking me *to*. Y'all got the number to my celly. Holla at your girl when you can."

The crowd laughed at her hip exchange. She'd be missed. Marcus backed the SUV out the driveway for the last time and went to the corner store to fill the gas tank. Once they were all settled again, he headed to I-40 West. Lettie reached over and grabbed her husband's hand. He looked in her eye's that had filled with unshed tears.

"I love you," she said without making a sound. He shook his head "yes" and drove westbound.

Mrs. Jefferson sat comfortably in the backseat with her hands folded across her lap. She softly sang the words to her favorite song.

"Never would have made it, never could have made it, without you. I would have lost it all." She stopped singing and asked quietly, "where are we headed son?"

He looked in the rearview mirror, then over to his wife, exhaled and said, "Seattle."

≈

Word on the street was that Leo killed Seven the reason no one saw him anymore and had threatened to do the same to his girl. So to protect her unborn grandchild, his mom moved them away. Many other scenarios were broadcast with all of them resulting in Seven's death. Leo didn't bother to correct anyone. It was best to let people think and believe what they wanted.

Leo told his wife what happened. Kim had never been more proud of her husband in her life. She cried until she was all cried out. At first it was hard for her to imagine him *not* killing Seven. He had held a grudge for so long. But since getting saved, he was a different man. The two of them could relax just a little bit more.

They agreed not to tell Honesty about Leo not killing Seven because they didn't know how she'd react. Since she was old enough to know what revenge was, she was set on getting it for her parents.

Honesty took great pains in finding the truth behind her parent's murders. She knew Seven didn't kill them. He was only a flunky. A pawn in someone else's game. When she overheard Leo tell Kim how old Seven was *now*, she did the math and figured out that he was her age when this all went down. But the difference between her now and him then is that she is a leader not a follower.

Yeah he could live, she thought. She was not that hard hearted. But D-Snake had to go. It didn't

matter if Leo tried to intervene and stop D-Snake's murder, Honesty was not having it. He did kill her parents. And when the time came, she would kill him. It wasn't Leo's responsibility to avenge her parent's. It was hers.

Over the years Honesty had picked up a thing or two about killing people. Whether it was through books, movies, or ear hustling on Tristan talking to Leo about his jobs. Tristan didn't know it, but he taught Honesty how to shoot gun, wield a knife, and even make a noose through all those conversations. *The boy was bad*, she thought. He was the E.F. Hutton of assassins. When Tristan spoke, everybody listened.

During the past year, there was not a place that D-Snake went that Honesty did not know about. The people who worked for Leo, worked for her too. But he didn't know it. He would pay them for their information, and out of loyalty to Goldie, they would give the same to Honesty. They had no clue that she was planning anything. Hell, she didn't even know what she was going to do. Her scheming mind was overloaded with ideas. All she knew was that when the time came she had to be ready to take him out like week old garbage. In his case, ten year old garbage.

I don't want to be a killer but if I don't end this, it will kill me, she thought.

Both sets of her parents, birth and adoptive, had been involved with drugs and prostitution. And even though Leo and Kim had given that lifestyle up, that was not what she wanted for herself. She had to find her own way. At 16, Honesty thought she was a G.A.W. Grown Ass Woman. She kept that to herself though. When she was with her parents, she was the sweet Honesty they expected her to be. But when she wasn't she was hell on wheels.

One of Leo's younger associates, Nitro, had opened a teen club that Honesty liked to frequent. The place was off the hook. Nitro was old enough to say "remember when?" But still young enough to know what a 'bust it baby' was. He was fine with a capital 'F.'

Each time he would come over to the house to see Leo, she would look for a reason to be in the same room he was in. She would "lose" things and go look for them but of course never find them. If Leo was in another room while she was looking around she would bend over so Nitro could see her *ass*ets. Often she would catch him checking her out. Once she walked by and leaned over in his face, wiggling her behind as she went down.

Like any red blooded man, he could not resist reaching out and touching her. She did not mind at all. It wasn't like he was an old man. He was only twenty-one. And that's what she liked, older than her but younger than twenty-five. The man was just her speed. Fine, financially fit, freaky, and fashionable. The four 'F's' every man must be. They especially had to have gear.

Honesty kept herself fresh to death. Every weekend she was in the club in something sexy and revealing. Low cut midriff tops prominently displayed the swell of her breasts. When she danced and worked up a sweat, little droplets of perspiration formed on her chest and trickled down between her cleavage. There were many a nights that some dudes saw that and envied the salty beads of water. Wishing it were one of their tongues.

The short skirts she wore barely covered her butt. If she bent over a person looking could get a view of the crease that separated ass from thigh. She had thick, shapely legs that had an athletic appearance to them. Many times her legs had been compared to one of those tennis playing sisters. Compliments like that made her cockier than she already was.

The only reason she dressed like that was to catch Nitro's attention. He usually sat in the upstairs V.I.P. lounge to watch all the action below. To watch her. She wanted him. Plain and simple. It was her mission to get him. This coming up Friday night was going to be d-day. Leo and Kim were going out of town and she was staying with her friend Desiree. The two of them planned to hit the club together.

She took her time getting dressed that night. Had even shaved a design in her pubic hairs. Baby boy would be seeing it if she had her way. She was still a virgin but she felt like she was ready for loving after the things she had discovered about sex.

Last week, Kim and her went to Dallas, Texas to shop and hang out. Honesty sneaked out the hotel room while Kim was asleep and walked to the strip mall a few blocks from their hotel off Interstate 635. There she found a XXX video store and bought some dvd's. The man behind the counter didn't even ask her age once he saw the stack of bills she pulled out her bra. His eyes feasted on the ripe melons that served as a temporary purse. Out of the corner of her eye she saw him rubbing his cock when she walked away from the register and out the store.

Once they had returned home, Honesty would hole up in her room to watch the movies she bought. The illicit sex scenes made her hot and bothered. Her skin flushed when she saw a woman on the screen masturbating. A pulsing throb began in her vagina and her pea-sized nipples got hard and started to ache. These feelings were unfamiliar to her at first and she didn't know how to stop them. The first several times she experienced them, she ended up taking cold showers because she overheard guys at school say that's what they did to calm down when they got excited in that way. That was cool for her at first. But she wanted more than that. Knew that she needed completion somehow.

She decided to do what she saw the women in the movies did to see if it was really as good as they made it seem. The overheated young woman popped in a DVD with a man and woman masturbating. Honesty waited for the now familiar ache to return and used her fingers to caress that spot. When she touched herself she discovered that creamy moisture settled between the folds of her lips when she was turned on. The moisture made it easy for one, then two fingers to glide in and out of her.

There was some moaning in the room and Honesty looked around to see who was in the room when she realized the moans were coming from her. She did not recognize her own voice. The friction from the rubbing caused heat to build up. Still she was not satisfied. She started to finger herself faster and her thumb accidentally brushed against a swollen piece of flesh she had never touched before. Her body jumped from the sensation. She took her wet fingers and began lightly massaging this button.

Damn, this shit feels better than anything, she thought.

Her legs began to quiver. Her breathing was coming in short pants. The heat that she had felt only in her center was now everywhere. Little electric shocks traveled up her arms and legs. The same that came when you touched a television with a wet hand. She was excited and scared at the same time. She liked the way this felt but was not sure if this was normal. There wasn't too much time to ponder her normalcy because after a few more strokes the invisible dam in her body burst and the cream started gushing and running down the insides of her thighs. Her toes curled up and legs shook with fury. A rushing wave overtook her and she screamed out. Her breathing was returning to normal just when there was a knock at the door.

"Chile, you alright in there?" Mrs. Louella, Kim's mom asked.

"Oh- oh yes Granny Lou. I just stubbed my toe on the dresser. I am ok."

"Okay then, just checking," and she kept it moving.

Honesty almost got busted. From that point on she pleasured herself daily, but after a while, she felt like she was still missing something. It had to be the 'D'. The girls in the movies went crazy over it and she wondered what made them act that way. Nitro's interest in her was what she needed to get what she wanted. Kim and Leo said she couldn't formally date until they sat down and discussed some things but they were too late, the time was now.

Desiree and Honesty arrived at the club looking hot. All eyes were on them as they walked past the people who had been in line almost an hour. The two girls walked past, looking for their friends. Honesty was V.I.P. She didn't stand in lines and neither did he friends. They spotted a couple of their home girls and pulled them out of line so they could enter with them. A few girls mumbled curse words under their breaths but they knew enough to know what was up. The bouncer pulled the velvet rope when she approached and let the fly girl crew cross the threshold.

The club was jumping but the true party didn't begin until Honesty got there. The speakers boomed and vibrated. Girls were grinding so close on the dudes it was hard to imagine them not getting aroused. They looked like they were having sex. Some of the dance moves she saw emulated things she had seen in her flicks.

Desiree found herself a cutie, leaving Honesty alone. She was cool with that. She had already found a place on the dance floor that would give Nitro a good view of her from his usual spot. The music slowed and R. Kelly's voice came over the speakers, telling the D.J. to slow the party down. The young vixen licked her lips, giving them a wet, glossy shine and began rolling her butt to the beat.

Nitro was staring down at her. He was mesmerized. She twisted her hips and bounced her ass just for him.

Omarion's "O" came filtering out the system and she really gave him something to look at. Her show must have been on point because before the song was over a security guard came and told her that Nitro wanted to see her. This was what she had been waiting on.

At first, there were some dudes in the room with him but he made them leave as soon as he saw her. He sat lazily in a huge red velvet chair with his leg propped casually over one arm. The massive big screen TV vibrantly displayed the latest videos. There were smaller screens flanked around it that showed different areas of the club. The dance floor, all four of the bars, the billiards area, and the entrance and exits.

With all that to watch, he should have been occupied, she thought.

He was looking good enough to eat but she played it cool.

"You wanted to see me?" She asked nonchalantly.

"Yeah. What you doing?"

"What am I doing?" Did you not see me down there getting my groove on?"

"Yeah, I saw that freak show you were putting on for me."

"For you? Pssh. Whatever. That was all for me. Don't flatter yourself."

"Whatever. I know you be checking for me. That's why you always come around when I am at yawls house. It's cool though. I be checking for you too." Flattery would get him everywhere.

"You do?" She questioned happily.

"Yep. I been wanting to holler at you but we always getting interrupted by Leo and shit."

"Well he ain't here now so what's up?"

"Shit, baby. You. How can I get with your program?"

"Hmm, you want Honesty, huh?"

"Damn skippy I do. I know you want me too."

" Yes I do. You have been the star in my dreams too many nights."

"Is that right? Well come over here and show me what you be dreaming about."

She walked to him and he circled his muscular arms around her. Her lips parted to receive his tongue but he moved slightly to the right and kissed her neck. He began to nuzzle the spot behind her ear driving her crazy. Her body came alive. His lips felt good on her. They were both breathing heavier when he stopped. She was disappointed.

He walked her across the room and unlocked a door which led to a bedroom. There was a round bed that sat in the middle of the floor, covered with a Chinchilla spread and lots of pillows. The carpeting was plush and soft and when she removed her high-heeled sandals her toes sank into the cool comfort of it. Soft music was piped in and the aroma of a brown sugar and vanilla scented candle filled the room. She was in heaven. Nitro walked her to the edge of the bed and started kissing her passionately. Before she knew it, her shirt, bra, and mini skirt were off, leaving her in her lace T-back panties.

"Baby you got a banging ass body. I'm going to enjoy this," he said admiringly.

His lips traveled from her mouth south on her body. He stopped at her breasts and took a hardened nipple into his mouth. It was like fire on her skin. She could not get enough of him.

"Touch me, my pussy is throbbing. Please touch me, baby," she pleaded.

His hand slid inside her panties and he stopped kissing her only long enough to smile at her. He moved his fingers skillfully like a pianist tickles the ivory keys of a piano. Small fires ignited all over her when he found each hot spot. Her hips bucked and gyrated under his tantalizing administrations. When she touched herself, she could bring about these same feelings. Honesty craved something more. She needed him to satisfy the unknown and she told him so.

"Nitro, please. I need you in me. This is crazy. Help me, baby."

He stopped cold. "Honesty, I want to make love to you but what if Kim decides to have you checked to make sure you are still a virgin? I don't want you to get into any trouble." He touched her womanhood. "Plus you need to save this here for your husband."

"What! You sat up here and got me all horny and now you gonna leave me hanging?" She was pissed off.

"Pump your breaks girl. I am going to finish what I started. Just not the way you expect."

"I don't know what you are talking about." Sexual tension caused her to become irate. She rolled her eyes in disgust at him.

"You trust me right?" He wanted to know.

"I guess."

"You guess. What the fuck?"

"Yes, Nitro. I trust you."

"Good. Then know that I'm gonna take good care of you tonight. Just do what I say and youll be fine."

She did just that. Nitro, whose real name is Sayvon, was going to teach her a thing or two. He alerted his security and told them he was out for the night and Honesty told Desiree that she was going to chill with Nitro for the evening so she didn't have to wait for her. After they took care of that, they picked up where they left off.

He pulled off her panties and laid her on the bed. His mouth moved over her body where his hands had once been, finally settling on her neatly shaved vagina. When his tongue darted out and parted her lips she scooted toward the curved head board. This was new to her. His hands grabbed her hips and pulled her into his mouth. He penetrated her and loved her with his tongue until she was almost out of her mind. Her hips bucked and raised off the mattress.

Sayvon's teeth gently bit and suckled the nub that held her passion until tears ran down her face. Her body exploded and she saw stars. Her thighs shook and body quaked. This was the first orgasm she had had without doing it herself.

"We're not done. I have more to show you."

Reaching over into the drawer on the nightstand, he pulled out a tube of K-Y Jelly and lubed himself.

He put her on her knees in doggy-style position and lubricated her anus. This looked familiar to her. She knew he was going to fuck her in her ass. His hands played with her pussy, stroking slowly in and out, working her up again. His fingers felt her vaginal muscles contract and he knew she was ready. He placed the tip of his penis at her back door entrance.

"Relax," he said. "When you feel me pushing in, I want you to push out like you are struggling to use the bathroom."

She obeyed. He continued to finger her, pushing in more, the wetter she got. She winced in pain.

"Baby it hurts," she whimpered.

"I know, but not for long. Just relax." He stopped pushing so that she could adjust to him and concentrated on her vagina. There were now two fingers inside her and he used his thumb to massage her clit. She was wet and wild.

"Ooh, baby. You make me crazy. Give me more."

"Yeah I'll give it to you. Push out hard and take this dick like a pro," he said and impaled her with his fullness.

Pain was replaced with pleasure and he brought her to another orgasm causing juices to run down her thighs. He pumped faster. She backed up in an attempt to get more of him. He screamed her name.

She yelled out his. They came together and collapsed in one big heap on the bed.

"Are you okay?" He asked.

"Yes. I am fine."

"Cool. We will make love like this from now on and your hymen will stay intact. You can't get pregnant this way either."

"Cool."

"What time you gotta be home?"

"I'm staying with Des tonight. Leo and Kim are out of town."

"So you can stay the night with me?"

"Yes. Can we do what we just did again?"

"All night long." His words offered promise. Honesty smiled. She was in lust.

CHAPTER EIGHT

D-Snake was coming back to Oklahoma City. And Honesty was going to kill him. Her mind was made up. Now not only did she have the means to do it, she would have the opportunity. Word was he was chasing some dope. *What else was new,* she mused. This particular day, she overheard Leo and Nitro talking about ten kilo's of dope, on its way to the 'O'. Some mules were bringing it in. They were coming in on the bus.

If Leo and Nitro knew the date and time, and now so did she, she figured D-Snake did too. People talked too damned much. No one should know that. No one! Her sources told her D-Snake was working for the guy who was sending the dope. Since Leo knew who he was, he guessed he was going to try to jack dude. She had a plan. If things went accordingly, this would be his last heist.

D-Snake was going to pull something. There was too much money and dope to be had in Oklahoma City to keep him away. Other cities were experiencing a drought on the 'white girl' but not OKC. People slept on this city. Thought that it was nothing more than country music, cowboys, and Indians. If they only knew. Dope was treacherous. It was because of that mess her parents were killed and others strung out. Broke, hungry and homeless. She was not going to sell or smoke dope. She was going to make a name for herself by herself. Not because of who her parents were or her adoptive are. Only close friends and relatives knew they adopted her. She did not allow anyone else that close to her to know otherwise.

Tired of ear hustling through the door, she walked into the room were Leo and his company sat, chatting. Neither man paid her any attention. Both of them were used to the hide and seek game she played by now. She grinned because now when he looked at her with those bedroom eyes of his, she knew what he was thinking. Probably the same things she was.

The men were trying to figure out who the man was in California so that they could put him up on game. It took Leo only two days to find out the man's name was Chuck and to gather his contact information. Once he spoke to him, Leo caught a flight to meet with him. Nitro told Honesty all this. If Leo knew how much he talked, he would stop fucking with him. He didn't like cats like that. But Honesty planned to use all that information to her benefit. Leo had his mission. She had hers. Both with very different results.

While Leo was handling business out of town, she handled it in town. D-Snake was here and she knew where he was. That man must have been stupid. She wondered what made him think that it was cool to return. Like people were slow or some shit and would forget him and what he did. She did not know much about him except what he looked like from pictures provided by her contacts. If he hadn't killed her parent's, she would have fucked with him. Baby boy was fine.

One of her contacts did say that he had an eye for beautiful women and would lose his mind over one in a heartbeat. She was about to be that one. On a warm Sunday afternoon, she and Desiree made their way to Edwards Park where all the ballers hung out. It was common for them to get together and cook out and chill in the park. D-Snake thought he was one so he would probably be there too.

Desiree was helping Honesty with different scenarios to "accidentally" run into D-Snake. But nothing worked better than fate. When they got to the park a cantankerous old man tried to push up on them when a young man intervened and sent the man on his way. D-Snake.

"Sorry 'bout that ladies. Y'all have to excuse Henry. He don't mean no harm."

The sight of him made her ill. Her stomach rolled and churned like it wanted to spew out her lunch. *Stay focused girl*, she berated herself and she gave him a sexy smile and walked over to him.

"Thank you so much. I didn't want to hurt his feelings."

"Awe you's a sweetie, huh? Shit, my name is Love, young'un. What's yours?"

"Saray."

"That's lovely. How your mama come up with a pretty name like that?"

"My mother. It's my dad's name said backwards. His name is Eric"

"Shit, I hope I get to meet your daddy one day. I want to thank him for convincing you."

"Convincing me?"

"Yeah. For bringing you into this world."

"Oh, you mean *conceiving* me." *Stupid ass*, she thought. "You wanna meet my daddy?" She continued.

"Hell yeah. For real. I want to meet the parents of my future wifey."

"Oh you will. Most definitely." *In death*, she finished silently.

He continued with the lame pick up lines for almost an hour. She told him that he could call her "Ray" when he said that she was his ray of sunshine. It was corny but she wanted him to feel a connection with her. His being comfortable was a major part of her plan. A couple of hours had gone by and it was an unspoken agreement the two of them were 'talking'. She pretended to like it. This fool was already talking about making love to her.

Her cell phone vibrated in her pocket and she told him that it was her mom telling her to come home. She went on to say that her parents were very strict and that she could not have dudes calling her phone. He offered to buy her one so he could talk to her when he wanted. Desiree was getting antsy and Honesty told him again that she had to leave.

"Let me get a good-bye kiss or hug or something." He sounded desperate.

"My dad will trip if he smells cologne on me."

Luckily he believed her and she was able to get out of that situation without having too much physical contact with him. She did agree to meet with him the next day to go shop for a phone. Of course he would have to have it connected in his name because she did not want anything associating her with him. Her plan was working. Soon the world would have one less snake slithering around. As much as she wanted to take him out right then, she knew she had to bide her time. The plan was for him to die *without* her going to jail for murder.

No one could have told her that he would fall for her like he did so quickly. After he got her the phone he called her every evening. He would send her kisses through the phone before they hung up. She thought that was so lame. The two of them had met for a few dates and each time he tried to have sex with her. He was fed a line that her dad had her checked periodically to make sure she was still a virgin. Technically, as far as vaginal penetration was concerned, she was. But he was persistent. So even though it pained her, she did allow him to eat her pussy.

She hated her body for betraying her because he made her come over and over again. His tongue worked like a magician's wand. It did wonders. During one of their times together, he confessed his love for her. Said that he never knew a woman like her. He thought she was nineteen. He went on to say that he could see himself settling down with her. *This has to end*, she thought, before things got out of hand and she was unable to stop it. It was time.

≈

Tameka and her sister Tranique were six hours away on the bus. They were the mules being used to bring the dope to Oklahoma City. Leo got to Chuck in time and they changed the drop-off and pick-up date. D-Snake would fail again. The day of the drop off, Leo met the girls at the bus station. The driver helped everyone with their luggage and once the girls had their bags they immediately went to the hotel and took care of their business. Chuck flew to Oklahoma and met the group at the hotel. Everything went off without a hitch. A Kansas dealer named Tre', got his product and Chuck got all his money. He kicked Leo down with some funds as a 'thank you' for looking out for him.

Leo took the money he had received and gave it to the young girls who turned out to be thirteen and fourteen years old. It shook him to his core to see babies transporting dope. The girls wanted to stay in the city and explore but Leo was not having it. He told them that for safety reasons he was putting them on the first flight back to Los Angeles. Before boarding the plane Leo told the girls about the dangers of the dope game. At the end of his speech, the girls were crying.

"And I don't want to hear that either of you are trafficking dope again. I have ways of finding out too."

He decided to help these girls and their family in California. Their older brother, who was only eighteen, was taking care of his four siblings, who ranged in age from nine to fourteen years old. He breathed a sigh of relief when he got back into his car after watching the girls board and take off. His work here was almost finished.

But Honesty's had just begun.

≈

D-Snake rented an apartment in a seedy complex on the south side of the city where all the junkies lived. The manager rented to anyone with money and didn't bother asking for rental or work history. His inattentiveness was just what Honesty was counting on today. She went to the apartment to spruce it up. Adding a few flower petals and lit some candles to give it a romantic feel. He had given her a key to his place the night she first let him give her oral sex. They still had not had any relations beyond that. Honesty had put on a pair of hospital gloves before she touched the door or anything in the house. Things were going well for her.

≈

The bus that the girls were supposed to be on pulled into the station as scheduled. D-Snake and a dude he had convinced to help him were there. Two girls who matched the girl's descriptions got off the bus. The dudes immediately went to them and introduced themselves. Because the men before them were so handsome, the girls did not think that they were in any danger. They were two hicks from Pine Bluff, Arkansas, looking to hit it big in the grand old State of Oklahoma. Men didn't look like this where they were from. *Wait until I tell the girls about this when I get home,* one of them thought. The guys offered them a ride to their hotel and they gladly accepted.

Once they pulled away from the bus station, all games were off. D-Snake gave his accomplice a gun and the young man turned around in the front seat and aimed at the girls. D-Snake laughed maniacally when they screamed.

"We gon' get a room and get the dope from y'all then we will let you leave. Cool?" The guy named Paul said.

"The dope? Wh- What dope? What are you talking about?" The short girl named Quan said nervously. "Don't be playing all innocent with me, we just want the yayo and we can bounce."

"You must have us mixed up with someone else. We don't have any dope."

Paul grabbed a bag and began to rifle through it. There were only clothes and shoes inside. Out of anger, he back handed, Sheena, the owner of the bag.

"Stop the bullshit, bitch. Give us the shit and let us move on. If you two cooperate you'll live," he said and then hit Quan in the mouth with the butt of his gun, busting her lip.

"Please don't hurt us. We promise we don't know what you are talking about."

"Man this is bullshit D-Snake. What the fuck is going on here? You said we were gonna hit a lick. Ten kilo's remember? If you done got me into some shit I swear I will kill you cuz!"

"Man fuck you. Check the other bag."

He did. Nothing. They were really pissed off now. Paul pounded the dash board with his fist so hard the glove box came open.

"Cuz, I swear your ass is full of shit!" Paul said angrily.

The car stopped at the red light, Paul said "kiss my ass bitch," and jumped out of the car, heading to the corner store. He was done with the mess. There he used the pay phone to spread the word about what D-Snake had done. He had no clue what he was about to do.

His leaving like that left an extremely angry D-Snake with two very frightened young ladies. He drove west on Reno Avenue and the more he drove the angrier he got and the faster he drove. In a matter of minutes he had driven them to a wooded lake. With his gun pointed at the girls, he led them into the thicket of bushes and trees. In a secluded area, he made them strip completely naked. They shivered in fear with their teeth chattering and skin growing chill bumps from the cold.

"I am going to give y'all one final chance to tell me what I wanna know."

Again they denied any knowledge of dope and begged and pleaded with him to let them go. D-Snake didn't believe they weren't the girls he was after.

Shaking his head, he said, "enough of this shit!"

He walked to the trunk of his car and got out some gray electrical tape. First, he made Quan tape Sheena's hands behind her, her legs, and cover her mouth with a strip of tape. Next he did the same thing to Quan. They were in a kneeling prayer position when he finished. Finally he shot one, then the other, execution style.

Back at the car he searched their bags and found their Arkansas state issued identification, clothes, shoes, and their bus tickets. His stomach dropped to his feet. They had been telling him the truth all along. He had killed the wrong girls and fucked up. Again. Still angry and now disappointed, he drove back to his apartment.

Honesty was waiting for him when he walked through the door, wearing a pink t-shirt and panties only, playing the popular song with the same title. Bad news traveled fast and word had already gotten to her what went down. She knew he killed the girls. But she pretended like she didn't know what happened and ushered him into the small dining room, sitting him in a chair that faced her.

"I have something for you, baby." A huge smile spread across his face.

She walked around his chair seductively and let him know he was in for a big surprise as she pulled the shirt over her head, revealing two very ripe, firm breasts. She placed a blind fold over his eyes.

"So you can't see when I am getting ready to touch you. Anticipation and the element of surprise will make this better baby. Trust me."

Unfortunately for him, he did. She pulled his hands behind the chair and cuffed them individually to the wrought iron bars.

"So you can't touch me," she explained.

He started to complain about that but stopped short when she touched his crotch and slid his zipper down.

"One moment, I forgot to do something."

With a couple of silk scarves, she tied each of his legs to the chair. He was now immobile. With him secure, she continued her mission. Soft fingers released his member through the opening of his boxer shorts. He almost tipped the chair over when he felt the hot mouth on the head of his hard shaft.

He started to squirm in his seat. His breathing became hard and ragged as wet lips gave his dick a bath. Slowly and gently he was sucked and caressed until he violently released his seed into his partners mouth.

"Did you like that baby?" Honesty asked seductively.

"Hell, yeah!"

"Good."

Leaving him blind-folded and secure, she asked, "would you ever lie to me baby?" As she dressed.

"Nah, girl. You know I wouldn't."

"Really? Then why did you tell me your name is Love instead of D-Snake? You are D-Snake aren't you?"

"What the fuck! How you know that? Untie me and get me out of these cuffs. We need to talk."

"Okay let's talk. Do you remember Goldie and his wife Silver?"

He inhaled sharply, making his chest puff up. But he did not answer.

"Yeah, I thought you would. Hell, you ought to. You killed them."

"What you talking about. I ain't killed no damned body."

"Tsk, tsk, Let's not lie anymore shall we? We can play a game. You like games don't you? A game like, I'll show you mine if you show me yours. But I'll call it, I'll tell you my truth if you tell me yours. Ladies first. I know you killed them, Gina, the two girls at the lake, and you *tried* to kill Giana in Dallas."

"How the fuck you know that!" Saliva gathered at the corners of his mouth like a rabid dog.

"You have been followed everyday for the past year."

"Why you doing all this? This ain't got shit to do with you Ray."

"On the contrary, boo-boo. This has everything to do with me. Tell me something, what did you think was going to happen to that little girl when you killed her parents?"

"What little girl? Goldie's? Hell if I know."

"You didn't care either. Well their daughter saw you kill her parents. Saw you and Seven come into the room that night and saw *you* kill them."

"Cuz how the hell you know this? That bitch ass nigga Seven told you didn't he? He talk to fucking much. I should have killed him when I had the chance."

"No, he didn't tell me. I know this because *I* am their daughter." Tears welled up in her eyes but did not spill over. "I was in the middle of them."

"What you just say? You were there? Cuz, you can't be that little girl. You nineteen. That little girl was like three or fo'."

"Silly rabbit. I am her. I was six at the time. Small, but six years old nonetheless, and now I'm sixteen. I lied to you about my age. You remember Leo, don't you? He called and had Chuck move the shipment up. It went down already. You don't play a very good game. You lose. Tell him what his consolation prize is, Bob." Imitating a game show announcer's voice, she said, "you have won a one way ticket to hell."

"Fuck you, bitch! When I get outta here, I'ma kill yo' ass."

She tuned out the string of curse words he flung her way and walked over to the stereo, increasing the volume full blast. Honesty looked at D-Snake with his soft, but still long, shaft lying on his thigh and shook her head. *What a waste. I bet he knew how to use that thing too,* she thought. Under different circumstances, she would have given him the time of day. Careful not to dwell on that though, she focused on the moment. She had something to do, and this was not business. This was personal.

The razor that had materialized was sharp enough to cut air. Gloved hands touched D-Snake and with the ease of a skilled swordsman, came down and sliced him. He could not see what happened but he knew. The pain coursed through his body. Tears ran down his face and his screams, no matter how loud they were, went unheard. His manhood was just detached from his body.

"Shut the fuck up, you pussy!" His penis was shoved into his mouth to silence him. Bleach then followed, poured into his mouth over his meat in an attempt to erase any traces of DNA from the blow job he received just moments before. "This is for my parents," she said and his throat was sliced from ear to ear. He was dead.

All traces of her ever being there were picked up and placed into a black duffle bag. With that done, she pulled a hooded sweatshirt over her head, gave the apartment a final once over, and left out. There was a black van on the corner that had been sitting there since she arrived. She walked over to it and the side door slid open.

"Get in," the man said. "We need to talk about what just happened in that apartment."

She got in and opened the duffle bag and pulled out two small bags. "What just happened in that apartment?" She questioned handing the man and his partner each a bag.

"Nothing," they both said.

"Thank you both. I could not have done this without you."

The woman spoke first. "Girl, that was the best dick I had in years. Believe me, it was my pleasure."

Honesty laughed.

"Don't worry lil' lady. We always had your back. Just like your folks had ours."

"You really know how to handle a knife."

"That's from all those years of cleaning fish and skinning 'coons and such."

She grimaced at the visual. The older coupled laughed at the face she made, then they all exhaled. It was over. But the black van was not the only vehicle out there for her. Detective Dunleevy followed her too. He was a self-appointed bodyguard of sorts. When he saw her come out the apartment he went in. He made sure there was nothing left behind that could implicate her. She had dropped her school I.D. card. He picked it up, put it in his pocket and called the crime in. Honesty was clueless. OCPD never did solve that case. Then again, they really did not try very hard. "Uncle Dun" had save the day.

That night changed her. Matured her. It was time for her to let go. In the few weeks to follow Honesty grew apart from Nitro and they called it quits. One night, a couple of years later, before she got into her bed, she looked at herself in the mirror and boldly proclaimed,

"I am Honesty Mitchell. And I determine my destiny."

CHAPTER NINE

She was the baddest bitch. In two weeks she would be twenty-one and moving on her own and her trust fund would be under her control. She couldn't wait. When Kim and Leo said that she could move out, she wanted to immediately celebrate her independence. But she'd have time for kicking it soon enough. The five bedroom, four bathroom ranch-style home she'd inherited was going to be her new home.

Desiree, her best friend, was moving in with her. Their parents were concerned about the two of them being in that big house by themselves so they asked their other friend, Essence, to move in with them. She was the other member of their click. They all met during their junior year of high school. That year, Essence introduced the two girls to a credit card scam.

Essence had asked them if they all wanted to dress alike at school. Agreeing that was a great idea they made plans to meet the next day. Honesty and Desiree were on an allowance and had already hit their parent's up for more than they should have that week. But Essence assured them she had it.

"That will be $3,157.89. Cash or Credit?" The clerk asked.

"Credit." Essence handed her the card, got the receipt and the trio was on their way.

They had already met Essence's mother and been to their house so they knew that they were living well and not hurting for money. But Ms. Lewis didn't play that. When they would be at the house looking at magazines that had expensive clothes in it and would say that they wanted something out of it she'd always say, "money don't grow on trees." Especially not three grand.

When folks said that that usually meant that you couldn't get anything that expensive. But the very thing that Essence's mother would say she couldn't have, would be the very thing she would come up with, within the next week or two. They were puzzled at how she got it. The clothes she wore were not sold anywhere in Oklahoma City. They were things one had to travel to buy. Rule out shoplifting. Something was crooked though. They just didn't know what.

"Yo, Essie, how come you didn't tell us your mom gave you your own credit card?"

"Cause you didn't ask."

"Come on now; don't just leave it at that. Tell us what's up. The real deal."

"You want the truth? Y'all can't handle the truth."

"Bitch please. With the things that me and Des have seen, oh we can handle it alright. So what's good?"

"Okay, I'll tell you. But not here."

Honesty and Desiree wondered why she was being so secretive. Essence was savvy. If she was making them wait on information then it had to be worth waiting for. What she had to tell them would change their outlook on a whole bunch of shit. It would make Honesty look at Kim in a new light too.

Understandably she didn't want to talk in public. They were hungry so they stopped by a fast food restaurant and grabbed some food and then headed home. Essence was acting weird. Like she was high or something. Her friends needed to know before they walked into the house and ran into Mrs. Louella. That woman could spot a person on dope fifty feet away and wouldn't mind telling Leo that her friends were junkies.

"Why are you acting so strange? Did you pop a pill or hit the joint when we were at the food place?"

"No, nothing like that. It's just that when I talk about this thing we do it gives me a rush."

"Who are *we*?"

"Me and my mother bitch, that's who."

"You have got to be kidding me. Your mom?"

"Yep. Listen, we're here at your house so wait a few more seconds and I'll tell you. Pinky swear. Since I bought the clothes one of you bitches pay the taxi."

Once they got into the house Honesty called out to see if Kalif or Ms. Louella were around. No one answered. When she walked into the kitchen she saw a note on the fridge saying that they all went to see Kalif sing at some program. They had the house to themselves. The girls headed towards the bedroom but Honesty suggested that they eat in the dining room. That way they could see who was coming up to the house through the window and know when to change the conversation.

"So what's this conspiracy that we've been waiting to hear about and how is it that your ass just dropped a small wad on us?"

"First things first. Did you know that Kim knows my mom?"

"My Kim? Naw, I didn't know that. She never mentioned it."

"Well she does. They used to do business together back in the day. Then your moms got out the game."

"What game? What are you talking about?"

"Credit card cloning. That's what I'm talking about."

"Credit card what?"

"Glad to know you're still among the living Desiree. You were a bit quiet there for a minute. Credit card cloning. That's what my mom does and she taught me how to do it. It sounds like small fries but it's really not."

"How is it done?" Desiree and Honesty asked at the same time.

"Well my mom has friends all over. She pays them a small fee to capture the credit card information of cards that they run. When they do that, they give her the information and she goes and produces a duplicate. It's that simple."

"You call that simple? Where and how does she make a duplicate?"

"Now that I can't tell you. Only because I don't know. But she has a friend from New York and he does all kinds of white collar schemes and shit. He is the one who actually makes the cards. He and mama are partners."

"Essence, won't your mama get mad at you for telling us all this? I mean, this isn't some shit that you really sit at the table and talk about with your friends."

"Girl my mama knows she can trust me. We've already had this talk. And let's face it, yawls parents ain't exactly on the up and up either. We all have skeletons in our closet."

"You're right about that. Forgive me for acting like a blond, but I just don't get it," Desiree admitted.

"Look here. Once we get the credit card number and all the other vital information, my mom gets it to dude. He then works his magic and turns that number into a real, plastic credit card. Once that's done, he then sends the cards back to my mother and we go and do whatever we want with them."

"So how much does your mom have to pay him?"

"Now you in her business," Essence said laughing. "Just joking. She doesn't pay him anything because he keeps half the cards for himself. It's a pretty good partnership that has worked for quite some time."

"Okay. So that's how you paid for our gear today?"

"Yep. Listen guys, I know you all don't know this, but me and my mama are on welfare."

"What the fuck? Bitch you're lying!"

They couldn't believe this. Essence and her family lived in a house right down the street from them and had almost the same shit, if not better, than they had. Her mom always had money and Essie was always super fly. So were her brother and sister. All of them looked like they had stepped off a page from the hottest magazine.

"I know it seems strange but it's the truth. Our house is not paid for like most people think. We're on Section 8. Our rent is only two hundred and fifty dollars a month."

"Two fifty? But that house looks just as good as ours and I know before Leo paid this house off they paid a high ass mortgage. Damn, your mama is a hustler for real."

"Yeah, she is that. She talked this couple into letting her use her voucher to get the house. They had never even heard of the program before but when she told them that it was guaranteed money they were all over it. We take care of that house because mama cut a deal with Mr. Lindsey and she's buying it now."

"Wow. This is something else. I didn't know that."

"Not many people do. I didn't want to tell you all at first but figured what the fuck. If y'all were my true friends then it wouldn't matter. If you weren't, then you all would turn your noses up at me right now and I would be on my way out the door."

"Girl, you're a part of us now. We don't care about anything so small as who pays the rent on your house or how your mom gets money. You're our dog. But tell me about Kim. I knew there were things about her past she wasn't telling me."

Essence explained that Kim used to do the same thing with her mother and the same guy. It was Kim who introduced her mom to, T.J. He was the guy who made the cards. Apparently he and Kim used to fuck around. They would go across the country using these cards in casinos and getting cash advances. Once all three of them had hit the same casino twice, they would move on. Each of them had a certain amount of cash that they were supposed to ask for. At the end of the day, they would sit in their hotel room and count up the loot. They split it three ways That way, one person did not get the lion's share.

Kim had been a very naughty girl. Essence said that Kim probably still had some cards somewhere around the house because when she quit, she didn't give her stash to anyone. That piqued Honesty's interest. If there were some loaded credit cards around this house, her ass was determined to find them.

They cleaned up their mess and went on a scavenger hunt. They were excited. This was crazy. Kim was doing it like that? Who knew? Her ass was sneaky though. Honesty should have known. That just goes to show that you never really know a person no matter how long you live with them. The first place they looked was the attic. Leo had been moving boxes from their room and storing them up there. What made her think about these particular boxes was that they didn't have any markings on them. That was not like Kim. She had to label each box so that she wouldn't have to open each one to find what was inside.

The attic was the only place they had to look. They hit the jack pot. In the first box they found it contained about ninety credit cards and a whole bunch of documents that meant nothing to them. The second box had calling cards in it. They took a few of those as well to sell around school.

With everything put back the way they found it, they went back downstairs. It was still a shock what Essence told them but it was starting to sink in. This was something that they could do together.

The three of them became closer as a result of that discovery. Over the years they hit up hundreds of stores. Them moving in together would only solidify their bond and they could hustle at leisure and buy what they wanted. They would no longer have to sneak things in and hide them. It was going to be great.

One of the greatest things about their house was that it sat on a nice parcel of land and they didn't have any neighbors directly next door. That is how Goldie wanted it when he had the house built for Silver all those years ago. It had never been occupied. Now it was Honesty's. Leo made sure the house received the latest upgrades and the in ground pool in the back was treated. There was also a gazebo that sat right next to it with a built in bar-b-que pit that he had painted. This summer was going to be off the chain for them.

On one of their most recent capers, they met a couple of fine dudes who were cousins. Devan and Delante' Campbell. Devan liked Desiree and Delante' liked Honesty. Essence was not with them that day. Delante' and Honesty had seen one another three times since their first date. He was cool people. Him and his cousin. Devan was exactly the kind of guy that Desiree needed. Hard enough not be a punk, but soft enough to be a real man. They were truly made for one another. Desiree was in love. That was something that Honesty longed to have one day, too. Devan said that they had another cousin who they thought Essence might like. When the girls told her about him she said that she would have to see.

"You guys know how much I hate being fixed up. Er'time I turn around it's the same things. That's one of my pet peeves. Ugh," Essence said.

The next weekend Delante and Devan helped them all move in. Leo was happy to have the male company. Rafael, Desiree's dad was too busy watching the golf network to help him do any serious lifting so he was happy for them to be there. The mother's were busy trying to picture this here or that there when it came to decorating ideas. They all looked sour when Desiree of all people said "This is our place and it's up to us and us alone to decide what we'll do with it. So thank you for your suggestions but no thanks."

Her mother looked liked she swallowed a canary. Kim looked proud. It was rare that Des had something to say so when she did, it was nice to hear it said so boldly. The day was shaping into a fun day despite the shutdown of the decorators. The mood was light. They were in the presence of good company.

Rafi had ordered some pizzas to eat. Essence heard some music outside and thought it was the delivery guy so Rafael gave her the money and she went to get the food. When she didn't come back in ten minutes Honesty went out after her. There standing in the front yard with Essence, was the eighth wonder of the world, Dante' Campbell.

So this was the other cousin that Devan tried to fix her up with? Da-mn, this bruh is fine too. The Campbell family had some bomb ass genes. And I can't wait to get into Delante's, Honesty thought.

While they were outside ogling this man, the pizza guy drove up. Essence didn't move. Honesty took the money out of her hand and paid the man. Dante' packed the boxes into the house and was introduced to everyone. Essie hadn't said a word. Honesty was tickled because Shemar Moore deuce had just rendered her best friend speechless. She hooked up with him that day. It was the three best friends with three cousins. They were all in.

CHAPTER TEN

Over the next few months, the girls spent a lot of time moving in and getting the house together. They were excited being on their own and the newness still hadn't worn off. The parents started calling their house the' Ranch'. It looked just like one. Each of them did their own rooms up in style. Essence and Desiree had such similar tastes that it wasn't even funny. Had it not been for Honesty, they would have ended up having the exact same rooms. Both of them had the nerve to be mad at the other when they came home with the same shit. It was funny because they had gone to two different places. Just goes to show you that great minds really do think alike.

Honesty had a gorgeous mahogany cherry wood queen sized sleigh bed with all the coordinating pieces. Her room had a more mature look. Contemporary yet old fashioned. She wanted her room to look good when Delante came to visit. They'd been seeing one another since January.

It was now almost the end of May. They still hadn't had sex. But the natives were getting restless. It's not that she didn't want to give it to him; she wanted to take her time. Ever since Nitro, she had a hard time even thinking about having vaginal sex. He had told her so many times that her kitty was supposed to be for her husband, she believed him. Honesty doubted that she would ever get married but she wanted to save that part of her for a man she truly loved. *If* he ever materialized. Dee was cool when they were together though. He was content so far just letting her jack him off. She wouldn't even go down on him because her brain game was the bomb

"What's it like?" Delante asked one day.

"It's like sucking marbles through a straw, baby," she answered seductively.

"Damn! I can't wait to find out." Yet, she made him wait.

Saturday they had a cookout. Everyone looked forward to it. Dante' had showed on previous occasions that he was the man to beat in the kitchen so they gave him free reign on the grill. Leo had called the pool guy out to come and fill the pool and balance the chemicals. But no parents were allowed. Kalif came though. They hadn't done much together since he started seeing stars and shit. He wanted to become an R&B singer. She thought this would be a good thing to share with her little brother. After all, he was growing up and pretty soon would be graduating from high school.

She let him invite a few of his friends from school so that he'd have people there his own age. He took it upon himself to invite ten of his closest buddies. They needed more food. Those growing kids were about to eat them out of house and home. Or try to at the very least.

Dante' had the grill working over time. The girls made the potato salad and baked beans. Everyone who was invited ended up bringing something good. Around noon the sun started to put in some work on its own. It was getting hot outside and Honesty wanted to show off her new two-piece Chanel bathing suit.

"I'll be back. I'm going to go in and change into my swim suit; it's time to take a dip."

Everyone nodded to let her know they heard her. Her plan was to rest for a few minutes when she got in her room. They'd been doing things around the house since eight that morning. That wouldn't have been a problem but they didn't go to sleep until five in the morning.

When she stepped in her bedroom to change Delante was right behind her. She gasped when she turned around because he was so quiet. She didn't say anything to him. His eyes had a strange look in them. He didn't say anything to her. Instead he placed his finger over her lips as if to say "sshhh."

He walked her to her bathroom and undressed her. He lifted her up and sat her on the vanity. She didn't know what he was going to do next until he bent down and sniffed her pussy. The man was a freak.

"You smell so sweet. I can't wait to see how you taste."

He loved on her gently with his mouth, keeping his fingers over her lips so that she wouldn't make any noise. That was not easy to do. He licked on her clit until it was stiff. She was so hot and wet for him. Her juices started to flow as she gyrated on the counter top. He really went to work then. Ate that shit up like it was his last meal. He couldn't get enough of her. She was losing control and needed to feel him deep inside her. This was not the way she planned their first time to be, but hell it would work for her.

She kept trying to pull him up to her by his shoulders but he wouldn't budge. She moaned to let him know she wanted to feel all of him. But she didn't know what the holdup was. His tongue was stiff as he stuck it into her pussy. *My, my, my, it feels like a small hard dick.* He rubbed his tongue over her clit over and over until she cried out in a pain like pleasure. Her head fell back and her thighs got tense.

"I'm cumming, baby." Like a volcano she erupted in his mouth.

He stayed between her thighs until her quakes subsided. She needed a cigarette. That was intense and she loved it. If this was his way of telling her that it was time for them to get busy then she heard him loud and clear.

Dee stood up and held her bikini out to her and prepared to leave. Before he left out the door he turned around, walked back over to her, and kissed her long and hard on the mouth. She groaned again. His fingers slid into her still drenched pussy as he worked her back into another frenzy. He stopped kissing her, licked his bottom lip and leaned into her and whispered, "It gets greater later."

Her head was spinning. The man had her going crazy. She could not wait to be with him. When she was done with him, he would not want to go anywhere. The question was, would she? She couldn't afford to be getting sprung off no dick. Nobody's. No matter how good it was.

She took a quick shower and tried to pull herself together. There were too many people outside for her to go out there looking like she had just been fucked well. Even if it was the truth. She didn't want her little brother to see her in that condition. Giving herself a once over in the mirror, she decided that it was safe to face the guests.

Desiree and Essence gave her the side eye when she joined them. They had questions. She didn't want to give them any answers. Unfortunately, there was no way around that. Her girls would demand to know what just went on. She'd have to tell them.

"Bitch, what was your ass in there doing? Let me look at you real good."

"Essence, please keep your voice down. I'm not trying to have half of Oklahoma City in my business. I wasn't doing anything either. Thank you very much."

"Don't give us that shit. Your ass was gone way too long. Now give us the scoop."

"Well, there's really not much to say except that he followed me to my room, undressed me and proceeded to give me the best head I've ever received."

"What the fuck you say?"

"You heard me."

"But I thought that you all hadn't, that you hadn't given him any yet?"

"We haven't and I haven't. I guess this was his way of showing me what I've been missing."

"Don't keep us waiting. Was it worth it? The wait, I mean."

"Yes and then some. My pussy was the main course and he was the fat man at the buffet."

"That's our girl. So what are you going to do? You gonna give him some or what?"

"Yes I is. To – night is the night," she sang.

None of Delante's boys questioned him during the time he was away. Either they already knew what was up before he left or they just didn't care. She was sure that he hadn't told them that they weren't getting down. He was too much of a player not to be getting pussy. And if he was getting it, he wasn't getting it from her.

They couple kept looking at each other all shy like. It was funny. She really liked him and thought that they had made a connection. Being with him was good for her. She hadn't had guys at her home before so this was new and exciting. She couldn't say that she loved Dee because she didn't use that word loosely, but it was something close to it.

She didn't know if it was time for her to love. She really wanted to. They had been doing so many scams since they moved into the house and stacking money, which was great, but she didn't have anything tangible to come home to. She wanted a family of her own. No one understood what she was talking about though. She tried talking to Kim about it but all she said was "you are too young to start a family."

Family to Honesty didn't mean having a baby and she knew that's what Kim was talking about. But she wanted more than that. She wanted a man to come home to who would welcome her with open arms. A man who put her needs ahead of his own and his homeboys. Someone who would love and cherish her for the woman that her mom, Silvia, started raising her to be. The woman that Kim had finished raising. What she really wanted was a husband. But she wouldn't find him until she was ready. Ready to be a wife.

Dee walked over to where Honesty stood and rubbed her shoulders.

"Your little bro has a good head on his shoulders."

"I know. I tell him that often."

"Yeah" he said, "I know, but it never hurts for him to hear from someone else." He added.

He was right too. Kalif was coming up a great young man. She missed her mom and dad every day but couldn't be mad at Kal for having some great parents by his side. Leo was doing a wonderful job with him. With both of them. The fact that Honesty decided to fuck with those credit cards and shit didn't have anything to do with them, it was all her. She was born to hustle. There was something deep inside her that drove her to get more. Do more. Have more.

It was getting late and Kalif had to get home. He was doing a show in Dallas, Texas the next day and he had to get home so he could get his stuff together. Delante offered to take him home. The guys ribbed him about it.

"Yeah you want to take little dude home so that your ass ain't got to help us clean up and shit. You ain't slick, man. We know your type."

"Cuz, it's not even like that. There are some things that I wanted to talk to him about. You know, one on one."

"Mm hmm, you trying to bond with the brother and get in good with Honesty so that you can *get in good with Honesty.*"

"Don't play me cuz. After what happened this afternoon, I'm already in good."

"Do your thug thizzell, we ain't mad at you."

"I plan on it. Now let me get him home before I wake up and have a gang of Rasta's standing over me."

He drove Kalif home and they talked about everything from sex and girls to music and sports before they made it. Dee was the first guy that Honesty had allowed to be around Kal so this was a milestone for the siblings. She didn't want just anyone meeting her family. There were some things that she wanted to keep private.

Even with Oklahoma being as small as it was, only a few people vaguely remembered what had happened to her parents. Things had a tendency to get old fast. Even though they did not know if all the people were caught, they never ran the piece on the news as an unsolved crime. She wasn't upset about that either.

One of her friend's cousins was killed in a dope house in the country. There were a few women over there and they all either sold dope, smoked dope or both. All of them ended up shot to death. It was said that they owed some Jamaicans money for dope that they received and never paid for, but no one really knew. Leo never said anything but he looked like he knew what happened. The news networks reran that story every few years. Still to this day, it goes unsolved and no one knows what happened to those five women in Spencer, Oklahoma. It was awful that none of the family's had closure. Honesty knew who killed her family and she still didn't have the closure she sought. She couldn't imagine how they felt.

Dee was hitting a nerve with her. As good as it was with them, there was something that was missing. Essence said that she was making something out of nothing but that was not the case. He was a great guy and they did great things together business wise and personally, but it wasn't all that it was cracked up to be. She wanted to get to know him on a serious tip and find out where his head was at.

As much as she wanted to learn about him, tonight was not the night. Tonight they were going to make love for the very first time. When she heard his car pull off she hurried to get her room together. It was about to be on. She placed candles strategically around the room so that the glow from them would cast a pretty light from her body when she walked into the room. She planned to come out in a black silk Kimono and nothing else. Her body was aching for him and been since that erotic episode in the bathroom earlier.

Right after she finished tidying her bedroom, she saw headlights from the drive way. Dee was back. She gave him her key to let himself in so that she wouldn't have to come out and ruin her surprise for him. The covers were turned back on the bed and the scented candles had the room looking and smelling good. This was it. Today's sampling was just a taste of what he could do. Soon, she was going to have him downtown like he was on an eight hour job. *I hope he ate his Wheaties today.*

"I'll be out in a minute baby. Get comfortable," she said from the bathroom.

"A'ight. Take your time. But not too much."

"Oh, I won't. Hey, will you push play on the CD player?"

"Sure thing."

The next thing you heard was some Usher playing. *Oh yeah, we were going to take it nice and slow tonight.* It didn't matter how old that track was, it was still certifiable baby making music. He didn't hear her come out. He looked good standing in his boxers. His back was nice and cut. The candles cast soft reflections of light off of it. So very sexy.

"I'm ready for you baby. Are you ready for me?"

When he turned around she let her robe fall to the floor. His eyes traveled up and down taking in a full view. She turned slowly so that he could see her round ass. It was an original apple bottom. Since he was enjoying the view from the back side she decided to give him a show. Her ass cheeks began to bounce up and down and then she made them clap for him. He was rock hard when she turned back around.

Slowly he walked over to her. She was so excited. With her two index fingers she slid his shorts down. His Mandingo dick jumped out at her. Someone was happy to see her. She dropped to her knees and looked into his eyes as she took his shaft into her mouth. Never taking her eyes off him, her head moved back and forth. At first she was going slowly. His eyes rolled back. Her jaws clamped down even tighter and she began to suck harder. She wanted everything he had.

He rested his hands on her head. It turned her on to see him reacting like this. Her left hand came up the inside of his thigh slowly. With the same hand she cupped his nuts in her hand and began to massage them like tension balls. Her long fingers squeezed and released in a pattern. Suck, squeeze, suck, squeeze. He never knew what hit him.

It was time to go in for the kill. Giving his balls one last squeeze, she took both of her hands, cupped his ass cheeks, and pulled all of him into her mouth. Deep throat. Her eyes never left his face. She could feel his body begin to shake. He was about to shoot. *I'm not like these other bitches out here. I finished the job. Every drop.* And she did just that.

Dee was still hard. She wanted to continue to show him what she could do. She took the condom out of his hand, opened it, and began to put it on him with her mouth. He never had that done before. That much was obvious. She put it on Dee like a porno star. She got on her knees at the edge of the bed and rolled her ass in the air, bouncing it up and down for him. Her knees slid apart to expose herself a little bit more. His skin brushed hers when he stepped up behind her. Just as the tip of his penis touched her vagina, she moved forward.

"No baby, not there. The other one."

He slid into her nicely. Fit just like a glove. It was wild. He loved her thoroughly. His thrusts were coming faster and harder. She called out his name. He grabbed her hair. They bucked until they both exploded. He wasn't through with her yet. She wasn't through with him either. They had sex all night long. But never vaginally. In the morning she was tired and sore. He had her legs going every which way but loose.

After they made love for the last time, Dee took her into his arms and kissed her. It was so passionate. She laid her head on his chest. He stroked her back and rubbed her ass. They let the ceiling fan dry their bodies. His lips caressed the top of her head. Before falling asleep, she heard him softly whisper, “I love you, Honesty.” Her heart stopped. She couldn’t say the same.

CHAPTER ELEVEN

Honesty had a dream last night. In it, she was in a store and had just written a fourteen thousand dollar check with ease. Everyone in the store was attentive to her and willing to do all that she asked of them. They smelled money on her. She walked like money and talked like money. It was time to make money.

While she was still dreaming she saw herself using checks with extremely high check numbers. That was how she was able to get the things she really wanted. There had to be a way to make that happen. Her dreams were not always just dreams though. They meant something. Usually they *meant* what she dreamt. Hopefully, this was one of those things.

She got out of bed careful not to wake Dee and she went to take care of her morning breath and hygiene. Stank breath and a stank cat early in the morning? That's a no-no. They used a half box of condoms last night and her little body was worn out. She needed a hot bath to soothe it.

Dee woke up just as she was getting out of the tub. He came into the bathroom with her. The toilet seat was up so he put it down and sat to talk to her. She figured that it was time to get some answers to the questions that she had. She would see if he was open and honest like she needed him to be.

"Baby, there are some things on my mind that I've wanted to talk to you about. Some questions that I'd like answers to."

"Okay. I'm an open book. Ask away."

"So tell me, how is it that a sexy ass man like you have been available for so long?"

"I don't like bullshit. Most of the females that I've been meeting have been coming with nothing but and I ain't down with that."

"So you haven't had anyone special in your life?"

"A few months before I met you there was a woman who I thought I was in love with, but that turned out to be infatuation."

"How did you know that it wasn't love?"

"When she started to show her true colors I realized that I wasn't in to her as much as she was in to me. She had a lot of things going on in her life. I had to ask myself if I was willing to stick around until she worked through her issues. I wasn't. I knew then that I wasn't in love with her. I loved her but I wasn't *in love* with her. When you love someone for real, you'll be there no matter what they're going through."

"So you just abandoned her while she was in the midst of an issue? Nice guy. Remind me not to cry around you."

"No, see it wasn't even like that. Her issues were not those kinds. It was her family. She has a bang of sisters and they're always in need of this, that or the other and they come to her when they need it. But when she's in need of something then she can't ever go to them. I told her that they were using her and that she needed to tell them no sometimes. She gave them her last and then wouldn't have anything of her own. I got tired of her letting them do her like that."

"I think it's funny that you speak of her situation in the present tense. Are you still involved with her? And are you mad at her for giving things to her sisters and not giving them to you? Surely you can't expect a woman to turn her back on her blood for a good lay right?"

"Oh, is that all I am to you? A good lay? And no, I don't want her to give me anything. I can take care of myself. I'm a hustler baby; I just want you to know."

"Funny. But you didn't answer my question."

"Which one? You came at me with so many."

"Are you still involved with her?"

"How can I be involved with anyone when I spend all my time with you? And when we ain't together you know where I am and who I'm with."

"That doesn't mean anything. You could still be fucking with her. She just might be getting the short end of the stick from you right now."

"What is that supposed to mean?"

"That means you're neglecting her to be over here with me. That she thinks you all are still together but you're just out doing your thing. It's possible that you all could've had a fight and you left to clear your head or something. I dunno. Anything is possible. I need to know if I'm the only woman in your life."

He stood up next to her and turned her to face him. "Honesty, you are the only woman in my life. You are the only woman who I *want* in my life. You are the only woman who I need in my life."

"Good answer. So we've covered you and the other woman question to my satisfaction. But just because you don't have a woman that you're with, do you have any baby's mamas?"

"Nope. Not a one. I don't have any baby's mamas or any babies. Period."

"Why not?"

"What do you mean why not? Why should I? A man can't be single without any attachments?"

"No it's not that. *Why* was not the right thing to say, I meant to say do you want any children?"

"Yes I would love some kids. A whole bunch of them. Do you wanna be my first baby's mama?"

"Bzzz. Wrong answer, buddy. If, I have a baby by you, I'll be your one and only. Understood?"

"I didn't mean it like that. What I meant to say was do you wanna go half on a baby?"

"Yes I do, but not right now. Kid's aren't in my immediate plans. I have too much that I want to do and playing mommy isn't one of them."

"I feel you. So can I ask you a question?"

"Shoot."

"Why were you still single before I stepped to you?"

"I'm high maintenance. Dudes in the 'O' know that they have to step with something other than weak ass lines and pretty cars. I ain't a car ho and material things don't impress me. I make the money, the money doesn't make me. In order to be with me, a man has to be confident. He has to have a good head on his shoulders and he definitely has to have goals and dreams."

"What kind of goals of dreams? Money making things?"

"Not only that. I just told you money doesn't impress me. Without a dream, people perish. That's what Ms. Louella, my grandmother, has been telling me my whole life. I get it now. If a person doesn't aspire to be something better or do something better then they'll die. They won't die physically per se, but their spirit will. And sometimes that can be worse."

"Your grandmother was a wise person."

"Is baby, is. Let's keep her in the present. Lou-Lou is not dead."

"My bad. So what do you want to do as far as your life is concerned?"

"Well, I want to go to college. I was in the top ten percent of my high school graduating class. I was going to go to Howard but my folks didn't want me to go that far away. I started acting out because I felt that they were being unfair. Basically I told them that if I couldn't go there then I wasn't going to go anywhere. And I didn't. I cut off my nose to spite my face."

"It's not too late to go to college. My mom's is still in college and she's old."

"I don't think your mom would appreciate you calling her old. She might break you off something."

"Nah, she'll be a'ight. I said it with love."

"Okay. So what do you want to do? What are your goals?"

"I'd like to have my own chain of fast food restaurants. I'm good at computers but I want something that's going to be a need every day."

"People need computers every day."

"Yes they do, but not everyone can afford one. Everybody has to eat and a person will scrape up pennies for food."

"You're right about that. What are you doing?" She asked Dee as he began to touch her.

"I'm giving you something you can feel."

He dropped his boxers to reveal that he had a condom on and was ready for her. Standing behind her, he bent his knees just enough to enter her from the back. Her hands held her up against the counter. Dee pushed her so that she was leaning completely over the bathroom vanity. Then he started pumping harder.

They were going at it like dogs in heat. He knew exactly how to please her and what she liked. Her hand reached around to grab his ass. She thinks she told him to do it harder but her words may have come out mumbled. They must have been clear enough because he started to do just that. They came together.

"I just got out the bathtub, baby," she said out of breath

"We can take a shower together."

"Are we going to shower or are you going to keep messing with me?"

"Umm, we'll shower eventually."

"Please let me shower. I have places to go and people to see. I have business to take care of."

"You're the hold up. The quicker we get in the quicker we can get out."

That 'quicker' turned out to be an hour. The man's sexual appetite was veracious. He was insatiable. And so creative. The things he could do with a bar of soap. When they finally made it out the room. Devan had fixed breakfast and the others were sitting down eating. Everyone was laughing and joking about something that he said. He was a character. Honesty stood back and watched him watching Desiree. He loved her friend. It was like he was seeing her for the first time every time he looked at her. Like he was in awe of her. Honesty wanted a love like that too. Dee only looked at her like he wanted to tear her clothes off. Which he did. But she wanted more than sex.

Dee and Honesty walked over and joined the group for breakfast. He held her chair out and told her to have a seat. He was going to cater to her. After their workout session, she was starving like Marvin.

Everyone finished eating and Honesty called the girls into the office.

She started the meeting off.

"Ladies, I had a dream last night that's about to take our hustle to the next level. We're about to have haters for real. Are y'all ready?"

"Umm, before we start with the meeting, I have something that I need to tell you all."

"What is it Des?"

"You guys know that I love you so much. There's nothing that I wouldn't do for you. We've been throu-"

"Just get to the point bitch we ain't got all damned day."

"Thanks Essence. You've always been patient. Devan asked me to marry him. I told him yes."

"What? Bitch you lying. Congratulations!" Essence screamed. Honesty looked on, smiling.

They jumped up and hugged their girl. This was great. Honesty was getting mad at herself though because she was not as happy as she should've been for her friend and she didn't understand why.

"I have something else to say so sit down."

"The next words out of your mouth better not be 'I'm pregnant' "

"No I'm not pregnant. I'm leaving the game. I don't wanna do any more schemes."

Silence. Neither Essence nor Honesty had anything to say. They couldn't believe their ears. They had been doing dirt together for so long that it was assumed they would continue until they all mutually decided to stop.

"Why do want to get out the game, Desi? Me and Honesty don't understand."

"Last week, when you almost got caught with that credit card that spooked me. I began to take stock of my life. Guys, we have money. Honesty, you and I both have trust funds. We have more clothes and shoes than the mall's themselves, shit I can't pronounce, and shit I'll never use. When is enough going to be enough? I'm tired. When the man of my dreams asked me to marry him, I knew that I couldn't continue down this path. Only two things can happen if we continue in this life, death or destruction. Let's get out now while we're still ahead."

"Devan put your ass up to this shit didn't he? His square, L-7 ass want you to be a fucking stay at home wife and mother and shit and he wants you to dis your girls. Fuck that bastard, Des. You don't need him."

"Essence, this is my decision. Believe it or not, I am capable of making my own decisions and

this is one of them. You're always trying to tell me what to do and how to do it and I am sick of it. I am tired. I don't want to go to jail. You've already been and it's obvious that you don't mind going back but I'm not trying to go."

Honesty just sat there and listened to them argue back and forth. There was nothing that she could say to her that would change her mind. They had been friends long enough for her to know when she was serious. Her friend was getting out the circle. And Honesty wasn't mad at her. She wanted to do that so many times. Too many times. But something kept pulling her back.

"Essence, Des, calm down. Arguing about this isn't going to solve anything. We're best friends. Sisters. Now is the time for us to pull together. Desiree, Essence and I love you very much also. We're so glad that you've met and will soon marry the man of your dreams. That's our desire also whether we want to admit it or not. I've known you long enough to know when you mean what you say. Getting out the game right now is good for you. We're still here for you. I'm not mad and neither is Essence. Are you Essie?"

"No. It's just that we're a circle and how can we be that when you're not here?"

"I'm not moving out Essie. I'll still be here. I'll just be doing different things. This fall I'll be starting school. I enrolled in college. I'm going the University of Oklahoma. Your girl is going to be a Sooner."

"Now that's what's up. Do your thing girl. We're here for you. Now let's get on with our meeting. Even though you're out of the game, Des, I want you to hear this too. I've come up with a new hustle. Bogus checks. Starting tomorrow, we'll go down to the homeless shelters and scout for people we can 'blow up.'"

"Blow up? What the hell are you talking about? I ain't blowing up shit. I ain't a killer."

"You're not intelligent either if you really think I'm talking about killing people. Blow up is going to be one of our new terms. It means that we'll get someone who doesn't have any active checking accounts, take them to the bank, open one, and write checks and get money on that account and boom, come up. Just like that," she finished, snapping her fingers.

"Okay, I see. That sounds good. But won't the banks be looking at that person funny when they mob in the bank smelling like last week's garbage?"

"Normally yes, but as an incentive to get their information, we will offer them perks. Set them up in a nice hotel, get them some fresh gear, and groom them. They will open the accounts, but it will be us who writes the checks. With the birth certificates they give us, we can get a picture I.D. in their names. It will have their names on it, but our face."

"Damn, that is good. If I was still down, I would do that. That's almost fool proof."

"I know right. When the checks finally make it to the district attorney, the cops will be after the person who opened the account. And like most criminals, they will say 'I didn't do it'. And in this case they would not have. The D.A. will more than likely give them a handwriting test and the signatures won't match. They won't get in trouble and neither will we."

"Bitch your ass is scary. You have some crazy shit going on in that head of yours."

"You're right Essie. Also, I know that we already dress fly but we're going to start doing bigger things. Going to better places. We're taking this show on the road baby."

"What?"

"We're going to start going from state to state. We still have good credit cards that we can use so we'll use them out of town since most merchants don't like taking out of state checks even with the new check system. We'll use our checks locally. I propose when we go out of town we take the Lincoln. It's a low key luxury car and it'll get us the attention we need."

"But we've always shied away from drawing attention to ourselves. Why do we want to do that now?"

"Not that kind of attention. When we take the Lincoln, we're going to take someone with us, probably Philip, he can dress in a black suit, put on a little black hat, and ta-da, instant chauffeur. We'll go to stores that have guards at the door. When they see us exiting the car with our driver holding the door for us, they'll think we're important. A celebrity or something. Then we'll have access to more things. Finer things."

"That's good. I think this can really work."

"It will if we work it. But we have to be on point. Don't bring anybody into this unless it's absolutely necessary. Not Devan, not Dante', and not Delante'. Y'all with me?"

"*I'm* with you. Des is out remember?"

"I know that, Essence. But just because you are not actively with us Des, we still need you to keep our business, just that. *Our business.*"

"You don't have to worry about me. I'm not going to say a word. I love you guys and you know you can trust me."

"Well then that concludes our round table discussion. Tomorrow we begin. Until then, enjoy your day and don't do anything that I wouldn't do."

The girls went their separate ways. Essence was quieter than usual for the rest of the day. Honesty called her cell to see what was wrong with her but she said that she was fine and didn't want to talk about it so Honesty let it go. Something was going on with Essence and she wanted to know what it was but she didn't push her. When Essence was ready to share, she would. She always did.

Desiree's leaving the group was a shocker to them but not a total surprise. Last week, Essence had grabbed a credit card out of the 'Do not use' box without the others knowing it. They had loads of things people had paid them to get on the line. When the clerk ran the card, the code came back stolen.

The clerk didn't say anything. She didn't have too. Honesty had seen the signs before. All of them knew how to read the signs. Essence wasn't even paying attention. She was on the phone with Dante'.

Talking nasty and shit. The clerk told them that they needed to wait a moment. The credit card machine was dialing slowly.

"The company must be receiving multiple requests at once. You know how those things go," the lying bitch said.

Whatever. It was time for them to bounce. Honesty gave Desiree the signal. She left out the store first. She tried to give Essence the signal too but she was too engrossed in her conversation. The next time she looked at her though, she gave her the signal. She thought she saw her. Honesty exited the store next. Out in the middle of the mall she waited for Essence. It had always been their custom to park as close to the nearest exits as possible. Desiree had already gone to get the car and was outside waiting. Honesty looked to the store where they were. Still no Essence. *What in the hell was this bitch doing?*

She called her phone. Essence answered.

"Bitch, get your ass out of that store. The card came back stolen."

"What? I've been standing here on the phone with my man and y'all just left me? Why you didn't give me the signal?"

"I did give it. You were looking right at me."

"I didn't see it. I can't believe that y'all wo-"

"Essie, run out of the store now. Security is running up the escalators. Meet us at the car. It's running. Hurry girl!"

She barely made it to the car. But now the little bucket of a car had been spotted. Desiree was so slick though. Instead of her pulling forward to take off, she reversed and sped the other way. Those fools didn't have a chance to take the license plate number because they didn't get to see it. Essence was slipping. She was losing her focus. Honesty hoped that she would be back at one hundred percent. If she wasn't, then she was going to have to cut her lose. It would be a one woman show.

CHAPTER TWELVE

Essence was late. The plane was scheduled to take off in less than half an hour and she was late. Honesty had been calling her cell phone and leaving message after message but no response. This was getting old and very tired to Honesty. Checks and credit cards were a hustle that was time sensitive. A credit card could only be used so much before it wasn't any good. Once the transactions started to catch up with the account, it would be all over. In order to get the maximum use out of that card, they had to hit places back to back.

The same thing went for checks. The best time to start writing checks was on a Wednesday. One account was only good for two weeks total. Honesty wanted to run an account into the ground if she could. That's why she was so careful about the things that she did. Writing checks was not the only thing that the girls did with a checking account. She also made empty envelope deposits. So before they even started writing checks on any account they had to make sure that certain things were in order.

After the account was opened, one of the girls went to a tag agency or office that held voter's registration cards and applied for one using the same name information they had used at the bank.

That was a valid second piece of identification to have in case a merchant asked. While waiting on that to come they would also be waiting for the Visa or Mastercard check card to come too. They would need to have that in order to carry out phase one of the plan. That was an integral part of the plan. The money portion.

With the bank card, Honesty would go to other banks and use their ATM machines to make deposits. She would enter an amount on the deposit envelope and would key the same amount onto the key pad of the machine and would make a deposit. Whatever bank she was using to write the checks at, they would see that a deposit had been made on the wire and would credit the amount of deposit to the account.

The wire is like a virtual bank. Once a deposit or transaction is made at bank 'A' the virtual funds would travel to bank 'B' and tell it that this money has been deposited. Bank 'B' will see the virtual funds from bank 'A' and go ahead and honor the posting by making the virtual funds real. Bank 'B' would then wait for Bank 'A' to send the money over via carrier. Wire posts took about two bank days. Honesty's deposits would never make it.

A bank day ran from two p.m. one day until two p.m. the next day. So if a deposit was made on Monday before two, then it would be available that afternoon. Anything posted after that wouldn't be available until Tuesday. This was the custom when it came to making deposits via the machine. Fund availability for deposits made via ATM machines would vary depending on the bank's policy. Some banks allowed the first hundred dollars of a deposit available immediately while some made a generous three-hundred dollars available.

There were some banks that held all funds. Honesty didn't mess with those banks. Deposits made in person that were made by check, were held for a period of five to ten days. Honesty didn't make deposits in person. Only withdrawals. She was getting to know banks very well. She was in its mind so to speak. To benefit her hustle the most, she started to ask questions. Honesty wanted to be the best.

She was already Oklahoma State's best check writer. The game changed when she entered it. There were other check writers in the city and they were pretty good at what they did, but she had perfected the game. She didn't brag about it either. It was a known fact. She ate, slept, and breathed checks.

The others didn't do it like her.

They snatched purses and got checks that way. Some would ask their friends to let them write bad checks on their account and then the friend could call it in stolen. That's cool, but not nearly as efficient as Honesty's system. She dared not ever snatch a purse just to get a check book. That was crime on top of crime. Robbery *and* forgery. If a person was caught stealing a purse the cops could take him straight to jail. With her system they had to build a case. By the time they did that a person could be long gone.

She had all the stores check writing policies down to a science. She knew which stores used which check system and how much a check could be before a clerk had to call for management approval. She knew how to do it all. No longer was this just a hustle. This was her job.

Her bank deposits were how she got her cash. She used to go to grocery stores and write checks over the amount of purchase and get cash that way but that didn't really pay off the way she needed it too. Making empty envelope deposits had a large return. The maximum deposit was nine grand because anything over ten would alert the feds. Honesty and the girls were not down with that. They chose a couple of different machines and hit them up a few times. They would make three or four deposits ranging anywhere from eighteen hundred dollars to eighty- five hundred. Honesty would make two deposits in one day so that they would post on the wire at the same time.

When that happened, she wrote herself a check made out to 'cash' and went and got the money. When the last transaction cleared the bank it was time to cancel the check card. That was inevitable. Making the deposits, waiting for them to clear, and withdrawing the money took a total of four days. Honesty started those transactions on a Friday.

Before the card was completely cancelled, she would use it for its intended purpose. To shop with it. She could only tell that the card had been officially cancelled when she tried to use it and her purchase was declined. Since it was not a regular credit card and was not stolen, no one had to worry about security codes coming up or even running out of the store to avoid being caught. Honesty hated having it declined though because it usually happened when she had picked something that she really wanted.

After the card was no longer valid, they started the checks. As long as a checking account number didn't have any negative information in the check systems, then it would clear. A check system could not determine if there were sufficient funds in an account to cover the amount of purchase. It only scans to see if any checks have been returned on that account or any derogatory information had been entered.

Every day there is something new to be learned about the check game. Every day, Honesty tried to be that one who learned something new. One day she was in an electronics store buying televisions and when she went to check out her check was declined. The clerk gave her the card to call the check system that didn't approve the check. She took the card she handed her. Usually when that happened, she would get this 'are you kidding me?' look on her face, play like she didn't know why it was declined and leave. But that day was a learning day. And the clerk really wanted that commission.

"Please give them a call. We have had to call them all day because their system is messing up. It may not be you at all," she said, handing Honesty the phone after she dialed the number.

Honesty took the phone and prepared to hear why she had been declined.

"Thank you for calling Equal Check, how may I help you today?" The customer service representative asked.

"Yes my name is Karen Atwood and I just had a check declined by you all and I would like to know why?"

"I'll be more than happy to assist you, ma'am. May I have the numbers at the bottom of the check beginning at the far left hand side?"

Honesty read all the numbers off to the man on the other end of the phone and waited impatiently while he searched for the reason she could not get the 52 inch big screen she picked out today. The sales clerk smiled and attempted to make small talk with Honesty while she held, but Honesty was not in the mood. All she did was smile back and nod her head when the young lady finished speaking.

"Thank you so much for holding ma'am. I found the information. It looks like yesterday we approved check number 3516 for you in the amount of $452.29 at Foot Locker. Today you are asking that we approve check number 3597 in the amount of $14, 632.01."

"Okay, so what's the problem? I have ample funds to cover all my purchases." Liar, liar.

"The amount of the check isn't the problem, Mrs. Atwood. Our system received a red flag due the span of numbers from the last check we approved and the one you're using today. It appears to the system that you have written 81 checks between yesterday and today."

"That's absurd. No one could do that." *But I can and I did, she thought before continuing.* "I see what has happened. My husband bought him and the boys some tennis shoes yesterday and he used his check book. Today I'm using mine. That's why the numbers are so far apart."

"I understand. We see this sort of thing happening all the time. Let me suggest that you all coordinate your check books so that the numbers are within a 50 check span and you all will not encounter this again."

"Thank you for that information. But what am I going to do about my purchase today? I can't very well go withdraw that amount of cash and have it on my person. That's not safe."

"No, of course not. I can issue an override in our system but it won't take effect until tomorrow. It takes 24 hours for requests to process. You can ask the clerk to set your items aside and hold them and if we haven't received any negative information in our system regarding your account, you can come back, present another check for purchase and we'll approve it."

"Oh, thank you so much, Sir. My husband will be so surprised when he sees this new television. He's going to go bananas over it."

"I'm sure. You have a very lucky husband."

"How nice of you to say. Thank you so much for all your help. I will let the clerk know what's going on. Have a nice day."

"Same to you and thank you for calling Equal Check. Goodbye."

Honesty ended the conversation with a huge smile on her face. She explained to the clerk what happened and assured her that she would be back tomorrow to complete the transaction. Both women were happy. Desiree, who was with Honesty that day, looked puzzled.

"What the hell are you smiling about? You hate getting your checks declined."

"I know Des, but dude just told me how not to get anymore checks declined prematurely."

"Huh? But you told me what he said and I don't remember you all having that conversation. I was standing right there."

"I know you were. Listen to this. He said that the computer thought I had written a bunch of checks because it reads in numerical order. You know, from one to ten. Too many checks with numbers going up will get your check denied. But I plan on doing it the other way around now."

"What are you talking about?"

"I am talking about writing checks starting at the back of the book and working my way backward. Instead of starting at one I will begin at ten and throw the system off."

"You got *that* from your conversation with that guy? Bitch, your ass *is* scary."

"I know, what I can I say?"

Honesty went back the next day and got her television and allowed the same clerk to receive that hefty commission. After that, she was unstoppable. She wrote more checks for larger amounts and the accounts lasted at least four days longer than they did before. The girl was the shit and she knew it.

Honesty sat in the airport and figured that Essence was out somewhere chasing around behind Dante'. Love was not that deep. Not for her. That's probably why she hadn't fallen in love or allowed anyone to get that close to her. Delante' kept telling her he loved her. It was cool at first but now it was beginning to get on her nerves. He said it like he expected her to say the same thing in return. She was not going to do that. She was not in love with him.

She heard the airline announce that it was time to board the plane. *Atlanta here I come*, she mused. She was going to do all that she said she was going to do, on her own. Philip, another one of her PIC's, partners-in-crime couldn't come because his girl gave birth last night and he wanted to stay with her which she understood. He was going to drive for her and be a tour guide of sorts.

She would have been tripping but she found out that people have drivers in ATL and that there were companies that she could hire. That was cool. A hired driver would not be in her business either.

Her eyes stayed focused on the door of the plane to see if Essence would make it. She never did. The plane took off without her. Honesty sat in first class alone, enjoying herself. She had brought along a book to read to keep her occupied though. She saw a young black couple across the aisle from her and they looked very much in love. Sighing, she turned her attention back to her book and began to read.

She fell asleep before making it through four pages of the book. That was a much needed nap though. By the time the plane landed in Georgia, she was refreshed. The sun was shining full blast by the time she stepped outside of Hartsfield-Jackson Airport. People were everywhere. She felt like she was finally home. There was something about that place that made her feel welcomed. A taxi pulled up in front of her and she asked him if he was waiting for someone. He said that he wasn't and asked her if she needed a ride. The man was nice. He sounded like he was of African descent. Her bags were loaded in the car and she told him that she would be going to the Ritz-Carlton in downtown Atlanta. He looked at her like she was crazy.

When she planned the trip she wanted to treat herself and Essence to something nice. Kim and Leo told her that taking care of herself was the best thing she could do. She was determined to do just that and that meant living her life like it was golden. Today, it was.

Atlanta reminded her so much of New York. Just more laid back. It was a more southern, somewhat slower version but the pace of the city was pretty much on point. They drove up Peachtree Street and the people were out in an abundance. Some of them looked like they were on their way to work while others looked like they didn't have a job and didn't want one either.

Traffic was crazy. The Marta buses were being disrespectful. Drivers would put their blinkers on and immediately cut in front of people. The police were out trying to direct the traffic and make some sense of it but they weren't having any luck. She was in downtown Atlanta. This is where she should have been all along.

Once they reached the hotel and the cabbie helped her out, she stepped into the hotel like she owned the place. The bellhop helped her with her six-piece Louis Vuitton luggage set after she checked in. Mrs.

Michelle Humphrey was who she was going to be that week. She had a Texas issued drivers license and Visa credit card that validated who she was. No matter where she went, whether it was to the club or to the mall, that's who she would be the entire trip.

Inside her room, she waited until the bellhop had set the entire luggage down and then she gave him a ten dollar tip. As soon as the door closed, she began to take her clothes off. She was hot. It gets hot in Oklahoma but it was a dry heat. The heat in Atlanta had a humidity factor associated with it, making it a moist, your-ass-is-going-to-be-sweaty type heat. Her clothes were sticking to her body. She needed to shower.

The water caressed her body when she stepped under the spray of the shower. The temperature was set to medium so her body could cool down quickly. When she got out the shower she stepped into the room naked and eyed the luxurious room. The bed was so huge. It called out to her. She was tired. It was serious nap time. She made a reservation at the Atlanta Grill while she was still downstairs checking in so she was covered for dinner. She pulled her alarm clock out and plugged it in so that she wouldn't oversleep. Before she got into the bed she hung up her clothes and took her toiletries out so she would not be scrambling for them later.

Her head hit the pillow like a ton of bricks. Honesty didn't realize that she was as tired as she was. Although, she could not wait to go shopping. It was time to put her skills to the test.

She took a nap and woke up to Sade playing on the radio. *This is definitely not Oklahoma*, she thought as she stretched. No radio station had played Sade in years. The song went off. The D.J. said that this was grown and sexy radio. He sounded so fine. Honesty had to agree with him. It sure was grown and sexy. So far, everything about Atlanta was grown and sexy. Honesty dressed and prepared for her evening.

She wanted to make sure that she looked good because she might run into someone famous.

This is my baby Luda's home town and he just might be out and about. It would be just my luck to see him too. Once he sees me he will want to take me home with him. He will be doing the right thing too. I could be his fantasy. Honesty laughed at her own delusions.

Dinner was wonderful and the ambiance was great. This was something that she could get used to. Eating alone was alright with her too.

"Why's a pretty woman like yourself eating alone?" That was question of the night.

"I prefer it that way. Thank you," she said blowing them off.

This one young executive came over trying to holler at her. He said that his name was Lorenzo. Honesty thought that he was fine as hell. For some reason, she asked him to join her. He accepted. They ate, drank and had a great time. They talked about everything. She even contemplated telling him her real name. At the last minute she decided against it though. There was something about him that told her he was not your ordinary guy. He didn't hold anything back from her either. He'd been single for almost six months, no kids; he lived on his own in a high rise condo in Atlantic Station (wherever that was.) He loved his sisters a lot, his mom was deceased, loved God and loved women. He included the latter after she asked him if he was gay.

Apparently that was a big issue in the A-Town; down low brothers. With all his good qualities she needed to know that he wasn't one of them. Lorenzo was quite a guy. The man was funny. Could have been a stand up comedian if he wanted to. He owned a couple of businesses and was always trying to do better. They hit it off.

She told him about her family and how they really died. He actually got tears in his eyes. Never in her life had she been that open with anyone and probably never would again. But for tonight Ms. Honesty was something she hadn't been in a long time, honest.

Their meal ended with him escorting her back to her room upstairs. She invited him in to continue talking which they did for another two hours. He excused himself saying that he needed to get up early the next morning. She did not want to let him go. He kissed her hand and told her that he hoped that he could see her again before she went back home. She told him "most def."

She went to sleep that night feeling better than she had in ages. It didn't even dawn on her to check and see if Essence or Delante had called her. She wasn't worried about either of them. Tonight she acted like a grown ass woman. She and Lorenzo had had a conversation and she hadn't cursed one time. Damn, that was a good man.

Her dreams that night were of him. She slept so well. So much hurt had melted away in one day. This was what she had been searching for. She was so into her slumber that she almost did not hear her cell phone going off. She did not answer it the first time but it immediately rang again. She turned the ringer off. It started to vibrate. Whoever it was trying to call needed her badly. She looked at the phone. She didn't want to answer it. Inside she already knew…so

CHAPTER THIRTEEN

Dante' had beaten Essence up. She was in the hospital. That was Desiree on the phone. The two of them had spoken briefly before she went to dinner last night and she told her friend that she had not heard from Essence. Desiree hadn't either. It was her idea to call and check on her. Essie didn't answer her cell phone for her either.

Ebony, Essence's mother was the one who called Desiree. Desi said that she was pissed off. Who wouldn't be? *Let some maggot ass dog put his hands on my child and see what happens to him,* Honesty raged. It was such a shame. Ms. O'Dell, didn't like Dante' at all. She said that he was a worm and he had too many women. On several occasions she had asked Honesty and Desiree to speak to her about her relationship with him but none of it worked. Their talks and disagreement only seemed to push her closer to him.

All this explained why she didn't get on the plane. *She should have called me. That's what friends are for.* Honesty did not understand what was going on with Essence and Dante'. It was not her policy to get in between what goes on between a woman and her man. But this here was different though. This was her sister involved in this mess. She wasn't going to stand idly by and watch him run her into the ground.

According to Desiree, Essence had caught him cheating. Again. She had to get her purse from his house because she left it over there the night before. It had her plane tickets and itinerary in it. She was just going to stop over there on her way to the airport. He was supposed to be at work. But he had given her a key to his place so she could get in. Brother man was not at work.

Des said that when Essence walked in she instantly heard moans coming from his room. When she walked in, he was in the bed with not one, but two tricks. He was fucking one chick from behind while she ate the other broad out. Desiree said that Essence told her that she wasn't even tripping out. She calmly had walked in and grabbed her purse off the night stand and turned around and told him that he was a punk and that she was through with him for good.

But that's not why he fought her. Des said that on her way out, she picked up this ceramic ball he had sitting on the glass dining room set that *she* bought him and slammed it down full force. The table shattered into a bunch of small pieces. That's when he ran out of the room and punched her.

She fell into the wall and he picked her up and slapped her around a couple of times. Trying to get away from him, she tripped and fell into the broken glass pieces. She got shards of glass in her hands and on the side of her face where she hit the floor. And even though she was on the ground in all that glass, Dante' still continued to hit her. The doctors said that she should heal without any scarring. Desiree was crying when she called Honesty.

"It's not over between them," she said. Dante' was at the hospital bearing gifts.

Honesty shook her head as she hung up the phone. Staying with Dante' was Essence's decision. Nothing anyone said would make any difference until Essence was ready to make that change. All they could do was be there for her when the shit hit the fan. And it would. When it did, it would be a truckload.

Surprisingly it didn't take her long to fall back to sleep. That was unusual for her. But it wasn't as late as she thought it was when Des called. The clock said that it was a little after twelve thirty. She had plenty of time to catch some z's. There were some key places that she needed to hit in the morning and she was also looking forward to seeing Lorenzo.

He was so nice. Maybe he was too good to be true. She didn't know. She liked being around him so much and that was only after one evening. Her girls would tell her that she was crazy if they knew how much she was feeling this cat already. Hell, she just might be. She couldn't put her finger on this but she knew that there was something different about him. He wanted to know her. The real Honesty.

She was honest with him last night but she didn't tell him about her "career." She was not that trusting, but with all that he already knew, he knew her better than Delante' did and they had been seeing each other for months. He could just be blowing smoke up her ass. He may not own the businesses that he said he did. He could have a wife and kids out there. But his eyes were the most sincere that she had ever seen in her life. They reminded her so much of her dads. Of Goldie's.

Lorenzo's eyes were deep and brooding. Piercing. Like they could see into your soul. Looking at him brought her pleasure. Not just carnal pleasures either, like those she got with Dee, but something real. Pure. His eyes were loving and warm. So were his hands.

When she was with him last night in her room, she wanted to lay her head in his lap and let him stroke her hair with those hands. She did not want to have sex with him, not yet anyway, but she just wanted to be with him. She called down to room service and ordered turkey bacon and a plain bagel with honey nut cream cheese spread for breakfast. When they sent it up, there was juice, fresh cantaloupe, honeydew, watermelon slices, and strawberries on the tray as well. The Ritz knew how to spoil her. It was a nice spread. Her hungry ass ate it all too.

It was time for her to get this show on the road. She called downstairs again and had the concierge arrange for a car and driver to come get her and take her around. She had a map of places that she wanted to hit up. Phipps Plaza in Buckhead was the first stop. She had heard many great things about the shopping there and was ready. Just thinking about all the wonderful stores up there turned her on. It made her nipples hard.

She didn't want to be under dressed but she didn't want to be over dressed for the Atlanta heat either. She chose a pink Ellen Tracy linen capri set with a cute white spaghetti strapped cotton camisole underneath. She kept the half-jacket to the capri's unbuttoned and open.

She wore the cutest Michael Kors pink and gold high-heeled sandals with a strap between the toes. She was working her outfit. She accessorized the outfit with a platinum tennis bracelet and matching earrings. She also had a pink diamond on her ring finger. Sister was fierce when she looked at herself in the mirror. Her skin was clear and she don't wear any foundation but she did put on a little translucent powder to give her skin a fresh look. M.A.C. made great products. Add a little eye liner and her favorite, Lip Glass and Honesty was hot to death.

By the time she made it downstairs the car and driver had arrived. She was on her way. The driver toured downtown and then straight up Peachtree Street at her request. She did not know if it was a quicker way to get there but she wanted to take the scenic route. He obliged. It was so nice seeing the sights. In Oklahoma, you didn't see many people outside downtown or anywhere else unless you were at a park or something. Everyone stayed in and stayed to themselves. Here, you saw people running, walking, laughing, and talking. She had even seen some people sleeping out on the street. You certainly didn't see that in the 'O'. Not in the heart of downtown anyway. You'd see the occasional panhandler here and there but no one sleeping in front of corporate offices. Not like they did here.

There were fountains all downtown and many beautiful works of art that adorned downtown Atlanta. Her digital camera was working overtime. They passed Club 112, Gladys Knight's Chicken and Waffles, of which she made a mental note to stop by there on her way from the stores, and the Fox Theater. There were so many sights to see.

The driver told her they were nearing Phipps Plaza. Her heart started racing. This was it. She was so excited. Then she saw it. All in a row were the places of her dreams. Nordstrom's, Saks, Bloomingdales. It was Christmas time in June. The driver pulled up to the entrance of Sak's, got out and opened her door. She told him that she did not know how long she was going to be so he gave her his cell number and told her to call him when she was checking out and he would come help her with her bags.

She gave those stores the blues. She called, Derek, her driver, and told him that she needed his assistance. By the time he came, she had six shoe boxes, three large bags, and four garment bags. And her day had just begun. He looked at her like she was crazy but he kept whatever comments he may have had to himself.

It was his idea that he stay near her so that she would not have to wait for him. When they were in Bloomingdale's, she saw him eyeing some cologne by Armani. He kept going back to that one fragrance. After he walked away from it, she went over and bought it for him. The girl behind the counter gift wrapped it quickly. The driver was being very patient and helpful. She knew that it was his job, but he was doing it well and it made her shopping experience more than she could have hoped for. He deserved the cologne

Six hours. That is how long she shopped. Derek hadn't complained once. He didn't look at his watch either. Truth be told, Honesty thought he was having as much fun as she was. The day was nice and so were the people. It was just like in her dream, people were running over themselves trying to help her.

She had not had lunch yet and she asked Derek if he knew of a nice place to dine for lunch. He asked her if she had wanted to go to Justin's and she told him no. She had been there and done that in New York. Then he suggested the Cheesecake Factory. She was down with the program. Since he hadn't eaten either she invited him to have lunch with her. He accepted.

While they sat waiting for their meal she told him that she had had a great time with him. He was a great person. During their chat he told her that he had plans to become a singer. She told him that her little brother was trying to do that too. He said that he had already been in the studio and was about to complete his first CD. She congratulated him on his hard work. Of course she wanted to put him to the test so she asked him to sing something for her. He wasn't shy at all. His voice was so nice and melodic. It was a cross between Brian McKnight and Usher. Sensuous. Tantalizing. Very romantic.

Derek told her that he was engaged and had one little boy. His fiancé was a hair stylist. She was Dominican. He said that she had just opened her own shop. Honesty told him that she would love to have her do her hair. Derek didn't understand that she meant today. When she told him that, he called her right away. She told him to bring her on.

Her name was Hetti. And she was the most exotic woman Honesty had ever seen. Their son looked just like her. He was going to be fine.

Hetti straightened her hair with a special tool of hers. Honesty had never seen an iron like this in Oklahoma. Or anywhere for that matter. Her hair was straighter and silkier than a Chinese woman's. It was bouncing and behaving. She even arched her eyebrows.

She paid her and gave her a nice tip. Derek took her down the street to get her nails and toes done. She wanted to look good for Lorenzo when she saw him. He had been heavy on her mind all day. Just when she really started thinking about him he called. She answered the phone in her sexiest voice.

"Hello."

"Hey you. How are you doing today?"

"I'm good Renzo, how are you?"

"Oh, so it's Renzo now is it?"

"Sorry. I'm bad at giving people nicknames. I'll call you Lorenzo if that bothers you. I don't mean any disrespect."

"No, it's fine. I'm flattered actually. Thank you. That made me a feel a way."

"What way is that?"

"Good. But enough about me, how have you been today?"

"I've been good. I'm on my way to the nail shop to get some girl things done. Today has been great."

"So how is Derek treating you?"

"He's been gre-. Hey, how did you know about Derek? Are you stalking me?"

"Nothing that psychotic, Honesty. That car that he's driving you around in just happens to belong to my fleet. Derek works for me."

"Wow. But, how did you know he was driving me? I'm not... Wait a minute, Renzo. What did you just say? This is straight bullshit..creepy."

"I know. I'll explain it to you later. Will you meet me this evening? I promise I'll explain it all to you. I'm not stalking you. Please believe that. Just give me a chance, okay?"

"Okay. I will. Listen, I have a call coming through on the other line. Call me later and let me know where you want me to meet you."

"I'll do that."

She didn't have a call on the other line. But she needed to get off the phone with him. Him knowing who she was with threw her for a loop. She really liked him and was kind of disappointed when he put her on blast like that. Was this man checking up on her? She didn't know. This whole thing was strange. She would give him the chance to explain this evening and then she was going to move around.

Since she was off the phone, she did give Desi a call to see how Essence was doing. She told her that all was okay with her and that she had wanted to talk to her. It was about Delante'. She asked her if he was hurt or in jail. She said no to both. She told Desiree that it would keep until she got home. That bastard hadn't called her once to see if her plane had landed safely or anything.

Her mind and thoughts had been so caught up on Lorenzo that she hadn't paid any attention to the fact that Dee hadn't called. Now the more that she thought about it the madder she got. *This nigga got me fucked up.* She was not the other bitch. She was the *only* bitch. Whatever he was doing and whoever he was doing it with he better make sure he enjoyed it because when she got home, it was going to be on and popping.

Lee, at the nail shop, hooked her hands and feet up. They were top notch. She went to work on her and had her feet looking better than they ever had. People in Georgia had it going on. Every service that she had performed on her or for her today was impeccable. *This is something to write down in my memory book.*

The bellhop who helped her when she checked in was there when she got back to the hotel. She felt like Julia Roberts in Pretty Woman when she walked through the hotel lobby. Minus the being prostitute part though. The bellhop helped her upstairs again. She made sure to give him a good tip. Yesterday she was too tired and only slid him ten bucks. She tried to give good tips. Never knew if she was going to need someone to give her one someday. This time she slid him fifty bucks. He looked like "damn." Her job was done for the day. She had spent almost twenty-thousand dollars in credit card purchases.

Again, she took a long shower. She needed to clear her head. Her mind was running a mile a minute. Lorenzo seemed like a genuinely nice guy. How could she have been such a bad judge of character? Where did she miss it? Their first meeting was so phenomenal. She was relaxed around this man. Was she letting her guard down? Getting weak?

Clearly she was fucking up. This trip was supposed to prepare her for working on her own. Obviously this was a sign of sorts. Right now, she did not know what it was a sign of. Ever since Desiree got engaged and quit the crew, Honesty had been going through some crazy shit. But she was no longer jealous of her friends' happiness.

That wasn't it. What she was feeling was longing and it was getting stronger every day. She longed to have that kind of love that Desiree did. Her and Devan dated as long as Honesty and Dee and already Desiree knew his whole family. She had met his mom and dad and every sibling, cousin, niece, and nephew he had. Hell, she had even met Dee's mom and Honesty hadn't even done that.

When she would ask him he would tell her that it wasn't the right time. The time was never right. Not that it was that important to her to meet his people. That wasn't the point. She didn't want to have to be nice to anyone. The point was that he had not even gotten around to asking her if she wanted to or not. He hadn't given her the chance to turn him down.

Lately, all he has wanted to do was fuck her in her ass, smoke weed and ask her for shit. She swore he was trying to get her pregnant too. Honesty didn't know it but one of his friends had told him that since the vaginal opening and anus were so close together all he had to do was fuck her deeper and she would get pregnant. When he was not asking for things, all he talked about was how pretty their baby was going to be and how he could not wait to see her carrying his child. The other night she even caught him trying to take his rubber off during their anal sex session. *This bastard was trying to trap me and set me up for failure.* Something was up with him.

Her crazy relationship with him was clouding her judgment. She could not have that. If getting herself back on track meant that she had to let Dee go, then she was all too willing to do that. It was time to cut him off like Elvis would have done to Lisa Marie if he was still alive after she married Michael Jackson.

She heard a sound coming from the nightstand. It was her cell phone. Someone was calling. Lorenzo.

"Hello," she answered wearily. She was so tired of thinking about this. Over thinking things.

"How are you doing? Are you tired?"

"No, I just have a lot on my mind right now. Are you ready to meet?"

"Yes, I was going to ask you if you were up for taking a walk. If you're not, I could hire us a horse drawn carriage and we can talk."

"No a walk will be fine. I don't want the driver to be in our business. Where would you like to meet? I'm already dressed."

"I'm downstairs then if you want to come on down. I'll be waiting in the lobby."

"I'm on my way," she said and hung up the phone. She checked her appearance in the mirror one more time before she left.

There was a couple on the elevator on her way down that looked like they needed to go back into their room. They were all over each other. It wasn't that bad really. She was just making more out of everything now. Life had been throwing her some curve balls that have been impossible to catch. She hoped that this thing with Lorenzo wasn't another one. Lorenzo walked over to her and gave her a hug. Before she had a chance to say anything he spoke up.

"I know that you are stressing out how I knew about Derek and some other things. Before we get into what I have to say, I do want to tell you how sorry I am if I have made you feel uncomfortable in any way. That was not my desire. You are an awesome woman and I would like an opportunity to get to know you better once this is all over. That is, if you would like that."

"I don't know Lorenzo. Today I was thrown for a loop. When you called me Honesty today I didn't pay any attention at first. That didn't register with me until after you told me that Derek was my driver. I thought that you had been stalking me or checking up on me or some shit. Like you was one time or worse, the feds."

"Again, I am so sorry. Here let me get the door for you."

They walked down Peachtree Street but didn't say anything then turned down Fourteenth Street and stayed on it. After they turned the corner, he began to talk. Before she knew it, they were at Piedmont Park. They sat on some steps and she listened to what he had to say.

"Honesty, we live in a crazy world. As large as we think it is, circumstances make it very small. I am twenty three years old and I have been through more than any man I know who's forty."

"I understand that much."

"I know you do. That's why talking to you is so refreshing. Anyway, I am my mother's oldest child. I have two younger sisters who I raised. Our mother was killed in Los Angeles when she tried to steal some dope from some gang member. He shot her in the back of her head as she ran down the street. I came out the store just in time to see her body hit the concrete and her head bust open. She died in front of me."

"How awful for you. I wish I didn't know what that was like." He gave her a look that said "bitch- stop- interrupting –me look. "I'm sorry, I'll let you finish."

"A few years before she died, my sisters used to run dope for this dude in L.A. One day they were on a drug run to Oklahoma City. After they made the transaction they had made a date with the homies of the dude they were doing business with. These dudes were going to cross their homeboy and jack him. They were going to kill my sisters. A guy found out about the drop and knew something bad was supposed to go down. He called the LA dude and they changed the plans. When my sisters came into town, he took them to a different spot, told them what was going on, and made them promise to get out of the game after that run. They did too. Well the guy who changed the plans ended up saving my sister's lives.

To make a long story short, he gave them his number and said should they need anything to call him. When my mother got killed we didn't have any money to bury her. He came to our home and helped us. Him *and* his wife. That man was your dad. It's Leo. Leo and Kim came and helped us out.

CHAPTER FOURTEEN

Honesty called to tell her about meeting Lorenzo and Kim told her some news. The doctors told Kim that she had a lump on her right breast. The announcement shook the young girl but Kim was cool. She said that she was fine and the only thing that it could be was a lump of fat. Everyone thought that she was just being optimistic. But deep down, they all wanted her to be right.

Leo was handling things better than his daughter. He hadn't seen any death or destruction in his wife's life. His thought's were that if he didn't see it, he didn't believe it.

Breast cancer. They had all been through so much in their lives; they didn't need anything else to add to it. Their story was already so unbelievable that if anyone tried to write a book about it people would see it as fiction. No one would believe that all that could have happened in such a short period of time.

Unfortunately, it did. Honesty's adopted parents were soldiers. Goldie and Silver were soldiers. She was a soldier. Every day she got up she put on war clothes. Living her life was like a fight and she was going to fight to win until the death. There was no other choice. Fight or die. She wanted to live.

Eventually she shared her news with her mom. Kim was excited about it too. She told her that his family was great and that she would like them. She and Leo had made it a personal mission to help them. If saving them meant sacrificing a few bucks or some time out of their schedules then they did it.

They took Lorenzo and his sisters in like family. She said that Honesty should too. But just because her parents were gung ho about something did not necessarily mean that she was going to be. She liked Lorenzo. He liked her. But merely liking him didn't give her reason to make changes to what she was doing. Kim kept hinting around about all the good things he had done and what he was trying to accomplish.

What about what I'm trying to accomplish? I'm trying to stack some dough the best way I know.

"Go back to school, Honesty. Get a job, Honesty," Kim said.

Get a job? Doing what? Flipping burgers? I ain't held down a job in all my life. Who would hire me?

She didn't want to do housekeeping. That might mess up her nails. Hands like hers were not made for being a maid. They couldn't be cleaning nobody else's toilets. She didn't even like cleaning her own. It only got done out of necessity.

Nothing about being a housekeeper appealed to her. Well, maybe the tips. But those were not guaranteed. That's like working in a restaurant as a server. Just because someone does a good job doesn't mean that the person that she has served is going to give a tip. Nothing was guaranteed in life.

All she wanted to do was make her own way in life. As crazy as it seemed, she was good at what she did. And she enjoyed it for the most part. Kim would tell her that having money and material things was not everything. She was right of course. But it is important to some folks. Honesty liked living a certain way. White collar crimes afforded her the luxury of doing so.

Leo and Kim went to Mr. Hall, their attorney and asked if they could have the money Honesty had, held in trust until she turned twenty-four. He told them yes. Goldie had put a clause in his will that said some shit like if she wasn't doing right then at Kim's discretion she could keep her from getting the money.

Imagine Honesty's surprise when she went to America's bank to finally make a withdrawal and was told that she needed a parent to accompany her. They needed to provide a signature.

"A signature for what?" Honesty asked.

"A signature approving a withdrawal from a secured trust," the teller said. Honesty was pissed off.

She knew that they were trying to get her to see their side of things but they wouldn't even try to see her side. The life that she has lived has been good as far as her not having to beg for anything. But other than that, that's where the goodness ends. Her soul was hungry and it needed to be fed. So until she found the things that kept her soul from growling, she would keep on looking.

It was hard for her to think about losing Kim to cancer though. She had seen the shows where women would lose a breast to the disease. The doctors would tell them that they got all the cancer. For a few months, the woman would undergo chemotherapy and be feeling great. Then on a follow-up visit, the doctor would drop another bomb. The cancer had spread to her other breast. It was a cycle that didn't end. Once you let the doctors start cutting on you to get that stuff out, it spread.

Straining her brain about this wasn't going to do any good for Kim or her. If Kim wasn't that worried about it, Honesty shouldn't be either. She was sure that when a cause for concern arose, Kim would let her know. Until then, Honesty was going to be as positive about this whole thing as Kim was. There was no other choice.

Deciding to make all her calls before she got out for the day, she called Desiree. Her phone rang for a while before she answered it. She was still asleep. Honesty forgot about the time difference. It was six in the morning there. Kim was an early bird. Desi was not.

Honesty told her that she could call her when she woke up. Devan was talking to her in the background.

'Devan said bring him a shirt with Atlanta on it," Desiree said. Honesty told her to tell him that she would. He was such a simple guy. Didn't ask for much and when he did it was something small like that. At first, Honesty thought that his simple life was a game. Especially since she knew that he was not hustling and his folks didn't have money. But he was a genuine guy.

His parents had tried their best with their kids. They did a good job. Although he didn't have the best material things, he had the best in everything else. Honesty would have traded in everything she had in order to be with her parents the way he was with his. Everything.

Sometimes it was hard for her to remember what her parent's faces looked like. Hard to remember what their voices sounded like. What their touches felt like. They were slipping away from her. She was afraid of losing them for the second time in her life.

Shaking her head she got up out of bed. It was a beautiful day and she was going to make the most of life and not concentrate on death. There were still some places that needed to feel her wrath and she wanted to get there early. The weather was supposed to be a warm seventy- five degrees today. She wanted to hit up as many stores as she could and then get back to her suite. There was no way that she was going to be out in the heat of the day. No, sir.

Today she decided to look virginal and innocent. She wore white silk. Her skirt was short. It rested about four inches above her knees. She wanted to show off her pretty legs. The blouse that she chose to wear with it was a halter that tied around her neck and around her back.

The back of the shirt drooped down and exposed her back. She wore white gold accessories and these gorgeous Gucci heels that had crystal G's on them. She was dressed like she was going out for a night on the town instead of shopping. Her white Versace big lens shades gave her a movie star look. *Watch out stores, here I come.*

During their conversation last night, she had asked Lorenzo if he could have Derek pick her up again. That guy was cooler than a fan and she enjoyed talking with him. He was one of the first men whom she had ever been around who didn't try to hit on her. Even though he was engaged, that wouldn't have stopped him if he was a dog. It was refreshing to know that he was not.

He was waiting in the lobby when she stepped off the elevator. He suggested that she hit the Mall of Georgia. This man could read her mind. It was on her list of places to go that day. Already having been to the Mall of America, she likened that mall to that one in her mind. Although it was a massive place, it didn't have anything on the one in Minnesota.

From there they hit the Perimeter. She saw a few celebrities while she was there. They were looking at her like *she* was one. One of them even came up to her and asked her how she was doing. He was sexy.

She told him that she was doing well. She asked him about his latest picture and he told her that it was almost complete. He asked about hers. She told him the same thing that he had told her. She was completely clueless as to who this brother thought she was. They gave one another a Hollywood hug, the kind were you don't put your arm around a person all the way, only use one arm, and you only lean in a bit, and went their own way. That was a trip.

Derek was cracking up. He was standing there watching the entire exchange. Some stars are so fake. Dude didn't even know her name. He just pretended that he did because she looked like she was someone that he knew. His ass was so superficial. She knew his and she might be judging him too harshly but she had let the whole thing play out to see what he was going to do. To see if he was going to admit that he wasn't sure who she was. He never did.

After hitting up thirty stores in four hours she was ready to call it quits. Period. She didn't want to do any more shopping the rest of her stay here in the A. If she had not bought it by now then it was not going to be bought either. Those cards were smoking. Later on, she would sit in her room and add up the totals for the two day's shopping she did. Right now, she was going to grab herself some eats.

Even though her girls were not able to make it on this trip, she looked out for them. Both of them. They were all going to be so fly in the Coach sandals that she picked up for each of them. Essence loved shoes. She was going to scream when she saw them. Honesty almost screamed when she saw them.

Bath and Body Works products are Desi's favorite. It didn't matter what the scent was, she loved anything and everything that they made. Honesty made sure to get her several new products that had just come out.

Because Oklahoma was about ten steps behind any major city, she didn't have to worry about her already having them. She was going to be excited. Overall her shopping turned out to be very productive and profitable. This trip was about Honesty only. She really didn't have anyone to shop for. Not clients anyway.

It was rare that she got a chance to shop and not have a list of things for someone else. This trip was supposed to be that for Essence too. Fucking around with that dog ass brotha caused her to miss out. Honesty felt that her life was worth so much more than that. No dude was going to be able to put his hands on her and think that it was okay. He would fuck around and catch a burning bed with her.

Just thinking about Essence and her situation got her heart rate up. It angered her badly. Her friend needed to wise up. If she didn't, she was in for a fall. No one wanted that to happen to her. But she had to want to get out for herself. What tripped Honesty out about Essence was that she is the one who was always spitting shit like "ain't no dick worth no ass whooping, and "I wish a nigga would step to this," and shit like that. Now it seemed that she was not so tough when she was faced with it, live and in living color.

Because she was on Honesty's mind so heavy she gave her a call. She sounded like she was hitting a blunt or something. Honesty heard Dante' in the background on his cell phone. Her stomach started to knot up. This shit was unreal. She wanted her conversation with her to be light and non confrontational. It was not.

"Essence, what the fuck is that nigga doing there? Why isn't he dead?"

"What you mean? He's my man, he has a right to be here."

"Essie, he beat you up. Doesn't that mean anything to you?"

"He said that he was sorry though, Hon. I forgave him. You should too."

"Forgive him? You want me to forgive the nigga that put my sister in the hospital? Bitch! Have you lost your ever loving mind? I hate that nigga and when I get a chance to I'm gonna spit on his ass. He's trash to me, Essence."

"Don't go there ho. I love him and we're going to get married. As a matter of fact, I'm moving in with him as soon as you return."

"Married? You gotsta be kidding me. Nobody is that damned stupid Essence. What? You gonna be having threesomes with him now. You gon' be dat bitch? The one who lets her man do whatever the fuck he wants to while you sit your ass at home crying and complaining. You're smart Ess. Real fucking smart."

"I'm tired of your ass always calling me stupid and shit. I am very smart. Smart enough to know when I got a real man to love me. What your ass got? Not shit. Bitch, Dante' told me that you were jealous of me and now I believe him."

"Jealous of what Essence? And why are you believing anything that fool says? I'm your girl. I was the one who stood by your ass when you thought you were pregnant by Chuck and scared your mama was gonna put your ass out if she found out. I was the one who helped you study late at night so that your ass could graduate from high school. It was me. *Me* bitch.

But I tell you what, since you gonna move in with that maggot bitch when I get home, do me a favor. Have your funky ass out today. I'm gonna have my daddy go over there and pack all your shit and change all my locks and my security code. Tell Mr. Wonderful your shit will be sitting out on the curb. He can get a truck and come get it. Have a nice life ho, our friendship is over!" And she slammed her cell phone shut.

That was not how she planned that conversation at all. Her friend was gone. She had just put her out. Derek looked at her through the rear view mirror.

"E'r thing a'ight?" He asked.

"No. No it's not. One of my best friends is fucking with this dude who puts his hands on her. She's in the hospital now because of this fool. Now she telling me she gonna marry the nut and move in with him. I just don't understand."

"Some things are not meant for us to understand," he said. "Sometimes we just have to live and let live. In time, understanding will come and it will all begin to make sense."

"You're right. Can you just take me back to the hotel? I'll eat later. All of a sudden I 've lost my appetite."

Upstairs in her room she sat on the bed staring at the television. It wasn't on. There was nothing that she wanted to watch. Her head hurt. How could this have happened? All she wanted to do was check on her friend. She should have kept her mouth shut. Desiree had called her crying because Essence had called her crying. Their friendship, their sisterhood, was being put to the test. Honesty didn't know if they would pass.

Lorenzo called and asked her if she wanted to go out. She told him that she was not up to it but he was more than welcomed to come up and visit her. He told her that he was on his way. Before they got off the phone she told him to bring her something to eat. She had regained her appetite.

When he got to the room he had pizza and cokes. Since he provided the food, she got the ice. They got their grub on. He didn't pressure her to talk even though he knew there was something on her mind. She wasn't ready to talk yet. The pizza was too good. If she didn't eat before they started talking the conversation might make her lose her appetite again. She couldn't do that to herself.

Honesty was stuffed. Her hand slid down in her pants and she burped out loud. Lo, said that she looked like a pretty Al Bundy. She threw a pillow at him. He threw it back. The fight was on.

She jumped up and ran to the sink and turned on the water. Lorenzo had the ice bucket. He ran to the bathroom and filled it with water. When he came out, she had the sprayer on the sink in her hand.

With a western styled voice he said, "go ahead darling, make my day." So she did.

Honesty turned the water on full force and sprayed him. They were wetting the room up. He ran up on her and soaked her with the bucket of water.

"Okay, okay I give up. You don't play fair," she said laughing, almost out of breath.

"What da ya mean, me? You're the one with the sprayer in her hand."

"Yeah but you got my hair wet. You never mess with a black woman's hair, dude. That's just plain dirty."

"Oh, whatever. This hotel provides blow dryers. And you don't hear me complaining about my hair do you?"

"Umm, if you did, then I would question your orientation. And you don't *have* any hair."

"Yes I do. It's just not as long as yours. But you could have messed up my wave pattern."

"Huh? Stop it; you're too silly for me."

"You ain't seen anything yet." And with that comment he tickled her until she fell on the bed laughing. Some how, he ended up on top of her. They both stopped laughing. He looked at her seriously in the eyes.

"I've never met anyone like you before, Honesty. You make me wanna..."

"I make you wanna what?"

"Leave the one I'm with and start a new relationship with you," he said giggling.

"Ooh, you stupid. Get off me clown."

"Nope. Not until I do this." His lips covered hers and he gave her a kiss that made her clit jump. Damn. This man was the one. They continued to kiss until they had managed to come up out of their clothes. She didn't know when he did it, all she know is that once they were naked, Lo had on a condom. He entered her slowly and he felt a barrier. She saw the look of surprise on his face. Her eyes told him that she would explain later and begged him to continue.

He was a gentle lover. His strokes were long and smooth. Slow and steady at times and then he would pick up the pace. She was going out of her mind. He was taking his time and working her slowly. Her body responded to his with intensity. It didn't take any music to get her worked up. No foreplay either. He had her right where he wanted her.

"Honesty," he whispered. His lips traveled down her body and he sucked her breasts. They both got equal attention from him. Her nipples were rock hard. His dick slid out of her and his hands began to gently knead her pussy. It felt so good to her.

Her moans were getting louder. His fingers slid inside. One first then two. His mouth traveled lower. While he was still fingering her, he began to suck her clit. This was total madness. She wanted to come all over his fingers and in his mouth.

He turned her over. She felt him enter her from the back. Loving had never been this good. This intense. Lo was still behind her when his hands came around front and started rubbing her clit. She leaned her head into his shoulder as she lifted her body up. It was magnificent.

Her gentle lover turned her back over and laid her down. The cool air chilled her body. She shivered.

"Are you cold baby?" He asked.

She nodded "yes."

"Well let me warm you up," he said softly. He pulled the covers back up on the bed and covered them up. Once he did that he entered her again and made love to her passionately. She turned him over and rode him. Up and down she slid on his dick. His hands cupped her breasts and he sat up enough to suck them again. Honesty was about to come apart. She screamed his name. He whispered "I love you." They both came and collapsed together.

As she lay in his arms she knew that she felt for this man. Something she had never experienced before. She would do anything for him. Had he asked her not to leave Atlanta, she probably wouldn't have. Like that pretty singer, she was so gone.

In the dark, she told him about why she had never had sex vaginally. She associated that with real love. Lorenzo took it to mean that she loved him. And if she didn't she cared an awful lot about him. She also told him what was going on back home. He didn't sound surprised about Kim. He must have talked to her himself. But he did sound shocked about the whole friend situation. The advice he gave Honesty was just to take it one day at a time and let the friends' love for one another heal any hurts. Smart man.

Honesty spent her last three days in Atlanta with him. They hit up the Georgia Aquarium and all the tourist spots and the hottest clubs and night life the city had to offer. This was the best time she had ever had in her life. Lo, didn't just make her feel special, he showed her that she was. Her last night in town they made love again and the morning she was set to leave. She couldn't get enough of him. He told her that he was going to come out as soon as he could. Until then, they would have to call, text, and email one another. He knew that she was with Dee but didn't care.

"That's only temporary," he said. "I'm the last man you'll ever need."

It was time for her to go. They had just announced her flight. He hugged her tight. She squeezed him back. She just needed a little more time with him. He asked her to consider giving the checks and hustling up. She told him that she would think about it. He said that he would be here for her always. She told him that he was her fantasy. They kissed. She walked toward the plane. It was time to come back to life. Back to reality.

CHAPTER FIFTEEN

Delante' has nine kids with three different baby's mamas. He had been lying to Honesty all along. When Desiree came to get her from the airport she told her that she had something to tell her. Desiree looked apprehensive.

"You can tell me anything," Honesty said.

Desiree looked at her as if she wasn't sure about that. While Honesty was away, Devan's grandmother had a big get together at her house. The whole Campbell family was there.

"Delante's mom was surrounded by all these kids. I went to see if she needed any help. May, his mom, told me know that when me and Devan got married that I should get my tubes tied," Desiree said.

"Why?"

"Because all those little monsters that were around were her son Delante's. She didn't realize that I knew him, Hon."

I can't fucking believe it. Then again she could. Dee tried to tell her this and that but nothing that he said ever added up. She just never called him on it. Damn. This was not what she expected to hear from Des but it wasn't as bad as it could have been. Honesty was cool though. It was over anyway. She wanted to be with Lorenzo. She would be okay, too. The question was, would Dee? She was going to rock his world.

On the ride home Desiree brought Honesty up to speed on what was going on in the city. Nothing but drama. Carla Ross had caught a dope case. She sold to an undercover and got hemmed up. The feds were talking about picking the case up. Marla was pregnant, again. She didn't know who the baby's daddy was. It was either Deuce's or Ice Tray's. Maybe neither.

This cat named, BJ took the police on a high speed chase down I-40. His car went out of control and rammed the side wall, hitting two cars in his path. He died and he killed a woman and her daughter. They were in one of the cars he hit. Her baby was five months old.

"They need to make it illegal for cops to chase people. That shit ain't safe. Every time they chase somebody now someone ends up getting killed. The shit ain't right. Just let the bastards go. Nine times out of ten they gon' end up doing something else and get caught. It's unnecessary to put innocent people's lives at stake 'cause your ass is having an adrenaline rush and think you can catch a nigga driving a Maserati and your ass in a Ford. It's foolishness."

"You're right, Honesty. This is crazy."

"So what's up with your girl? She move out yet?"

"Well, you know you called Leo and had him pack her stuff up. Girl he cleaned her room out too. I didn't know you told him to break her bed down."

"Yes, I called him and told him that everything must go. I was serious. If she wanted to leave then I was going to make it a clean break. Now her ass ain't got any reason coming back to our shit."

"Hon, don't be so mean. That's our sister."

"I know she is, but fuck dat bitch. This is not about her being our sister or our friend. This is about her allowing some penny ante ass nigga to come between us. When I called her, I know I came at her the wrong way. But she knows I only did that 'cause I care about her."

"That's true. But she doesn't need us telling her what she needs to do. She already knows that whether she does it or not. What she needs is for us to be there for her no matter what. To support her."

"Girl you sound just like Lorenzo. You been talking to him?"

"Now that's what I want to hear about. The elusive Mr. La' Fleur. Tell all."

Honesty told Des about everything that she and Lo did in Atlanta. She was smiling from ear to ear. It was evident in her voice that she really cared for this man. Life had never felt so good. Her friend was genuinely interested in her life. Being happy, safe and well were important to her. Des was the kind of person who wanted everyone to be happy because she was. She told her that she made love to him. The right way. Because she was the only one who knew about her hang-up, she was stunned.

"Bitch, you did what?"

"I made love to him?"

"You had sex once with this man that you just met and hardly know?"

"No, I didn't say once. As much as we did it, I can honestly say that I know him pretty good now."

"You slut. I knew you had it in you. Good for you."

Huh? Where in the hell was this coming from? Honesty thought. This could not be the same girl who is saving herself until marriage. She wasn't a virgin. She and Devan had already been together. But once he asked her to marry him they mutually decided that they would not make love anymore until they had jumped the broom. *Both of them are stupid. I don't think I could hold out.* Their wedding was still six months away.

"Des, wait until you meet him. He's going to be down here soon. Lorenzo is different. Really. It's not like how Dee was, you know? He appeared sincere and all that but under the surface he was just full of shit. You can tell Lo is different by his eyes. They speak to you."

"All hell your ass is sprung. He has you open like 7-11."

"Yes he does. And I ain't mad at him for it."

They laughed and talked more about him and Essence. Desiree wanted to get them all together for a round table discussion. Honesty told her that she would think about it. It wasn't time for anything like that. Her head began to hurt just thinking about hitting Essence in hers.

No, I needed to cool down first. If I don't, I will beat her ass.

The house was quiet when they arrived home. Honesty could tell that Essie's stuff was gone. Leo had gone through the house and packed everything that she had ever put up in the house. He was just following his daughter's instructions. She didn't realize that Essence had had such a presence in the house. Going from room to room she saw things of hers missing.

Intentionally she made her room the last stop. It was right across from hers. She saw the print in the carpet where the bed frame had made an impression. There were white spots on the wall that were square shaped. Those were places where her pictures used to be. Her walk-in closet was empty. Not even one hanger was left. It was cleaned out. Desiree came into the room while Honesty was still standing in the closet. She had tears in her eyes. So did Honesty. Their friend was gone. They had to get her back. *She* had to get her back. Before it was too late.

Honesty let Desiree set the round table discussion up. Essence wasn't going to get out of the hospital until the next day. She didn't want to do it that soon. No one blamed her. She needed to rest. Des set it up for two weeks out. That way it would give them all the time they needed to heal and cool off. Essie was still heated.

Honesty's focus shifted from Essence to Delante'. She was heated with him. It was time for her to get on it. *This bastard was not going to play me and get away with it.* He had fucked with the wrong one.

With Desiree's help, Honesty located one of his baby's mama's houses. Her name was Katrina. She had seven kids by this fool. Not one, not two, but seven. *No wonder el cheapo was always asking me for shit.* He didn't have any money to buy shit feeding all these people. Des and Honesty sat outside Katrina's house, in the parking lot across the street, for a few minutes. They were about to pull off when Des spotted Dee's black Mustang come down the street.

He pulled up in the driveway. The house was a dump. It looked like it needed to get some foundational work done. The porch was sagging and there were missing pieces of concrete off the steps. The roof was sagging on one side too. Maybe it looked better on the inside. Somehow the girls doubted that.

The yard didn't have one stitch of grass in it. It was all Oklahoma red clay dirt. The kind of dirt that does not come out of clothes no matter how much they get washed. Not even bleach can get out red dirt. Not the dirt in the 'O'. It was a small house but the yard was bigger than the house was. The fence around the house was in an 'L' shape. It didn't come passed the driveway. From the street, they could see that the house had a detached garage. The doors on it were the kind that opened out like a door instead of lifting up like most garage do. The screen door on the house was missing the screen at the top. It was a half door. This bitch even had the nerve to have it open. Like what was it protecting? Isn't a screen supposed to keep things out of the house while allowing cool air in? Not on this house it wasn't.

Desiree and Honesty were cracking up. This nigga was living in squalor. When he got out of the car, he had a small sack of groceries. Taking care of home. That's what he was supposed to do. *He shouldn't have lied to me though.* It was time to fuck with him. Honesty called his phone. He stopped in his tracks when his phone rang and looked at his caller I.D. A smile spread across his face. He answered it.

"Hello," he said.

"Hello, baby. How are you doing?" Honesty asked in a silky voice.

"Shit, I'm fine. You back in town yet?" He started looking around like she was close.

"Not yet. I'm on my way though. My plane's about to take off within the hour. Where are you?"

"Where am I?"

"Yes, where are you? Can't you hear me?"

"Uh, yeah, but you cut out for a little bit. I'm over at my homie Kyle's house. Hold on a minute." He put his hand over his cell phone receiver. "Tre'! Tre! Come get this sack and take it in to your mama. Okay I'm back. So you want me to come pick you up from the airport?"

"Nah, Des got me. We have some errands to run for her wedding. Baby, who's Tre'?"

"Oh, he's my god son. You should see him. He's real cute. People say he looks more like my son than my god son."

"You don't say? Did you ever mess with his mother?"

"Naw, naw. Nothing like that. Kyle and I look alike is all."

"Well honey I gotta get off the phone. I'll call you when I'm on the road. I have something special planned for us both later on. I'm going to call your phone and leave you a message so don't answer it."

"A'ight. Love you."

"Unh, hun." Honesty hung up the phone and called him right back. He didn't answer. She left him an erotic message telling him all the things that she wanted to do to and with him sexually. She even went as far as to tell him that she thought she was ready to have his baby.

"When you come over tonight baby, don't bring any rubbers. Tonight, we're gonna to go half on a baby."

He listened to the message before they pulled off. His head was bobbing up and down like he agreed with what she said. Coming out of the house behind him was a thick girl. She was cute. Her hair was in a cute ponytail but she looked slouchy. She had on this stretched out thin white t-shirt, some dingy boxer shorts, and raggedy house shoes. *He laid up with that?*

She grabbed his cell phone and held it away from him. She was dialing numbers. Honesty's phone rang. This was too good.

"Who da hell is this? She yelled.

"Who do you want it to be? Honesty countered.

"Is this one of his bitches?" She was trying to get to her. It wasn't working.

"No, I'm not one of his bitches. I'm *the* bitch. Who is this?"

"This his motherfucking girl Tina dats who dis is."

"Oh, well how are you doing today?"

"Fuck da dumb. You fucking him, bitch?" He was trying to get his phone. She had a small pocket knife keeping him at bay. He was a punk. Scared of a blade no bigger than a minute.

"Whatever he and I are doing you will have to ask him. And please refrain from calling me out of my name. Not once have I said anything to disrespect you."

"Shit, you disrespect me by fucking with my man. Did he tell you that he has nine kids. Yeah dat's right. Nine."

"As a matter of fact, he didn't tell me that he had any kids at all. A woman either for that matter. I was under the impression that I was his one and only. Silly me."

"You probably be giving him money don't you girl. You hear me, you girl?"

She was so intelligent this chick was. How in the hell did he meet someone like her. This was way too funny. Desiree was about to pass out because she couldn't breathe. She was laughing too hard. Of course Honesty had to put the phone on speaker so that Des could hear everything.

"What he and I do is none of your business. If I do give him money it's because I have so much to give. I know you don't have any money to spare with all those kids you have."

At that moment three kids ran out the house in nothing but underwear. One of the kids had snot running down his nose and he was wiping it with his hand. The other kids were running from him because he was chasing them with it. Honesty used that to her advantage.

"I do have money you girl. You don't know what goes on over this way."

"Sure I do. He tells me all the time how he hates your house. It's a dump. Nothing more than a dilapidated shack. The house is falling apart inside and out. You don't clean it good and you don't take care of the kids or yourself."

"Have you been telling this bitch shit about me? Huh?"

"What you talking about. Give me my phone back Tina before I slap the taste out of your mouth." She kept it away from him and came back on line with her nemesis.

"He also tells me that the kids be running around in their underwear all day and you can't cook."

She didn't respond to that. She snapped his phone shut and started hitting him upside his head. He was a punk for real. But before Honesty blinked, his hand pulled back and he socked her in her eye. In front of her kids. She ran into the house crying. All you could hear was the two to them screaming and yelling.

Desiree pulled away from the church fast. Dee came to the door to see what that was. He was so stupid. Tonight Honesty was going to let his ass have it. She had formed a plan in her mind. Des was going to help her carry it out. Dee called and told her that he wasn't going to be able to make it that night. Something had come up. She played like she was sad and shit but was happy about it. Today couldn't have gone any better. Everything was working out better than expected.

At the house, she went through all the pictures that she had taken of Dee. She found one that they had taken the night before her Atlanta trip. He was posing naked. Perfect. She and Des went to the print shop and had them make one thousand flyers with that picture on it. They began to staple them on poles all over the city and putting them on car windshields. When it got dark, they went back over to Katrina's house and put some all over her yard and taped them to her house. They almost got caught over there because Desiree was laughing loud and hard.

Desiree had gotten the addresses of the two other chicks he had kids with and they went and hit them up too. There were flyers everywhere. At the malls, in the grocery store parking lots, fast food places, clubs. You name it, they put it there.

"Honesty, you know your ass is wrong for this right?"

"Yep. But he shouldn't have messed with me. He fucked with the wrong one, Des. I know I wasn't in love with him but I cared for him. I thought that I could learn to love him and that we could have made a great team. This shit hurts."

"I know it does. I'm just glad that you are not sticking with him like your sister is with her dude."

"Naw. That's your sister."

"Whatever. Do you wanna go get some ice cream?"

"Sure I do. Let's bounce."

They rode around for a while to make sure that they had passed out all the flyers. If nothing else could be said about Desiree, she was thorough. The girl was just as crazy as Honesty was. It was fun with her. *This is my nigga if she didn't get no bigger.*

They talked about what they wanted to do for her wedding. Desiree was getting nervous. Her mom was trying to take over too. It figured. Honesty told her friend that she was going to have to stand her ground with her wedding the same way that she did when they moved into their house.

She knew what she had to do. The colors were not decided yet. Honesty told her not to stress out. Everything would all fall into place. Desiree wanted Honesty to be her maid-of- honor. Honesty appeared shocked.

"Why wouldn't you be my maid of honor? After all, you are only my very best friend in the whole wide world."

"Oh thank you so much. If and when I ever get married you are going to be mine. I love you girl. I am so glad that we are still tight."

"I'm not going to let our friendship go that easy. You couldn't have put me out. We would have been fighting when you came home. I don't care if that is your house, shit, I pay bills there too."

"Listen at you with your little potty mouth. I don't think I could have told you to move. Honestly, I didn't think Essence would have either. That surprised me about her."

"Did you ever stop to think that you telling her to get out was actually giving her an 'out'? Maybe Dante' had told her she had to move."

"Do you think that he did that?"

"I don't know. Anything is possible with El Foolio."

They finally made it to the ice cream shop. The last five or six flyers they put outside of the store. Desiree had walked to the counter. Honesty went to the restroom. By the time she returned Desiree she had ordered for them. Honesty got Black Walnut on a waffle cone and Des got Butter Pecan. They liked their nuts. This kid was holding one of the flyers when Honesty turned around. He was reading it.

"Mommy, what's AIDS?"

"Timmy what are you reading?"

"This paper I found outside."

"Let me see that."

The flyer said: "Caution, the man in this picture has AIDS. Please do not mess with him. When you see him coming, run as fast and as far away from him as you can. He won't tell you the truth about his disease. He is a down low brother."

The girls laughed all the way back to the house. Honesty blocked his number out of her home phone. She cancelled his cell phone service she set up for him and she packed what little shit he had at her house. It was over. He tried calling her the next few days but she was not interested. There was nothing he could do. He knew that Leo would do him in if he tried to harm her so he chilled on that note. Honesty was a dirty bitch and proud of it.

CHAPTER SIXTEEN

Dee continued to call weeks after the flyer incident. He was angry and wanted to fight someone. Honesty. Who could blame him? Anyone would have wanted to fight her too. The only thing, or person rather, that held him at bay was Leo. Because Devan and Dee are cousins, Honesty kept tabs on him.

The morning after the flyer was put out was the main thing that she wanted to know about. Devan said that Katrina was on her way to the county welfare office that morning. One of her sisters came to pick her up. When her sister, Monica, got there, she saw the flyers posted up all outside. She was laughing so hard and loud, Tina opened the door just to see what the commotion was.

She saw that it was her sister and stepped out on the porch. That is when she saw the paper for herself. Homegirl was pissed the fuck off. Devan said she cussed Dee out so bad. Told him that it was bad enough that people on the outside were going to be laughing at her, now she had to contend with her own family laughing at her too. Word is that they had a knock down drag out fight over that.

Devan said that the little tiff that the girls witnessed that day wasn't nothing.

"They fight like cats and dogs on a regular," Devan said.

Des has seen her up close and personal. She said that Tina had all these old scratch marks on her neck and that she looked old. Apparently she's in her mid twenties. *I'd look tired too if I was that young, had all the bay bay kids, and a nigga who didn't work but lived off me and my welfare check.*

The Campbell family men were some abusive bastards. Devan was quick to remind us all that he was a 'Drummer'. He said he wasn't born out of wedlock. His mother got a man and kept him. That must have been the pinnacle of their family history to see one of the girls married off.

Des said that Dee was leaving Tina alone. She was too crazy. Him leaving her didn't ring true to Honesty but the other way around. And in the end after all that mess that they went through over the years and with the flyer, they were still messing around. Tina wasn't that mad at him after all. They were still together.

So was Essence and Dante. That was an ugly situation too. They finally had their heart to heart. It didn't get them anywhere though. While Honesty's and Des's main focus was getting their sisterhood back on track, Essence was busy trying to sell them on the good points of Dante. Like the bastard had any.

"Essie, we didn't come here to talk about him. We came here to talk about us. Our friendship."

"Okay then, talk." She was not going to make this easy.

Honesty knew that she was not going to say anything until she did so she broke the ice. Essence was waiting on an apology. Honesty was waiting on her to do the same thing. They were at a crossroad. Neither one of them wanted to be the first to say 'I'm sorry'. Tired of just sitting at the table rolling her thumbs, Honesty spoke up.

"Essence I am sorry. I never should have come at you sideways. Especially while you were in the hospital. You are my sister and I love you very much. We miss you. I miss you. Will you please come home?"

Essence was teetering. It looked as if she wanted to say "yes" but something was holding her back. She started to rock nervously. No one knew what to think. This was a new thing for her.

"Dante said that if you all were my true friends then you wouldn't have abandoned me when I needed you the most. He sa-"

"I don't give a fuck about what Dante said or thinks. He's booboo to me. I care about you. You alone. He can kiss my ass after I shit and lick my bloody pussy but I'm through with him and your ass needs to be too."

"See that's why I didn't want to come over here today. I knew your ass was going to have smart shit to say about my man. He said that you would too. Your ass is jealous of what we have. Jealous, Honesty!"

"Here you go with that shit again. If anything I pity your stupid ass. That motherfucker must have some gold on his dick and crack for sperm cause baby your ass is addicted."

"Man whatever. You can't tell me about *my* relationship because your genius ass doesn't even have one."

"Right. You right about that. But I'd rather be single and have to get my own self off every night than to lay up with a sorry, disease packing, no bathing, maggot mouth bitch like Dante."

"Ooh, that was original. I see why you graduated at the top of your class. You are so quick on your feet."

"Don't choose now to finally get smart Essence. What happened to you? You used to be the toughest one out of all of us. What changed? When did it change?"

"I don't know what you're talking about. I'm still the same person that I was a year ago. It's you who's different. You've always been stuck up and stuck on your damn self. It's always been about you."

"Don't hand me that shit. It's always been about *us* bitch. Us! Not just me and you know it."

"Man, I don't have to sit here and listen to this shit. I have a man at home who's waiting to make love to me."

"He doesn't make love to you dummy. He'd have to know what love is in order to do that. All y'all do is fuck."

"Fuck you bitch."

"Fuck with me, ho."

"I'm gone."

"Kick rocks then tramp."

Essence ran out the house slamming the front door behind her. Desiree was sitting in the same spot dazed and confused. She didn't know what just happed there. Honesty didn't either. Desiree spoke first.

"Well, I think that went pretty well. How 'bout you?"

"Mmm hmm. It was good for me."

"Hungry?"

"Starved."

"Let's go get us some dinner. My treat. We'll go to Friday's. I need a drink. A strong one."

They both needed a strong drink. Honesty was going to get into that restaurant and throw a few back. If she was sober when she came out of that place then she was going right back in and fix it. Des would have to be the designated driver or else they would be driving home drunk. But Honesty was getting twisted tonight no matter what.

At Friday's they ordered some potato skins and mozzarella sticks for appetizers. They didn't want to eat too much because they were going to get their drink on. Desiree ordered a Long Island Iced Tea. Honesty had a double Crown Royal with coke. It was party time. Desi's phone rang while they were munching and drinking.

It was Ebony, Essence's mom. She sounded upset on the phone. Ms. O'dell wasn't the hysterical, cry all over the place type mother. She was one of those bitch-you-must-be- crazy-I'm- about-to-kick- your-ass- type of mothers. Tonight she was in rare form. Apparently Essence had come over there to borrow some money from her. Ms. Ebony knew that Essence had money stashed away of her own so she didn't understand why she was at her door with her hand out. Essie had told her that she didn't have any more money like that. She was down to a few thousand and she needed some money to put with it so that Dante could come back up.

That made her go off. She didn't know that Essence had even moved off of the Ranch with the girls until that moment because she asked her why she didn't just ask them for it. Essie had to tell her that she moved out and told her that they were all into it. Her mom was ballistic. She knew that there was shit in the game. This woman was talking so loud on Des's phone people in the next booth could hear every word she was saying.

"And why in the hell is she trying to raise money for a nigga to come up? Is my baby on dope and y'all just not telling me 'bout it?"

"No, Ms. O'Dell. Not to our knowledge. One day she wigged out on us too. It was all over him. I think he has her brainwashed."

"Brainwashed my ass. The nigga whooping on her dat's what he's doing. Oh lawd. My baby done turned into a dumb ho. The very thing that I told her not to become. What is I gon' do?"

"I don't think that there is anything that can be done. We've tried talking to her several times and it hasn't worked. Maybe you can try talking to her to see if it will do any good."

"Fuck dat. Essence is a grown ass woman. I didn't have no nigga's in this house that beat on me so I don't know where she get dis bullshit at, but I tell you what, until she wise up, girl gon' be on her own."

"So I guess that means that you didn't give her any money?"

"You damn straight. I didn't give her ass shit. If she was trying to help a man who helps her in return then dat der is a different story. But buzzard lips ain't done nothing but drag her down since she done been wit' him."

"I have to agree with you there."

"Hell baby. It don't matter if you agree with me or not. Right is right and don't wrong nobody. Now I gotsta get off dis here phone. My chi'ren need to be fed. Holla."

Honesty laughed herself back sober. Des was laughing too. Ms. O'Dell was a trip. That woman wasn't afraid to speak her mind. She was a good mother. Regardless of what she did to make ends meet, she provided for her kids the best she could. Ms. O'Dell's feelings were on point. After all, she did what she was supposed to with Essence. Her daughter was a hustler like her, but for the most part, she raised her right. By her standards she did anyway. Ms. O' Dell was not perfect. No one was. But she came through for her children.

Now it was Essence's turn to be the adult. She had to grow up and figure this thing out on her own. They all did. Their parents could only take them so far. It was time for them to fly solo. Hopefully Essence's wings would hold her up through the storm. *Hopefully, mine will too.*

Lorenzo called Honesty. He sounded so sexy on the other end of the phone. She told him that she was at the restaurant having drinks and eating with Desiree. He had just finished his evening workout. She imagined the he was looking mighty delicious. Chest glistening with sweat, no shirt on, baggy shorts loose enough to let him all hang out. What a beautiful sight.

There were three bedrooms in his condo in Atlanta. One was his master bedroom and it was nice. It looked like a dude's room but classy. He had chosen bedroom furniture that was rich in color. For a guy, he had some good taste. The other two he used for a gym and an office.

His gym had the latest state-of-the-art equipment in it. He had things that you could hang from, pull on, stretch on, the whole nine. The free weights he had ranged from five pounds to one hundred. He had a weight bench that they used when she was there. Although not for its intended purpose.

Desiree kept pulling her arm. "Lemme talk to him, lemme talk to him. Ple-a-se."

"Oh alright." The girl was being a pest. "Hold on, Desiree wants to talk to you." She was earth disturbing.

"Hel-lo Lorenzo. How are you?"

"I'm cool, thanks. And you?"

"I'm fine. But not as fine as I hear you are." Honesty kicked her leg under the under the table. She continued, "Umm, I've heard a lot about you. Can't wait to finally meet you in person."

"I know. Same here. I'll be down there real soon."

"Okay. Well I'm going to give the phone back to Honesty now. She's looking at me like I'm spending too much time on the phone with you."

"Why would you say something like th- hello? Don't pay any attention to her. She has a few screws loose."

"I miss you Honesty."

"I miss you too."

"I can't wait to hold you again. It seems like a lifetime since we were together."

"I know, right? This thing between us is..."

"Is what?"

"Don't know. Can't find the right words. It just, is."

"My sentiments exactly. I'm going to shower and get this sweat off me. Enjoy your dinner and don't drink too much."

"That's a lot easier said than done. I've got a lot on my mind. We both do. That's why we came here. To take our minds off what's going on."

"Alright. Be safe. I'll talk to you soon."

"G'night."

Her mind stayed on him after they hung up. The man was like whoa. Something in the way he made her feel. No words could explain what he was doing to her. His mother did a great job bringing him up while she was alive. And whoever his daddy was, Honesty wanted to thank him too. Brother man was blessed.

The rest of their meal was filled with light banter and easy conversation. A couple of dudes tried to step up but Ms. Des kindly told them to step off. This was their night. Neither of them brought up Essence or any of the Campbell men. They wanted to stay as far away from gloom as possible.

"Hey, before I forget, one of Devan's friends needs someone who can make some pay stubs and stuff like that. Do you think that you can do something like that? He'll pay you whatever you charge."

"Hell yeah I can do that. This is me remember. Queen of copy. If I can see what the original looks like, I can duplicate it."

"Well that's just it; he doesn't have any stubs at all. He needs someone who can make him some and have them look professional."

"Not a problem. I have check making software that has a stub attached to it. All I have to do is input the information and it will handle the rest."

"Cool. I'll call you tomorrow and give you his number. I'll tell him that I did so that he will be expecting your call. He's cute too, Hon."

"Bitch DO NOT try to fix me up with any more Campbell friends or family. I am through with all that. All of them."

"For your information, I am not trying to fix your crabby ass up. I was merely saying that he was cute. But not as cute as Mr. Lorenzo is. You never showed me any pictures of him. Why not? Is he really ugly?"

"No. And I thought that I did. I have my camera here in my purse. You can see him." Honesty pulled a digital camera out of her purse and let Desiree scroll through the pictures. She stopped when she got to this tall dark guy.

"Is this him? He is cute." She had stopped on this picture that Honesty had taken of Derek the first day they were in Buckhead.

"Naw, that's Derek. He was my driver while I was there. That's one of Lo's cars. He owns a limousine and transportation service. Derek works for him."

"That's what's up. Is this him then?"

"Yessur, that's my baby."

"Damn yo' mama fine," she said to the picture. "Honesty this man is beautiful. He looks better than Devan and my man is all that and then some."

"I know. He was so gorgeous and so classy I had to ask his ass if he was gay or bi. The man has so many things going for himself I thought something was wrong with him because he was still single. It's crazy. Oklahoma women aren't the only ones who are crazy. That seems to be universal."

They continued to talk about Lorenzo and alsoDesiree's wedding. Things were going better for her now since she put her foot down with her mom. Her dad backed her up with it too.

Neither got as drunk as they wanted to be. Des almost did though. The girl was throwin'em back like a trooper. Since she was having such a good time Honesty decided not to drink as much so that they could make it home safely. Friday's was just down the street from their house but she was not willing to take any chances with either of their lives.

Desi had gotten drunk enough to the point where she needed help into and out of the car. She couldn't even take her own shoes off. All of her words were slurred so Honesty had no idea what she was even talking about. Dee had taken her video camera with him and never returned it so she could not tape her. This was not like Desiree at all. .

The girl had started stripping out her clothes. She was singing way off key. Poor girl didn't even know the words. She was just making them up as she went along. Her performance went to another level when she started dancing on the table. The bitch had lost it. Honesty finally managed to get her down and put her to bed. She would have a serious hangover in the morning..

Honesty hurried up and put on her pajamas. She would bathe in the morning. Right now, she was too tired to do any things other than relax. Lying in the bed, she thought about what was going on in her life. *Here I go again.* She hated being reflective. It made her think of all the things she had done in the past. Made her think of D-Snake. It was going to be a long night.

The next morning she got up and showered and then went to check on Desi. She was in her bed passed out. Her legs were hanging off the side. *Looks like she had a long night as well.* Honesty walked over by her and quickly backed up. Desiree smelled foul. All the liquor that she drank last night was coming out of her pores. She needed a bath.

She exited the room without waking her. *I'm sure she would not have appreciated that. She might be an angry drunk. Start swinging on me or some shit.* She did want to take that chance.

Luckily, Desiree gave Honesty the number to the dude that wanted the stubs. His name was Bernard. She gave him a call and set an appointment to meet him later on. He sounded very professional. They didn't discuss over the phone what he needed the stubs for. She just assured him that she was the one for the job.

Kim called and they had a long talk. For the first time in a long time, she was not trying to tell her wayward daughter to leave the game alone. Most people didn't think that white collar crimes were a part of the game. But truly they were. White collar criminals were just on the other end of the rainbow.

She told Honesty that she was going to have surgery soon. It was almost time for Kalif to start school again and she wanted to make sure he was settled into that before doing it. Her spirits were still high. Honesty did not know what to say to her. It had been a while since they had spoken.

She did tell her what happened between her and Essence. Kim said that Ebony had called her with the money story too. Honesty almost forgot about that. Thinking about it made her laugh. Kim must have been remembering too because she guffawed like a hyena. They laughed and talked about many crazy things.

By the time they got off the phone it was time for her meeting with Bernard. They made plans to meet at his office which was ten minutes from her house. She pulled her hair back in a bun and put on a business suit by Prada that she had picked up in Georgia. She looked like she was ready for corporate America.

This meeting with Bernard was going to be the beginning of something new. Depending on what dude was talking about, she might add this to her repertoire. She was always down for networking and making new contacts. There were many places that she wanted to go. This just might help her make it there.

CHAPTER SEVENTEEN

Bernard Coleman was fine. When Honesty walked into his office her breath caught in her throat. He was standing up behind his desk when his assistant escorted her in. She had to do a double take. Ol' girl saw her looking at him and reading her mind she said, "I know. I feel the same way."

He was in the mortgage brokering business. One of his clients was trying to buy a house but couldn't get financing because he didn't have proof of employment. That's where Honesty came in. She would provide the paper that he needed to fax over to the lender. He already had someone on the phone end who could verify that he worked there. All they needed were stubs.

She asked him some pertinent information that she felt would be needed for this. The clients name and last four digits of his social security number. What address needed to be on the stub. How many dependents. Filing status. Things of that nature. With all the questions that she asked he assumed that she'd done this before. She allowed him think that too. *No need to scare him off by telling him I was a rookie. This could be a profitable business venture for me.*

Bernard said that his client was going to come in for a meeting with him if she wanted to stick around and meet him. She told him that it would be her pleasure. It was important to her to know who she was working with. His assistant knocked on the door to announce that his next appointment was here. He excused himself for a moment and came back with another fine ass man. Then two more came in. They must run in packs. She wanted to ask him if it was one of his requirements as a friend or client to be fine, because these men were sexy as hell.

"I hope you don't mind that a few more of my clients dropped in," Bernard started off saying. "it's just when I told them that I had found what we were all looking for they all wanted to meet you."

"I can understand that. Hello gentleman, my name is Honesty Mitchell. I look forward to working with you all." She sounded very professional.

"Let me go around and introduce everyone. This here is Terrence Palmer, Zane Trudeau, and Michel Bose."

They all extended their hands for a shake and said "hello."

"Now which one of you needs the stubs?" She asked.

"Actually, they all will eventually, but Zane's are needed first. We're trying to close on his house in the middle of next month and I need to get everything put into play."

"Okay, so how soon do you need them?"

"Yesterday. But how fast can you get them to me?"

"Yesterday." They all laughed. "Seriously, I can have them for you within the hour's time. I can go to my office and do them and fax them over for your review. If you have changes that need to be made you can call me and I'll redo them to your specifications."

"Wow. That would be great. How much is this going to cost me?"

"How many check stubs do you need?"

"I'll need the most recent three but they have to show year to date on all of them."

"Of course they do. Well, I usually charge two hundred dollars a stub but for you one hundred."

"Okay that's cool. Do you take checks?" Oh boy. Here this man was asking a check writer if she takes checks. All she did was pass bad checks on a regular.

"Not usually but as long as it's good I will."

"Don't worry, my money is good."

"Then that's all that matters isn't it?"

She stayed a few more minutes and then went home and got to work. Making the check stub turned out to be tougher than she expected. Initially, she thought all she had to do was input the information and print. That was not so. The software that she had did not calculate the deductions the way she needed it to. She ended up digging through Desiree's stuff and finding one of her old pay stubs and those numbers as guidance. She saved a template for future reference.

The pay stubs that she made were good. She couldn't tell that they weren't real. No one else would be able to either. These were top notch reproductions. She would know if they passed the test after she got final word from Bernard. After she inspected them one last time, she printed them and faxed them over. Ten minutes later, the office phone rang.

"Hey, Honesty. These look great. Can you do a verification of rent?"

"What does it need to look like?" She hadn't seen one before so she didn't know how to duplicate it.

"I'll fax one over to you that I had used before. It doesn't look too hot. Maybe you can update it or something."

"Sure, send it on over. I'll fax it back when I'm done with it."

Shortly after they got off the phone she received a fax from him. The verification of rent was nothing more than a spread sheet type document that showed when a person moved in, how much rent they paid, and when it was paid. The copy he had sent over was ugly. But on it, he had written all the pertinent information that she would need for Zane. Fifteen minutes later, she faxed back a cleaned up to date form. He called her back as soon as he got it and was so excited. This man was a loon but in a good way.

The other guys there wanted her to be the one who did their documents as well. She was going to have to raise her prices. Bernard said that he had never seen anyone make documents so fast and professional looking. He asked her if it was okay to give her number to some other mortgage brokers. That was fine by her.

Their business was concluded for the day. Everything he had asked her to do, she had done in less than an hour. She told him that she would come pick her check up in the morning. It was time for her to take a nap. She was tired but she hadn't done anything all day.

Just when she was beginning to fall asleep the office phone rang again. Who in the hell was it? They'd better be glad that this was the office phone ringing and not her cell phone. Otherwise she would have let them have it. She hated having her sleep interrupted.

Putting her anger aside, she answered in a polite manner. "Hello, Creative Documents." Damn, she gave the business a name just that quick and it had a nice ring to it. *Reminder to self; get business cards made.*

"Um,yes, may I please speak to Ms. Mitchell?" The strange voice asked.

"This is Ms. Mitchell speaking. How may I help you?"

"This is Zane. I'm a friend of Bernard's. We met today."

"Yes, I remember you Mr. Trudeau. How may I help you?" She didn't want him to think that she was not professional. This man was fine. Definitely someone she could get to know better. But she didn't want to come at him like that though.

"I know this might be out of line, but I was wondering if you would like to have dinner with me? I have a few things that I would like to talk over with you."

"What date did you have in mind? My calendar is pretty full. I don't have that much time available." She was lying like a rug. What calendar? The one on her office wall? It was important that the men thought that she was at the top of her game.

"As soon as possible I guess. I really hadn't thought that far in advance."

"I'll tell you what. I have some time available from seven to nine this evening. I can schedule you in that time if you are able. If not, I'm afraid I won't be able to see you until next Wednesday." And today was only Thursday.

"Would you like me to pick you up? I can. It's no problem."

"Thank you so much for the offer. However, I don't make it a practice to get into cars with men I don't know. I hope you understand."

"I'm straight. So where can we meet?"

"We can meet at Pearls on the Lake. Seven thirty sharp. If you are not there by seven thirty one, I won't be either. My time is valuable, Mr. Trudeau. I don't waste it and I don't allow others to do it either. Are we on the same page?"

"Absolutely, I'll see you at seven then."

"Seven - thirty."

"No ma'am. I don't want to take the chance of being late. I'll be the early."

And so he was. She walked into the restaurant at fifteen after and he was already seated. The hostess escorted her to the table. He was looking nice in a pair of chocolate brown slacks and a pink shirt. His hair was long and black. It had a natural wave to it. He must have been mixed with something.

When she got to the table he stood up. He was tall. Maybe about six-two. Nice. Just the way she liked them. He was a gentleman and came to pull her chair out. After she sat, he did too.

"Would you like to talk first or eat?" He asked.

"Since you are the one who wanted to meet, I will let you decide. This is your time, "she replied.

The server came over and introduced herself.

"I'm Mandy. I'll be your server for the evening. May I start you all off with something to drink."

He asked Honesty what she was drinking and then he gave Mandy both orders. Out of professionalism she ordered water with Lemon and he ordered a Corona. Zane proceeded to tell her about the things that he was trying to do. He wanted to buy up a bunch of properties and rent them out. His plan was to get as many in a short period of time as he could. That way, he would have multiple loans going at the same time before he closed on his first one.

With that happening, none of the lenders would be able to see what he was doing because none of the transactions would hit his credit report yet. Indeed he was intelligent and had a good head on his shoulders. Honesty's nosey ass asked him what he did for a living. He told her that he was into pharmaceutical sales. A dope dealer. *No wonder he needed the pay stubs. This fool ain't got no real job.*

They talked about him going legit. That was his goal. His grandmother was a preacher and she had been trying to get him to clean up his act. Doing this property management and investing was his way of doing it. That was admirable about him. Honesty was all up in his business. She wanted to know if he had children, a woman, women, a man, all that.

She liked him and was not afraid to show it. But she needed to know the deal. No more trick bags for her. Life was short. Too short to be playing kid games with dudes. Just be honest. That's all it takes. Shit women will date a man with kids. They did not discriminate. It's a fact that if he will take care of his kids, then he will take care of that woman.

He had two children. Same mother. One son. One daughter. The kid's mom and he were friends only. She was married now. He was just a father to the children. The kids were six and three. She didn't ask their names. Didn't want to get *too* personal. He didn't volunteer their names either. .

She liked listening to him talk. He told her about his life on the streets. His mom died when he was little and he had been raised by his grandparents. When he was in junior high he started hanging out with some gang members and kicking it tough with them. He started selling drugs in the eighth grade and had been doing it ever since.

He did some time in the Oklahoma correctional system for three years. During that time was when his ex-girlfriend got married. When he got locked up, she was pregnant. She didn't tell him. Only after she had gotten engaged to her husband did she write him and tell him that she was pregnant. The little girl is his though. They took a blood test. But she has the other mans last name. That's fucked up.

Their time together was nice.

He wanted to meet again and she told him that that was fine. It was nice being out of the house. She was scared by what she felt for Lorenzo so she wanted to stay as far away from that as she could. She did not tell Lorenzo that she was not messing with Dee anymore. Her being with someone else kept him at bay.

Kicking it with Zane would do the same thing. She was not looking for a long term relationship or anything for that matter. All she wanted to do was have fun and enjoy the company of a man who didn't mind spending money on her every now and again. She was worth it. It was time for her to leave the restaurant. She didn't want dude to monopolize too much of her time just yet. The last thing she wanted to be was 'convenient' to any guy. She wanted them to have to wait to see her sometimes. That way when they did, they would appreciate her more.

In the days to come she was busy with forms and faxes. The word spread quickly about what she could do with paper. Bernard was promoting her business without her even asking him. She had requests from several companies wanting bills, pay stubs, w-2's, and divorce decrees. She was hot. Her price to the other people was high as hell. For a w-2 alone she charged five hundred dollars a pop. That was fucking with the feds and it needed to be worth her time.

Zane was trying to court her so she let him take her out. He was cute and she was alone so what the hell, she figured. Her house was off limits though. She took him to a condo that Leo owned and hadn't rented out yet. Zane didn't need to know where she lived just yet. She wasn't going to make that mistake again. Lorenzo was going to be the next man to step his feet on the Ranch. No one else.

The condo was cool though. It was fully furnished because she had taken her old but still new furniture there instead of paying to have storage for it.

Leo was going to rent it as a furnished unit. Sometimes she would crash there when she was too tired to go home after the club. That used to happen a lot. She offered him something to drink and they sat down to talk. Zane wanted to buy a new car. It was an old school Chevy and he wanted to get custom paint and interior.

"It may not be my place to say but I don't think that's a good idea. Due to your line of work, having a car that noticeable could be a hazard."

"It's cool, yo. I'll be alright."

" Okay. You're grown."

They changed the conversation. He started talking about sex. Her pussy was throbbing. *I am acting like a ho.* She needed some dick bad though. If he wanted to give it to her tonight she was surely going to let him. Zane must have been a mind reader. Her little skirt was riding up her thighs. They were sitting on the sofa and she draped her legs across his lap. They spread open just enough for a hand, his hand, to slide between. The more they talked and laughed the higher her skirt went. She caught him looking at her. He was breathing heavy.

She took his hand and helped him out. While she was in the back room she had taken her panties off. Easier access. His fingers touched her and he jumped a bit, shocked that she was naked underneath her skirt. She grabbed his arm and moved his hand in more. He was fingering her as he leaned over and pulled her shirt up. Her bra snapped in the front and he used his teeth to get it undone. Titties spilled out everywhere. His mouth covered one breast and he sucked on it with passion. Her hips were moving around.

She asked him if he was carrying. He told her that he wasn't. The disappointment must have shown on her face. He told her not to worry that he would take care of her. When he pulled his fingers out he licked them. Her skirt was lifted all the way over her hips now. His mouth came down and covered her pussy. He was on his knees and she was on the sofa. She draped her legs over his shoulder. Zane loved on her until she exploded. He was good at this.

After that she was ready to go. All she wanted was to bust a nut and that's it. It was like she was telling him "hate to have to eat and run but I must." she was hard. He gave her an out and told her that he had to go get his kids before it got too late. This was fine with her. She showed him to the door and went to shower. Leo wanted her to come to the house and she didn't want to be smelling like she had just been sexing.

Between working with Bernard, writing checks, doing credit cards, and fucking with Zane, she was tired. Every day she had something going on. The mortgage people were calling every day all day. It got to the point that she was spending all day in her home office. Like she had a real job. Her movements were restricted. She and Desiree hadn't even kicked it and they lived together.

One day, Zane asked her if she wanted to go to church with him. That was a new one for her. She had many guys ask her many things and that has never been one of them. Of course she accepted because she was always willing to try something at least once. Her family didn't go to church much. Ms. Louella said they were trifling for that and called them CME Christians. Christmas, Mother's Day, and Easter. The only times they attended church.

Since Zane didn't know where she really lived she had him pick her up from the condo. He looked nice. His shirt was a nice yellow and navy cotton polo shirt and he had on some navy slacks and Tims. She wore a simple white dress with silver heels and coordinating accessories. Her hair was pulled in a pony tail that was to the side. The hair hung over her shoulder. They visited his granny's church. It was cool. She didn't fall asleep like usual. The people in the church were running around and jumping up and down. A woman next to them started speaking in tongues and when Honesty heard that she wanted to scream.

She had NEVER heard that before. The woman sounded like she was possessed. After church Zane wanted to go to the store to get a blunt stick of all things. His grandmother had invited them over for dinner and they were on their way to her house. He needed to make a pit stop first. They pulled up at a corner store less than seven houses down the street from his grandparents. She told him that they could have walked down there since it was so close. He went into the store to get his stick and the juice that she asked him for.

When he got back in the car he started rolling his blunt. Neither saw the car pull up on the side of him. Nor did they see the dude who crept up on the side of the car. All Honesty heard was a cannon going off. That's all she remembered.

Honesty woke up in the hospital. Zane was dead. Some dudes he had been beefing with finally caught up to him. They were able to find him now because of his car. His name was painted on the side.

There was something strangely familiar about this place to Honesty. Leo was by her side when she woke up. Kim was in the chair next to him sleep. Desi and Essence were both standing at the foot of her bed. Kalif was lying across the foot of the bed. Her whole family was there. Later she would come to find out that this was the hospital she was in after her parents' death.

Honesty was okay. The shock caused her to pass out and the doctors just kept her for observation. They released her the next day.

Kim and Leo wanted her to come home but she wasn't hurt and didn't need that. Even Essence was acting normal, Honesty noticed.

Zane's funeral was five days later. She cried for him. He wanted to get out of that life. Make a way for his children. Give them something good to look forward to. Now he was gone. She sat with his family. So did Delante'. She didn't even know that they knew one another.

Dee couldn't take it. He got up and walked out the church. She went out there to comfort him. Zane was his best friend. *How did I not know that?* Probably because Dee never did share that part of his life with her. He let her hold him while he cried on her shoulder when she reached him outside. Whatever had happened in the past between them was long forgotten. There was only now.

When she walked back in the church she noticed Katrina sitting on the other side of the church. She kept staring at Honesty. She felt her eyes burning a hole in the side of her face.

The bitch can't mourn properly for looking at me.

Honesty was exceptionally beautiful that day, too. This was her friend's final hour and she wanted to show the city the reason why he fucked with her. Among other reasons. The crazy thing was that Dee and Honesty had on the same colors. It's like they coordinated on purpose. He told her that she looked nice. She said the same. They hugged. She had to go. Her girls were waiting outside for her. He kissed her on the cheek. Katrina stood on the sidelines fuming.

If looks could kill Honesty would have been dead. She didn't have to worry about Honesty, she didn't want her man. She had one. The girls were on the steps outside the church when she came out. She needed to get some air. They both knew that although she wasn't in love with Zane, she loved him. He was a great guy. She was going to miss him.

They decided to get some food. It had been two days since Honesty had last eaten. For some reason she couldn't bring herself to eat. Now she was starving. Des let Essence choose the spot. They already knew where they were going to go…Chili's. That was her favorite joint. The place looked to be pretty crowded. They waited to be seated.

While they stood in line, Des commented on Katrina's behavior. She was a low class bitch to bring that drama to a man's funeral. Essence was laughing at her clothes. She did look a hot, funky mess. Her sisters were fly though. The hostess was about to seat them when behind them they heard a commotion. A woman had passed out. It was Essence.

CHAPTER EIGHTEEN

Essence was pregnant. She was going to have a baby for the demon's spawn. Dante' didn't know yet. It was her secret. She wanted to figure out what she was going to do about the baby first before she told anyone else. The only reason that Desiree and Honesty knew was because she fainted and scared the crap out of them.

Her greedy ass didn't even want to leave the restaurant after she passed out. Desiree asked her what was going on the reason she fainted. At first she was tried to avoid the question. She wouldn't look either girl in her eyes. But they could tell that there was something she needed to tell them. *A*fter the waitress took their drink orders, they began to talk. It took her a minute but she broke down and let them know what the real deal was. Her story started off slow but she got it all out.

"I'm devastated about being pregnant. Believe me, it wasn't planned. On the contrary, I've been doing everything I could to not get pregnant."

They didn't fully understand what was going on with their friend. All they knew was that she needed them. They would make sure to be there for her. They laughed… talked… sat and cried at the table, thinking about everything that had gone on with them the last few months. Honesty having to be in the hospital, even for that short period time, shook her up. When Zane got killed, she was not prepared for everything that would follow. There were many emotions that she tried to suppress that were associated with the deaths of her parents. His death brought them up.

Mental things. Being back in that hospital brought back memories. Bad ones. She was able to see her parents again, very vividly, before they died. Her mind went back to that night. The killer, D-Snake, slithered in. Even though it was dark, she could see his eyes. Through the mask they looked haunting. In the hospital, she saw them again and they pierced her heart. She wanted her mommy and daddy.

Honesty did not know if she would ever reveal to Lorenzo that she was responsible for D-Snakes death. She still could not believe that she did it herself. It had been so long since she thought about it. Her being a hustler was one thing but would Lo accept her as a murderess? A part of her wanted to tell him the truth but she did not want to lose him.

Everything that she went through these past years hardened her. She didn't want to get too close to people. Other than her girls and those in her immediate family, she really hadn't gotten to know anyone. Even her relationships with Dee and Zane were superficial.

She didn't realize until after he was gone that she hadn't asked him any significant questions that told her who he really was. Of course she asked basic questions. But not once did she ask him any leading questions to find out about him. Who he was or what was going on in his head. Yeah, she listened to him. Heard him tell her that he wanted to get out of the game. She listened to his ideas and they were all wonderful.

She even shared a few of her own but that was just her making conversation. Fronting like she cared when she really didn't. He was fine. She is beautiful. He was doing his thing. She was doing hers. She just wanted them to be able to do it together. *What am I trying to do? What am I trying to accomplish?* She kept asking herself that. Internally, Honesty was trying to be like her parents and did not realize it. She sat up and listened to stories about them and wanted to emulate them. Kim even has video taped footage of them together. In the film she saw two people who were born to be together. They made their own way. People from back in the day who knew them were still talking about how they put it down. She would like to recreate that. But in her own way.

Kim and Leo had their own legacy as well. She looked at them and knew that before they hung up their hats, they did the damned thing too. Devan and Desiree even had a thing that no one could touch. She desired to have that also. This quest that she was on was leading her down a destructive path.

Once the food arrived they stopped talking long enough to eat. The food looked and smelled so good. Honesty could not remember how hers tasted though. It was chewed and swallowed. Poor food didn't have a chance to touch her tongue. When she looked up all her food was gone.

The girls were laughing at her. Laughing with her. Inside Honesty didn't feel like laughing. She would smile with her lips but it would never reach her eyes. She was tired of feeling that way. Of being sad. Searching for something that she never seemed to find. Not even knowing what she was searching for. All she knew was that there was something missing. That her life had something better intended for it.

There had to be something better than this. *And if it's not here in Oklahoma than I am more than willing to travel wherever it is to find it. Willing to do all that I deem necessary to have it.* Love.

That's what she needed. A love that she could hold on to. It did not have to be from a person. Did not have to be a man. If she could find something that she loved more than herself then she would be good. Someone who was not a parent, or brother, or relative.

They sat at Chili's for almost three hours, enjoying the meal and conversation. The date of Des's wedding was approaching soon. Their focus shifted to that. It had been hard for Desiree to make all the plans and do all the things she saw fit that concerned her bridesmaids because Honesty and Essence were out of pocket. Now that they were back on track, it was a lot easier for her to do that.

She looked across the table at them and they looked back at her. Her hands lifted up and stretched across the table to them. They knew what that was, what it meant.

All of them locked their pinkies and said "Unbuntu." That's Swahili for 'we're all in this together.' And they were. They were her family. Never again would they allow an argument, a man, or anything else come between them. Life was too short to be dealing with bullshit. Like Ms. Louella would say all the time, "it's time to straighten up and fly right." They did too.

For the next several weeks every free moment that Honesty and Essence had they devoted to helping Desiree. They threw themselves wholeheartedly into helping her plan her wedding. There was still so much to do. The dresses had to be altered and they still had to find matching shoes. Honesty wanted to wear the Gucci shoes she had bought in New York. But the other girls didn't have any and those shoes had to special ordered. Plus they cost almost three g's a pair.

Desi was so excited as was her mom. One would have thought that it was her wedding instead of her daughters. Her father was cool. He was the typical father of the bride. All Des really wanted him to do was to keep the checks coming. His bank account was going to be lighter after this event.

Devan was looking great. He was getting his dudes together as well. Since Desi was only having the two girls standing beside her, Devan didn't have any choice but to comply. Honesty just knew that his best man and groomsman were going to be Delante' and Dante'. He didn't choose either. He said that they were his cousins, not his friends.

That too surprised Honesty. She thought that they were close. Goes to show you how much she pays attention. His friend's James and Leonard were going to stand up next to him. She had met them and seen him hanging with them on more than one occasion. Come to think of it, she had never really seen him with his cousins unless they were all at the house with their girls.

Des said that Devan had been promoted on his job. It was going to increase his annual income over forty large. His promotion came with a relocation. *They* were going to have to relocate. He and Des had already talked about it together. She was down. They had also spoken to her parents and his. Every one was okay with it. Except Honesty.

He didn't know where he was being transferred. The company was in several major cities and the choice was his. Must be nice. Those were the type of perks that you get when you had a Masters degree in business like he did. Des had landed herself a good one. She didn't care where they went as long as they were together.

Honesty was going to miss her friend. It was hard trying not to think about her moving. For so long it had been the three of them. Since they were losing a roommate soon they would be splitting the bills two ways instead of three. It was great that the house was paid for. Essence hadn't moved back in yet officially but they were going to do that this weekend. Her bedroom furniture and knick knacks had all been put back into place. The only things that were missing were her clothes and her.

She didn't just want to pack up and leave. For some reason she was scared of Dante'. Terrified. Some things did not have to be said out loud in order for them to be true. Essence had been getting her ass beat just about every day from him. Honesty told her to tell Leo but she wouldn't and she made Honesty promise not to tell either. That was the hardest thing for her to do. She did ask her if they could have Leo and his friends help her move. She obviously needed protection and help and Honesty was not down with manual labor. *I didn't move my own shit in my house. I'll be damned if you catch me moving someone else's.*

Leo called before Honesty had a chance to call him. He told her that Kim was going in to have her biopsy in a couple of days. She wanted her to be there. She agreed but didn't know if she was cool with that. It was possible that Kim was facing the big "C." But since she was counting on Honesty she would make sure to be there. She did get a chance to ask Leo if he would help Essence move. It was all good. He said that he would. Essence was so busy trying to keep people from knowing what was really going on with her and Dante', that she wasn't aware they already knew. Leo did.

"I'm so glad that she is leaving that punk alone," he said furiously.

"I know. It's been a long time coming. Daddy, can I tell you something?" Honesty asked.

"If you gwon say Essie with child, me already know. Gul, got a glow about her."

"Okay. So you already know."

"When she be needing me to help her move?"

"This weekend. She wants to do it while Dante' is out of town. I dunno why but the girl is scared of him."

"Tell her not to worry. Me and the boys will come and help her on Saturday. There's a call on the other line for your mother, gotta go. Love ya'."

Essence was grateful when her friend told her that Leo and his guys were going to help her get the rest of her things out of the apartment. They were the ones who moved her stuff out of storage back into the house. Other than packing, she won't have to lift a finger. That's the way it's supposed to be. Women are supposed to be pampered.

Lorenzo called Honesty on Thursday night. He was aware that Kim was going into the hospital in the morning and wanted to offer some support. She hadn't spoken with him in a week and a half. When he would call, she would just look at the caller I.D. and let the phone ring. He would end up leaving a message. She wouldn't call him back. Tonight she needed him. Maybe it was selfish of her to only talk to him on her terms, but right now, that's how things had to be.

There were some things that she needed to talk to him about anyway. It was time that he knew she stopped messing with Delante'. For some reason, she was hoping that would please him.

He called her on her cell phone. Her stomach was nervous with butterflies. Since she hadn't called him back any of the times that he called she did not know how their conversation would go. Hopefully, it would all be to the good.

"Hello, Honesty. How are you doing?" He asked. His voice sounded like he was down.

"I'm good, I guess. How are you? You sound kind of down. Are you okay?" She really was concerned.

"Yeah, I'm good. What's good with ya'?"

"Is that how this conversation is going to go? Us asking how we are back and forth?"

"How do you want it to go? I have been calling you, texting you, and leaving you voice messages but you haven't bothered to call me back. Shit, I'm at a loss for words."

"Look, I know that I was wrong for not calling you back but I had a lot on my mind. A lot going on."

"You don't think I know that? Damn, Hon, I thought that you and I were trying to develop something here. You just left me standing out in the cold."

"I'm sorry baby. You're right. I think I'm ready now."

"Oh, so I'm baby now. And you're ready for what? Cause you're certainly not ready for me."

"Lo, you are my baby. And I'm ready for us to be together. I need you. I was scared"

"Naw, you ain't ready for me. You ain't ready for no relationship. I don't need someone who just needs me. I need someone to love me in return. Someone who *wants* me. Can you do that, Honesty?"

"Lorenzo. You know that I have never felt for anyone the way I feel about you. Yes, I fucked up. I should've called you back. No, I don't know if I am ready to love. But what I do know is that up until five minutes ago I thought that I was cool on my own, until I picked up this phone."

"So what are you saying, Honesty?"

"I'm saying that I need you to be patient with me. We've only just begun. Please don't give up on me just yet. I promise I'll be all that you need me to be. Please, Lo. You know I don't beg."

"Honesty I know what you've been through. I know that every time you get close to someone that they end up leaving or something. But life is short. Aren't you the one who always say that?" He asked pleadingly.

She mumbled "yes" on the phone.

"Don't you believe that? Do you practice what you preach? If you don't you need to. It's time for you to take a chance. Not just on love but on yourself. You don't give yourself enough credit. There is so much more to you than you know. Will you try to let your guard down? For me, baby? Because I need you too."

"I'll try, Lo. I will."

"Good. That's all that I am asking. For right now. So guess who's coming to dinner tomorrow night?"

"You? Baby you're coming to town tomorrow?" Oh, hell yeah! It was going to be on now. Honesty needed to feel her mans touch. And she had to admit that she missed Lorenzo. They used to talk for hours about everything. She wanted that back.

"My flight will make it into the airport about nine your time in the morning. You gonna come pick me up? I'm flying Delta."

"Yes! I'll be there with bells on and very little else. Make sure you eat your Wheaties."

They talked about his trip and what they'd do while he was there. Oklahoma didn't offer much concerning night life but they would do what they could. She really wasn't trying to go out at all. It would have been fine with her if they spent the whole time he was there in her bed. She was sure he wouldn't mind that.

She got off the phone with him because Kim called. She told Honesty that her cousin was coming back to Oklahoma and needed a place to stay. Honesty was okay at first until she told her which cousin it was. Cheyenne. She was Kim's sister, Karla's hating ass daughter.

Kim volunteered the Ranch. Honesty was mad as hell. *Why in the hell did she do some shit like that. She could have let her stay at that condo.* Lorenzo was coming that weekend and Honesty had not counted on having to entertain anyone other than him. Now she was stuck with this bitch. When Kim got better, she was going to have to get her told. This shit wasn't right.

Cheyenne was a gold digger. Aunt Karla was too. That's where 'Shine', as she was calling herself now, got it from. They didn't care who it was or how the dude looked, if he had some cash, he could get the ass. Shine was pathetic. Her outlook on life was fucked up. If it wasn't about her then it wasn't important. She was more superficial than Honesty was. She felt sorry for her two little boys. They had it bad.

Yeah, Shine dressed them nice and gave them nice things but she was a stupid mother. It was more important to her to have things like clothes and shit than lights, water, and gas. She'd buy clothes with her light bill money. Intelligent, right? She was mad at Honesty for a long time. There was this D-boy who liked Hon named Marco. He was fine and had a hard ass hustle about him. Honesty liked him too. They weren't a couple officially but they kicked it. Shine liked him also. But he wasn't thinking about her ass. One day he came over to visit Honesty up but she wasn't there. Only Shine was. Later, Marco told Honesty that Shine asked if she could roll with him because she was tired of being stuck in the house and he told her that she could. They went back to his apartment where he fucked her and then brought her home.

Next thing Honesty knew, Shine was saying that she was pregnant by Marco. Honesty wasn't angry with either of them. He didn't mean shit to her and neither did her cousin. But the ho was already pregnant before she started fucking with Marco. She even admitted it to Honesty with her own slimy ass mouth. Said that the only reason she did it was because she wanted her baby to be taken care of. Marco had loot.

Shine wanted to trap Marco. Thought that since he was balling he would take care of her and the baby. The baby's real dad was working for his uncle as a professional mover. She chose the dude with the most loot. But when Joseph, the real father, got a dope sack, he was the daddy. Honesty told Marco that he wasn't the daddy. The little boy was his real fathers' twin.

Later, Marco caught a case and was taking care of the baby from inside the pen. When Shine had another little boy, he took care of him too. He knew for a fact the second one wasn't his. Shine didn't try to pin that one on him. She couldn't. The bitch was trifling. Honesty did not want her stinky pussy ass staying at her crib. All the dudes in the hood would talk about this odor she carried and how nasty she was. But that didn't stop any of them from fucking her. So that made them nasty too. If Honesty had to put up with her for one day, she could do that for her mom's sake.

CHAPTER NINETEEN

The cancerous mass in Kim's breast turned out to be fatty tissue. It was benign. Honesty did not realize that she had been holding her breath until she exhaled. Her mom was okay. Their family was still intact. Kim's surgery was at seven that morning. It was now almost nine o'clock. Leo knew that Lo was coming into town that morning and that his plane would be landing soon, so he understood that Honesty had to leave. After the morning that she had, she needed to see her man. Bad. *We might have to take a detour before heading back to the hospital.* She needed to release some tension.

Traffic was slow going to the airport. The time according to the clock on the dash was nine ten. She was late. Hopefully Lorenzo would understand. It wasn't her fault. Pulling up in front of Will Rogers Airport, she realized that she didn't have her purse. No purse meant no money. No money meant no parking. What was she going to do? This could not be happening. How was she supposed to go into the airport and find him, if I couldn't get out of the car? There was no way that she was going to leave her vehicle unattended. If she did, it was a strong possibility that she could come out and find it towed away.

She had to do something so she figured that she would run in and have him paged. Her message would be for him to meet his party outside in front. Once he heard that, he should come on out. Only problem with that idea was that once Honesty got inside the airport, there were forty or fifty people waiting in that same line probably to do that same thing. Looking despondent, she walked out the airport. On her way out, an officer stopped her.

"Hey young lady, what seems to be the problem?"

"I left my purse at home so I can't pay for parking and now I'm not able to go inside to tell my friend that I am outside."

"That's something I can help you with you. Come with me." The officer escorted her to the front of the line and she was able to have Lorenzo paged. Beauty did have its advantages. The cop gave her his number and told her to give him a call any time. Having a connection like that might prove to be beneficial. She would keep his number just in case.

Lo heard his name over the loud speaker. She wasn't outside in the car ten minutes when he came out. He had a lot of luggage. More than she did when she left Atlanta. The man had packed like he was staying for a while. He looked so good when he walked out. His chest looked bigger. The t-shirt that he had on was nice and white. His jeans were baggy and his Tim's were neat. He looked straight thuggish. Honesty loved it. Just looking at him turned her on.

"Hey baby. How are you? I am so-o-o-o sorry that I'm late. Traffic wasn't that good and this lady almost hit me. It's been a crazy morning." She said trying to pacify him.

"Don't sweat it. My plane just landed. I hadn't even gotten my bags when I heard my name called. How you do that?"

"Oh, I know somebody who knows somebody." She told him about the cop and how he helped her.

"Oh, so my baby is macking law enforcement officers now, huh? I'd better watch out then. Keep my eyes on you while I'm here."

"You need to do that anyway. I missed you Lo, "she said seriously.

"I missed you too. Glad to be here. How's Kim and Leo."

She told him how the surgery went that morning. He was happy for the family. Kim's health and recovery meant more to them than her just being alive. Right now, she was the glue that held their family together. It wouldn't be the same without her. Although she wanted to stop and make love before going to the hospital, Lo didn't. He wanted to head straight over so he could see Leo. They had some things to discuss. He wouldn't tell Honesty what it was though.

The first person that they saw when they got to the hospital was the last person that Honesty wanted to see. Shine. She had on a pair of shorts so short they looked like denim panties. And she had the nerve to be bending over when they pulled up. She was standing outside talking to some other broad. She saw them pull up. Honesty thought she probably bent her nasty ass over on purpose.

"Ooh la la. Who's this Honesty?" She asked in this fake as voice of hers after she sashayed over.

"Lorenzo, this is Cheyenne but we call her Shine. Shine, Lorenzo, *my* man." she introduced them grudgingly.

"What's up," he said.

She looked down at his crotch. "Not you, but I'll see what I can do about that," she said.

I'm gonna kill her. "Look, Cheyenne. I'm trying to be here for my mother today and don't want to have to whoop your ho ass but trust that I will." Honesty said angrily.

"That ain't ya mama bitch no matter how much you call her that. And Leo ain't ya daddy."

Honesty was about to reach out and touch her but Lo held her back. Inside she fumed.

Lorenzo spoke up first. "See all that wasn't even called for. Now if I were to let her go and she kicked your ass then you would think that I did you wrong. At least she knows who her daddy is. Come on Hon. Let's leave the trash outside. Your mother needs you."

From that moment on, Honesty knew that Lorenzo Semaj LaFleur was the man for her. If she knew what it felt like, she would think that she was in love with the man. He had her heart. The way he handled Shine and that situation impressed Honesty. He kept his voice nice and low, letting Shine know that he meant business. Cheyenne didn't say anything else when they walked off. What could she say? Honesty didn't know if Lo knew, but Shine really didn't know who her daddy was.

Leo was out in the hall when they made it to Kim's floor. He was talking to the doctor. They had their heads together and they were talking in hushed tones. It looked serious. Leo wasn't smiling. *'Oh no'*, Honesty thought. *Please don't let it be something else.*

"Hey, Lee. What's going on?" Lorenzo said. He looked worried too.

"Hey, Zo. Nothing much. Come on in here with the others. We have some tings that we need to talk to you all about."

"What is it Leo? Is Kimmy gonna be alright?" Honesty asked, getting choked up.

"Gul, I haven't heard you call my wife dat since you were but a wee child," he laughed using an Irish accent. "Come on in here and I'll tell you all what's going on. You know I hate repeating things."

Kim was sitting up in her bed when they walked in. She looked good. Her skin was glowing and she looked healthier than she had in a long time. Waiting to come here and have this biopsy and then having to wait for the results had taken a toll on her. The good news that she was well did her a world of good.

"I'm glad that you're all here. My wife and I have some tings to tell ya." Shine chose that moment to walk in, annoying Leo. "Glad dat you decided to join us, Cheyenne. Anyway as I was saying. Kim and I have a word about her health from the doctor. Go head wife. Tell them what he said."

"Well guys. The lump in my breast turned out to be just some fatty tissue. That was good to hear. But the doctor said in seven months..."

She didn't even have a chance to finish, her sister Karla went crazy. "Oh, Lord not my sister. Please don't take my sister. Seven months to live? She's too young. Oh, no. Why lord, why?" Karla was so dramatic. She was falling all over people and putting her hand up against her forehead like she was getting ready to faint. Honesty hoped she didn't. In the last couple of years she had put on a significant amount of weight. She was standing by Honesty but there was no way Honesty was going to catch her.

"Calm down, gul. Nobody's going anywhere. Let her finish." Leo was the voice of reason.

"As I was saying. Overall my health is pretty good but in seven months, well," she paused and took a deep breathe. "Leo and I are going to have another baby."

"Aw hell. Here my ass is thinking that you getting ready to kick the bucket and your ass is just knocked up." Karla said. She sounded like she was upset. Like she wanted her sister to die instead.

"Well had you let me finish before you went into that performance that you put on then you would have known. It's your own fault that you always jump the gun and fly off the handle."

"Excuse me for living. Next time I won't be concerned about your ass I'll just let you be sick."

"Whatever Karla, didn't no body ask you to ev-"

"Shut that mess up!" Ms. Louella screamed. "Now I know I didn't raise y'all to be up in no hospital arguing. God done just blessed your sister to be healed of cancer and doubly blessed her with another baby. Instead of y'all arguing we should be up in here praising God and rejoicing. Don't make me show my ass up in here. You here?"

"Yes ma'am," they both chorused.

"I'm not just talking to them; I'm talking to all y'all."

"Yes ma'am," they all said. Ms. Louella knew how to get some act right when she put her foot down.

The door opened and the nurse walked in. "Sorry to break this up but we need to take you for some tests," the nurse addressed Kim.

Honesty noticed that Shine didn't say anything to her when she was in the room. Leo had pulled her aside and asked her if all was okay between the cousins because he saw Shine look at Honesty like she was sad and then drop her head. Quickly Honesty let him know what happened outside. Honesty could not believe that she would say something so mean like that? Even though they didn't share the same bloodline, they were raised to be cousins. Honesty had always thought of them that way even after she betrayed her with Marco.

"Shine is going through some tings. Pray for her," Leo told Honesty. "But you don't have to let her stay with you if you don't wanna. She can go elsewhere."

"Are you going to let her stay at the condo?"

"Can't. I rented it already and I have workers over there getting it ready. She can come home with me and your mom."

"Uhn uh. I don't want her negative butt around my lil' bro. She cool to crash at the house, I guess."

Both Karla and Shine were together when Leo approached them. Karla's old snake ass started smiling all seductively and shit. It didn't matter to her that Leo was her only sister's husband. If he had a dick, some money, and was breathing, he was fair game to her. Karla even tried to get at Leo before. He didn't respect her at all. And he felt sorry for Shine to have Karla as a mom.

From where Honesty and Lo stood they could see that the smiles that the mother and daughter once had on their faces were now frowns. Karla didn't want her daughter to come live with her. Shine didn't want to stay with her mother either. Shine was furious. She cut her eyes at her mom and walked off. Honesty saw Karla's mouth move. "Bitch" she said without making a sound. All Honesty could do was shake her head and thank God that Karla was not her mother.

Lorenzo looked beat so Honesty offered to drive them home. Before she took him to the house, she stopped by the grocery store and picked up a few things. Desiree sent her a text telling her to pick up a few necessities. Necessities to Desiree were zoom zooms and wham whams to someone else. Chips, cookies, soda, ice cream, and chocolate bars. The girl had a sweet tooth that just wouldn't quit.

"Babe, will you be okay staying at the house with my girls' there too?"

"Yep. Long as we have some privacy."

"We do. Trust. And Devan is there so you'll have some male companionship."

Lo said that he wasn't that tired so they drove to the park and sat and talked for hours. It was time for her to come clean with him. Honesty decided to tell him about D-Snake. Lorenzo understood why she felt the need to avenge her parents' deaths. He said that he would have done the same thing if he was able. It was hard for her to tell him about Zane though. Although they hadn't declared themselves 'official', Honesty needed to tell him everything. She didn't want there to be anything between them. He was worth the whole truth to her.

By the time they got home it was almost six in the evening. Essence was the only one at the house when they got there She was in the kitchen cooking her famous lasagna. The girl had been eating up the house. The baby was going to weigh fifteen pounds fucking with her. Nothing was off limits to her. If it was edible, she ate it.

Honesty introduced her and Lo. They hit it off immediately. He commented on how good the house smelled. That made her blush. She was always self conscious about her cooking. Honesty did not know why either. The girl could hang with the best of them.

They talked for a while and Honesty went and changed clothes. When she came back, Lo was outside getting his luggage. Essie was fixing plates. It was going to be the three of them for dinner. Essence seemed genuinely happy tonight. Honesty asked her what was going on. Inquiring minds wanted to know.

"So what's up with ya chick?"

"Nothing. I just feel good that's all. Dante and I had a long talk today. And before you fly off the handle, it wasn't like that. He told me that he was going to leave me alone. I still didn't tell him about the baby though. I'm not sure if he was serious or not. But I felt at peace after the conversation."

"I thought you were about to tell me that you two were getting back together. Had me worried there for a minute."

"Honesty, you're not the only one who needs someone to love them. I need that too. With Dante I thought that he and I had something special. Even with his cheating. I thought that if I could show him how much of a real woman I was then he wouldn't want anything or anyone else. I was trying to show him a different type of woman."

"I understand that. But in the process you allowed yourself to get hurt and suffer. No man is worth that. He was dragging you down. For a minute there, we thought that yo' ass was on crack or some shit."

"Honesty, Dante is fucking with the telly. He be getting shermed out all the time. That's when we fight. When he on that shit."

"Bitch don't you know that shit's like some jet fuel or something? That'll fuck his mind up in the worst way. How long he been doing it?"

"I don't know. I found some small brown vials in his drawer and when I opened one up the smell almost knocked me out. No one had to tell me, I knew what it was right off."

"Damn. Your ass is lucky you got out when you did. He could've gone to west world on your ass and we be without a sister."

"I know. I wanted to tell you guys but I didn't know where to begin. That's why I was always so defensive about him. He really is a good guy. When he's not high. At first he was only doing it on occasion, now all he does is smoke that shit. He stole my money. That's why I was broke."

"Shit. That's a lot to take in. I'm just so glad that you're back home where you belong."

"Me too, Honesty. Me, too."

They hugged at the same time Lo walked into the house. He was looking delicious. The ladies helped him carry in his two small bags.

"Damn you got a lot of luggage," Essence observed.

"Sure am," he joked.

They all sat down and had dinner. Lorenzo couldn't stop complimenting Essence on the food. She told him that if he kept that up, she was going to keep feeding him 'til he was as big as a house. They all cleaned up the dinner dishes after it was over and retired to their separate places. Desiree and Devan came in just as Honesty shut the door to her room.

She heard them giggling trying to be quiet. Her door swung open real fast as they crept past it. They both looked stunned.

"What y'all doing?" She asked in a deep voice.

"Girl you scared the mess out of us," Desi said.

"Sorry. I just wanted you guys to meet Lo, before you turned in for the night."

"Aw dag, I forgot he was coming to town today. My bad homegirl. Me and Dev been out looking at flowers. I'm getting married next month. I'll be Desiree DeLynn Drummer. Triple D. Like a bra."

"Not your bra with your little ass titties," Honesty laughed playfully.

"Hey now. Those are now my titties you talking about. And I think anything more than a handful is a waste," Devan said defending Des's honor.

"That's because you haven't tried it yet. Now take these right here that I have. This is double 'd' at its best," Honesty boasted.

"What the hell are you talking about Honesty?" Lo said, looking at her like she had lost her fucking mind.

"Oh baby, I was just joking with Devan and Desiree. It's a running joke she and I've had for years. This is my other sister and best friend Desiree and this is my new soon to be brother -in -law and good friend, Devan."

"What's up," the two men said, giving one another dap.

Devan seemed interested in Lo and they went back into the living room to talk. Since Essence was by herself, Honesty and Des went in her room to chat. She was up writing. Essence liked to keep a journal. She was always trying to get the others to keep one, too. They sat on the bed with her and talked about Desiree's wedding and her baby. Each of them had something going on in their lives. Honesty sat back and watched them get excited over the great events that were about to happen. Other than being with Lo tonight, She didn't have much to look forward to.

It had been an hour since the dudes went into the living room. Essence was dozing off so they let her go to sleep. When Des and Honesty got into the living room, the guys were playing Grand Theft Auto on the PS2. The girls made them end the game. It was bedtime. Des took her man and Honesty took hers. They said that they would pick up the game where they left off in the morning. Devan looked like a kid in a candy store. He was excited to have a new friend. So was Lo. Why was it that a dude could meet another dude and in five minutes they were like best friends? But with women, they instantly started off judging one another and make each other jump through hoops before becoming friends. It was a conspiracy.

Honesty lit some candles for Lo and pulled back the covers. Lorenzo wanted to talk. His voice was so soothing. Honesty listened to him while he held her. The progression from them talking to making love was gradual. He said something sweet; she rolled over to look him in his eyes. His voice got lower. She licked her lips. He kissed her. She touched him. When he entered her moments later, she didn't remember a thing he had just said. Her mind had drawn a blank. New thoughts of passion and bliss had replaced the old ones.

Lorenzo loved on her so good until her eyes crossed. His skills seemed to improve. Each time they made love was better than the last. She didn't know that was possible. Before she fell asleep that night, she whispered "I love you, Lo" so low, she didn't think that he heard her. He did. That night, he went to sleep with a smile on his face for more than one reason. The woman he loved now loved him in return.

CHAPTER TWENTY

Bitches seem to experience memory loss when they want something. Shine wanted something from Honesty. To be put down with her game. Become a part of her hustling crew. That is what Honesty found out when she woke up the next morning. Shine had the nerve to be sitting in the living room like they were cool. The girls didn't know what had happened yesterday. Honesty hadn't had the chance to tell them yet. Had they known, they wouldn't have opened the door for her and let her into the house.

Essence saw Honesty coming in the living room first. She acknowledged her straight off. Her stomach was beginning to pooch out. If anyone told her that she would have a hissy fit. The girl wanted to have the baby but she didn't want her stomach to get big. She was scared she would get stretch marks and mar her perfect skin.

"Good morning Essie," she returned. "What the hell you doing here Shine?" She said frostily. Her morning was great until she saw her cousin's stupid ass.

"Good morning to you to cousin dear," she said syrupy sweet. That let Honesty know for real that she wanted something. She was easy to figure out.

"Don't cousin dear me. We weren't related yesterday remember? And I repeat, what are you doing here?"

"I came over to visit you. And to apologize. What I said yesterday was fowl. It was uncalled for and I'm sorry. I was just mad at some things that had gone on earlier and was taking it out on anyone in my path. Will you forgive me?"

"Of course I forgive your ass, but I won't forget it. Snakes do shed their skin fairly quickly. I don't believe you're really sorry though. What do you want? You have to want something because that's the only time you come around or call. This is not a social visit or a visit just so you can apologize. You could have done that over the phone."

Before Cheyenne started speaking though, Essence got up and ran out of the room. Morning sickness was still getting the best of her. She was almost three months along.

Shine was getting ready to say something. Her mouth was opened to speak and then nothing came out. It just hung open so flies could get in. She was looking at something intently. Honesty turned to see what the new focus of her attention was. It was Lorenzo.

He came out of the bedroom with a pair of cotton pajama bottoms on and nothing else. The pants drooped since they were loosely tied. You could see the grooves where his waist and legs met. The sexiest part of a man. His chest was exposed to show how cut he had gotten since the last time his woman saw him. The man had a heavenly body.

When he saw that they had a guest he turned around and went back into the room. He came back with a shirt on and his pants were fixed. Honesty told him that the girls didn't get up early so he was probably thinking it was okay to come out of the room like that. Normally, it would have been.

"Good morning baby," he said as he leaned over and kissed Honesty.

"Mmm, minty fresh. I like."

"Well, you know, what can I say? I know how much you like it so I did that just for you."

"Aw aren't you so tweet,"she said in a baby voice. They exchanged light conversation and forgot about Shine being there. She could tell they did too because she cleared her throat loudly.

"Excuse me; y'all do have company in here. Y'all acting like it's just the two of you," she said trying to sound offended.

"Well had you not come over, it would have been just the two of us," Honesty replied haughtily. "What do you want Shine? I'm not going to ask you again."

"What I need to talk to you about is private," she said looking at Lo. She was expecting him to leave the room.

"Lo is my man. He and I don't have any secrets. Whatever you have to say to me you can say in front of him." She wasn't going to have the chance to dis her again. He was going to be here for whatever Shine had to say.

"This isn't personal. It's business. I have some questions to ask you regarding business."

Honesty looked at Lo. He understood how Honesty felt about her business so he kissed her on top of her head and went back into the room. This was not her ideal way of waking up. The best part of waking up is supposed to with coffee in your cup. Not a snake on your couch. Strike one.

"He's gone. Talk." Honesty didn't have time to listen to her bull shit.

"I want to be down with you and Essence. Word on the street is that Charlie's Angels are now down to two since one is getting married. I want to be the third angel."

Did this bitch just say what I think she said? Did she just ask me to allow her to come into my inner? Aw, hell naw. She had to be out of her mind. Honesty looked at her crazy before even speaking.

"Let me get this straight, you want *me* to let *you* be down with the ultimate hustle? Why in the hell would I want to do that? I only work with people I trust. And I don't trust you."

"Are you still salty about that Marco shit? Girl don't trip over that. Blood is thicker than water any day. We can't let no dude come between us."

"Blood *is* thicker than water, but you and I don't share any blood lines. Remember? And I am not tripping off of Marco. He and I are still friends. I just got a letter from him two days ago. Regardless of what your ass tried to do, he still wants this over here. He knows he fucked up. But I'll be damned if I run behind you. I don't do sloppy seconds. And after having you, his dick is sloppy."

She didn't like that one bit. It caught her off guard when Honesty told her that Marco still wrote her. There was a look of surprise in her eyes. His grandmother, with her messy ass, had called Honesty to tell her that he only spoke to the boys when he called home, he didn't talk to Shine. The only time he wanted to talk to her was when he needed something. Cheyenne looked jealous. The green eyed monster had reared his ugly head.

"Look, fuck Marco."

"You did," Honesty spouted.

"Forget him. This is business. You know I don't have any money or anything. I need to get some dough so that I can get me and my kids a place to lay our heads at night. A place of our own. I'm doing bad here. I thought that things would be different when I came home."

"Why didn't you stay your as in Houston? I heard you were doing well down there. If that was the case, then why come back to this? You were out of Oklahoma. Why you come back?"

"I didn't have a choice."

"What happened to the dude you were fucking with? That ballin' nigga Troy? Did he leave you? Last I heard, he was setting you up in mansions and shit."

"Me and him got into it. When we left Oklahoma I was pregnant with Jaquan. He was happy about it because that was his first baby. We was gonna get married and all that."

"So what happened? It looked like he really cared about you."

"He did. And I really cared about him. But I was stupid. My mama told me not to get my feelings involved and just get what I could get. She told me that I could get some big loot from him if I used the baby as leverage. So I did. I would play these games with him all the time. Threatening to have an abortion, telling him the baby wasn't his, all kinds of dumb ass shit. Shit, he had asked me to marry him and all that. Got down on one knee and shit. The whole nine. He went all out when he purposed. Had flowers all around and e'rthing."

"Proposed."

"Yeah he did."

"No, the word is proposed. You said pur –posed."

"Whatever. You know what I mean. We was going to do it too."

"So what happened? I mean, it sounds like things were cool. Why did you come back?"

"He wanted my mama to come down there for the wedding. I didn't. She always trying to fuck my shit up. But he wanted her there and that's the way it was. When she got there she tried to fuck him."

"Bitch you lying."

"Naw, I'm serious as a heart attack. I was downstairs reading to the kids in they room, cause only the master bedroom was upstairs. It was like we had our own world apart from the kids. Anyway, mama was down there with us too and she said she was going to go on to sleep. I didn't think anything of it.

Troy was upstairs knocked out. He likes to sleep butt ass naked too. That way when he wanted to hit this then it would be easy access. I slept that way too."

"T-M-I bitch. I don't need any visuals of you naked this early in the morning."

"Sorry. Anyway, mama went into our room and got undressed. She pulled the sheet up just enough to expose his dick and started sucking my man off. The sheet fell over her head and he didn't see her face. He had put his hands on top of her head and she was really got into it. I tucked the boys in their bed and came upstairs and walked in the room just in time to see him busting in her mouth. He didn't even know it wasn't me until I started yelling at both of them.

It was so fucked up. He reached over and pulled the sheet back and I turned on the light. His eyes were bigger than frying pans. You should have seen mama. She was sitting there like she had won a gold medal or something. He was mad as fucking hell. Yelling and shit asking me what was going on. I didn't know my own self. What was I supposed to tell him? He pulled the sheet around his waist and came over to me and slapped the shit out of me.

Mama was laughing and shit. Saying mess like 'I told you not to get your heart involved. You was just supposed to fuck him, get what you could get, and leave. But naw, you had to go fall in love, give him a baby and shit.' "

"Girl I can't believe your own mother would do that to you." Honesty was completely stunned. She knew that Karla was slimy but this shit was unreal.

"Girl, mama fucked Marco. That's why I be telling you not to trip off that. Yeah I was wrong when I did that to you and honestly, I didn't care. Until my own mama did it to me. Every guy who had money that I ever brought around her she has either fucked or sucked. Possibly both. Troy was so angry, he threw us both out that night. I haven't seen him since."

"He threw you and your kids out in the middle of the night?"

"Nope, just me and mama. The boys are still in Houston with him. He won't let me take the boys."

"But only one of them is his. How you let him take a baby that don't even belong to him?"

"The night he put me out, I didn't have any money on me so I figured I would just let them stay for a few days until I made some money. Those few days turned out to be a week. Mama drove back to Oklahoma that same night. I was all alone. All the friends I had down there were Troy's friends. I was alone. Anyway, I was going back over there to get the kids on a Thursday evening. That morning when I was at the shop doing some heads I got served with some papers saying that Troy was granted temporary sole custody of the boys. Bitch I was up in that beauty shop showing my ass out. Crying and screaming and all dat.

Michelle, the owner, pulled me into her office and I told her what happened. I was so devastated. Girl don't you know that the bitch fired me right then. Said she would have someone else finish up the heads I had left. Come to find out, that ho was Troy's step sister. All the time I had worked there, I never knew. She paid me a week's pay and sent me on my way. That's when I ended up back here. I need to get some money so that I can show Troy that I can take care of the boys. He won't let me have them otherwise." Tears were streaming down her face.

Honesty wanted to believe her but she was leery. Experience had shown her that Shine couldn't be trusted. *Nobody can act this good though, could they?* Her boys weren't with her. And Karla was a weasel. But then so was she, maybe she was saying this to get Honesty to let her guard down. What's a girl to do? She was honest though. Lying to her wouldn't do either of them any good.

"That's a helluva story you just told. Fucked up is what it really is. I want to believe you. I even want to help you out but something inside is telling me not too. Leo always told me to follow my gut. I'm having strong feelings about this."

"I know and I understand," she said, "and honestly I don't blame you. But what I'm telling you is the truth. I need this. I want my baby's back."

"We'll see. I'm not going to make you any promises. The decision is not mine alone to make. I have to talk it over with Desi and Essie. Even though, Desi doesn't actively participate, we still take care of her. So the word on the street is wrong. It's still the three of us. She's just more of a silent partner. Would you have a problem kicking her down with some things that you get?"

"Hell naw, it's all free to me right?"

"Exactly. Wait here. I'll go in the back and talk to the girls and then I will come and let you know what we all decided to do."

The girls, with their nosey asses, were in the office already when Honesty walked to the back. They had the room monitor on and had heard the whole story. They were burnt up. Honesty was glad that they did that, that way she didn't have to tell the whole story herself. It was rather long.

"Okay, so y'all heard what was going on. Tell me what you think?"

Essence spoke up first. "That's fucked up what her mom did. I'm so glad that my mama don't get down like that. We'd be enemies."

"I know. My mother thinks she's too good to give my daddy some booty, she surely wouldn't be giving it to anyone else," Desiree said laughing.

"Look, Hon, I know you have reservations but this about her kids. Not her. Not you."

"Leave it up to you, Essence to be the voice of reason. Ugh. If you guys think it's okay, then I guess."

They all went into the living room to tell her as a group what they decided. She was jumping up and down when Desiree told her she was in. Essence told her that there were certain things that she would need to know before she could come out with us. First thing was for her to learn how to speak proper English. And class began immediately. Shine was like a sponge. Absorbing all the information that she could.

The girls took her into the conference room and showed her the whole operation. She knew how to operate basic office equipment. That was good. Now they wouldn't have to start from the very basics. Essence liked her a lot. Since neither of them had a man, they could talk to one another. Des and Honesty left Essence to explain the rules of operation to her. They both had men to attend to.

Since it was their rule not to discuss that part of their business with anyone, Honesty couldn't tell Lo what just happened. He asked her what was going on and she told him that Shine came over to apologize and they made up. Knowing how attached he is to family, she knew that he wouldn't ask any more questions after that. She told him that they talked and she was beginning to see her differently. It was true, too. Cheyenne had been raised to be slimy. Karla was a trip.

Now that she was doing business with them, Shine ended up staying at the Ranch anyway. Leo and Kim didn't understand why that was though. Neither of them fell for the okie doke that she told Lo. They knew something else was up.

Leo was puzzled. "Follow your gut," he told her a few days later. He knew something else was in the atmosphere. And it wasn't good.

For the next few weeks they worked diligently with Shine. She was so loud and boisterous.

"Use your inside voice, honey,"Essence told her. Shine didn't get mad either. She was taking things seriously. Honesty had to give her credit for that.

Devan and Lo were busy entertaining each other when the four of them were out and about. The two men were busy doing things for the wedding that Devan couldn't seem to find time to do alone. Like what was that? He just wanted to kick it with Lo. They hit it off well.

One day the girls were taking Shine out to do her first check at this small strip mall. Before they pulled in front of the store Essence spotted

Lo and Devan. They were going into the Game Stop. *Wedding details my ass, they were buying video games.*

Shine turned out to be pretty good. All the lessons had paid off. Her speech had changed and even the way she walked. Of course the things that she wore had to change too. The clothes that she brought over to the house were stripper clothes. She was ready for the pole. Honesty still had reservations concerning Shine. There was something inside telling her to leave her alone. But the girls felt that she was exaggerating the whole thing. Thought that since Shine and Honesty had conflicts growing up that she was still harboring ill feelings against her. That wasn't the case. Honesty wasn't holding a grudge. Well, maybe just a little one.

Being suspicious of her every day wasn't going to make their working relationship better. She had to let it go. So she did. Once she did that, they all worked together smoothly. They could really get the job done now. They had a meeting at the round table. It was time to take the show on the road. Even Devan and Lo were down with taking a trip.

Desiree made travel arrangements for them all to fly to Minnesota. The fellas had never been there. Neither had Shine. They were all in for a treat. The Mall of America was a hustlers dream. Stores spanned for miles. There was no way a person could make it around the whole mall in one day without being in shape. Honesty couldn't wait for them to see it.

The morning of their departure came quickly. Everyone was excited. This would be the first time in all of their history of messing with checks and credit cards, that they allowed anyone outside the crew to come along.

"Hell we feel privileged coming along, don't we Lo?" Devan said.

"You should," Desiree replied.

Desiree booked three suites at the Marriott. It was right across the street from the mall. Essence and Shine shared a room and the couples had their own. Once the plane landed, a shuttle took them to the hotel.

From the time they landed in Minnesota things were off to a wonderful start. Everyone they came in contact with was helpful. They treated them all like stars.

"I could get used to this treatment," Shine told Honesty.

"I already have."

Shine had called Troy and told him that she was doing better. He had told her that he would bring the kids to see her. They missed her. He said that he missed her too. She was happy. Troy admitted that he had acted harshly with the situation involving her mother and told her that they could try to work things out. She told him that she was hustling with the girl's. That made him happy for some reason. Maybe now he would have a woman who could contribute instead of taking all the time.

Between the six of them, they gave that mall and the city of Bloomington the blues. Desiree even had to come out of retirement for a moment. She found the shoes that she wanted to get married in. They cost eleven hundred dollars. She wanted her bridesmaids to have a pair. Shine even got some.

The credit cards they used had limits on them ranging from five to fifteen thousand dollars. Each person had eight cards apiece. There was no way that they were going to run out of cash or stores. Those cards were saved just for this mall.

Seeing Honesty in action did something to Lo. He had formulated a plan all his own. She could see the wheels turning in his head. A light bulb had come on inside. Just because he owned legitimate businesses didn't mean that he wasn't still a hustler. When they got back to O-City he started to put his plan down. Lo had taken five grand and opened two business accounts at local banks. Then he 'hired' some homeless people to work for his mock, landscaping business. The bank had given him some business checks.

He had his employees going all around the city in one day cashing check after check. They did this on a Friday. The merchants would call the banks verification number to make sure the check would clear and that it was good. It would and it was. They would give the people the money.

Lo had made the checks range anywhere from five hundred to nine hundred dollars. He would keep half of whatever the check amount was giving the other half to the 'employee.' On Saturday morning he was in the bank before twelve noon, pulling out the five grand that he used for an initial deposit. In one weekend he had made almost twenty five large. The boy was a shear genius.

Devan started writing dudes in prison he knew who were lifers. He would write them and ask for the information that was on their birth certificates and the social security cards. Once he had that, he would be at vital statistics getting birth certificates a plenty. Then he would take it and have one of the homeless people they had worked with before go take the ID picture. They would start an account and it would be on again.

It was funny and also sad how the ladies corrupted the men. Devan wan an engineer and Lo was a business owner and they had them doing dirt right along with them. It is true what the Bible says; EVIL COMMUNICATION DOES CORRUPT GOOD MANNERS. All those times the guys were playing video games, this is what they were talking about. Coming into the game with their women. Goes to show that there is a little bit of hustle in everyone.

For the next couple of months, the six of them worked hard getting money. They knew that this was not going to last too long. It was better to quit while they were ahead. For all of them, even Shine, this had turned out to be more than any of them expected. Desiree and Devan would be getting married in October. Three weeks to be exact. They all wanted to have the operation completely shut down by then. When it closed down, all of them planned to move. The game would be over.

CHAPTER TWENTY-ONE

Her best friend's wedding was just around the corner. Honesty was so nervous. They all were. This wasn't just Des's wedding anymore it was all of theirs. She was just the only one getting married. Lo was still in Oklahoma City. He had to decided to extend is trip. Now that he was working with Honesty that made sense. He did have to fly back to Atlanta though for a couple of days. There was a problem with one his drivers. Dude had gotten pulled over for speeding and Fulton County cops found a loaded weapon in the car. The idiot had it sitting in the seat. They took him to jail and impounded the stretch Hummer that he was driving. Lo had to get it and him out of jail.

Dude should be glad to have a boss like Lorenzo. He was professional enough to deal with heads of states but still hood enough to understand the streets and handle the cops. He knew how to handle business for real. The driver was released without incident after Lorenzo showed them he had a permit to carry the weapon. The 'permit' was Honesty's handiwork.

Since he wasn't going to be gone that long, Devan flew out with him. The company that he worked for had an office in Atlanta. He figured that he could check the office out and have a look around the city. It was important for him to see if that was a place he would be willing to go. Lo had been trying to sell him on the good points of his city. It seemed to be working.

While they were gone for those two days the girls kicked it. They got their hair and nails done. At the beauty shop, Kita, Desiree's hairdresser gawked at Cheyenne. Shine's hair was long. It looked like she had weave in it. But all of it was hers. Her hair touched the top of her butt. Her hair was almost prettier than Honesty's. And she looked like Pocahontas. Just like her mom did when she was her age. Hon was happy with herself for once because although Shine was getting attention, she was not jealous of her. Ms. Honesty was growing up.

Desiree wanted to go the club Friday night. This was going to be her last hurrah before she was a married woman. She had called Devan and asked him if it was cool that she went. He told her that it was fine and he and Lo would be back by then. At first Honesty didn't understand why she checked in with him like that. It's not like he was a control freak.

"I do that out of respect for him," Desiree told her.

With her, having a man meant treating him the best she could. She knew that she didn't have to ask him anything. It was her way of showing him that he was the head of their family. She was letting him know that every thought and opinion he had was important. The things she did for him were spirit building she said.

Her heart went out to men. Especially black men. All too often she would see how they got beat down. It pained her to witness that. Desiree worked as a counselor and had seen the effects that mere words could have on a man. She felt it was her duty as a black woman to help build black men up. Not tear them down.

For years black men have been on the receiving end of put downs. Whether it was in the work place, on the streets, or at home. They were suffering. The injustice that many of them faced on a daily basis was enough to make them feel worthless. Some of them had even been told that. It was disheartening to her.

So, Desiree, the advocate decided that she was going to build black men up one man at a time. She would start with her own. When he would come over, she would have his slippers waiting for him. He never had to fix his own plate or draw his own bath. This bitch would even scrub his back. He was spoiled and pampered by her. But whatever she gave to him he gave her right back. That's what made them so good together. They took care of each other.

They had lunch and shopped. It seemed like all they ever did now was eat. Every other place they went Essence was popping something in her mouth. She was now five months pregnant and showing. There was no way she could deny being pregnant now. Ebony was finally getting used to the idea of being a grandmother. She had been talking to Kim about it and was finding understanding. It was hard for her at first because she thought that she was too young to be a 'granny' as she called herself. But Kim had made her see that both of them had lived their lives and had raised some good kids. It was time for them to let the girl's grow up.

Dante' called Essence and was being sweet to her. Too sweet. He was telling her some shit like how much he loved her and missed her. She still hadn't told him about the baby. But Oklahoma was small and eventually he would find out. There was no way she could go nine months without him finding out. For now, he was in the dark. Honesty told her to blow him off. They were having a wonderful day and didn't want it ruined because of him. Today was not going to be one of those days. And today it would be happy. Unfortunately, that was short lived.

Less than twenty minutes after she got off the phone with Dante', she ran into Shanequa, Dante's current girlfriend. She was also one of the girls Essence had caught him in the bed with. Her stomach was just as big as Essence's was. He would know for sure she was pregnant now. This bitch was bound to tell him. She hated Essence with a passion. And who should Honesty see coming up on the side of her? Katrina. The girls had just been pampered and they did not feel like fighting. Shine and Desiree walked up next to them to make sure that they were chill. They could tell by the looks on their faces that it was about to be something.

"Who knocked your stupid ass up, Essence?" Shanequa said tartly.

"As usual Shanequa, you're in my business. I guess you can't help it since you have none of your own. And my husband and I created this baby thank you very much", she said in return.

"When did your ass get married and to who? He must have married you only because he found out you were pregnant."

"If that's the truth, then that makes him an honorable man. Unlike the piece of shit who got you pregnant. You all have two kids and he still hasn't married you. It must be something with the Campbell men.

They have all these kids by these stupid ass women and they don't marry any of them. Such a shame."

They all knew that she was throwing barbs towards Katrina as well. Trina knew it too. That's why she rolled her eyes. She was smart and kept her mouth shut. They stood there for a few more minutes exchanging insults before Honesty had enough.

"Let's leave these welfare bitches alone. They are so beneath us," Honesty said and pulled Essence's arm as they walked away together. Shine whipped her hair around like a white girl and gave them a funky ass look. They were heated.

The confrontation wasn't bad . All Essence and Shanequa did was argue a bit. Shine thought that it was going to come to blows when they first saw them. And Honesty hadn't dealt with Trina enough to know what she was capable of doing but she knew herself and she wasn't having that shit. Desiree had asked Essence if she felt that Shanequa was going to tell Dante' she was pregnant.

"Probably. The bitch can't hold water. She knows how possessive Dante' was about me though. I'm sure she'll tell him I got married first."

They were all laughing about what Essence had said. It was too funny. Her? Married? None of them could see it.

"What made your crazy ass say that you were married?" Shine asked.

"I dunno. It just came out. In a way I'm glad that I did though cause now he might think twice about approaching me. He's not one to step to a man. His thing is hitting women."

"He's such a punk then. Bastard," Honesty said heatedly. He made her so angry. Just thinking about him made her want to do some bad things to him.

It was getting late and the girls and made plans to watch a movie. It was girl's night in. They each chose a movie at the store and bought plenty of junk food. When they got home Shine made a huge pallet on the floor for them in the family room. The others got the stuff out the car while she did that. Desiree and Essence fixed the popcorn and drinks and they all changed into their pajamas and got comfortable.

The first movie that they watched was School Daze. That was an all-time favorite. Honesty loved the music. Shine and Essence loved the fine looking men in it. Des loved Tisha Campbell. She was her biggest fan.

That was the only movie that they watched. Instead of them watching television, the television ended up watching them. All of them passed out on the floor. Shine snored very loudly. Honesty left them and went and got into bed. Sleeping on the floor was not for her.

She woke up to the smell of frying bacon and brewing coffee. Which one of the girls' was cooking she did not know and really didn't care. All she knew was that she was about to get her grub on. After brushing her teeth and washing her face she made her way to the kitchen.

Imagine her shock when she went into the kitchen to see that the cooks were not her girls. They were not girl's period. It was Devan and Lorenzo. She ran up to her man and jumped in his arms. The other girls were still passed out in the family room sleep. It was like they were drunk or something.

Her big mouth woke them up. Honesty didn't understand how they could sleep through that delicious aroma anyway. Essence of all people should have waked up. Her greedy ass dreamed about food.

Every one was busy talking and fixing plates.

Devan gave Desiree a look that said "meet me in the bedroom." They left the room for twenty minutes. Nobody noticed but Honesty. When they came back, Des's hair was out of place. She looked at Honesty who stared back at her. Desiree knew that her friend knew what had just happened. They both started laughing. *Wait for the wedding night my ass.*

Honesty told Lorenzo that the girls had planned to go out that night but she was willing to change her plans if he wanted her too. Desiree's behavior was rubbing off on her. Lo said that he wanted her to enjoy herself and kick it with her girls. He wanted to hang with his dude.

The guys played video games and the ladies sat around and talked. Essence said that she had to take a nap. She was always tired now.

Desiree, Shine, and Honesty played scrabble. At eight o'clock they started to get ready to go to the club. There were enough bathrooms so that each lady could do her make up with comfort. Honesty had a double vanity so Shine did her hair and makeup with her.

The fellas decided to go too. Devan had on some black Prada jeans with a clean white Prada button down shirt and a black leather jacket. He wore some white leather kicks on his feet. Dude was clean. Lo was Sean John'd from head to toe. Navy jeans, yellow and navy shirt, and navy hiking boots. He looked good.

Essence was modest with her outfit. She didn't want anything to show too much of her stomach. The black dress she wore was short but tasteful and it concealed her stomach. Her black strappy heeled sandals were nice. She wore silver accessories. The girl looked elegant. It didn't matter that it was October. Shine wanted to let it all hang out. The girl had a nice shape. Her shorts were more like panties. The six inch heels she wore showed off her long legs. She had chosen a strapless tank top which looked great because she let her hair hang down over her shoulders.

Needless to say they were all hot to death. At eleven o' clock when they finally stepped out the house they were looking too good for the city. The fellas had already gone ahead of the girls. They were taking too long to get ready. They made plans to meet up later . Shine had bought herself a new Nissan Armada. The piece was nice. It was Candy Apple Red with smoke gray leather interior, a vista roof, ten CD changer and other perks. They arrived at the club in style. She drove through the parking lot slowly so people could get a good look at her shit. This was her first time driving it.

They parked and got out. The club was packed. Honesty was going to call Lo and ask him where they were but they had just gotten here. It didn't make sense to hook up right now. There would be time for that later. Club Infinity was the place to be on a night like tonight. The city was jumping because the Lil' Wayne concert just ended. Everyone was looking their best. People were supercharged. But there were more people outside the club than on the inside. The girls were outside parking lot pimping. There wasn't anything better than that. Everybody who was any body was at the club tonight.

"I gotta pee. Let's go inside and then come back out," Essence said.

"You're pregnant Ess and always have to pee," Des said.

"You mean to tell me that you want to pay fifteen dollars to go into the club and pee and then come out? You know if you have to pee again, you'll have to pay again?" Honesty spoke up.

"I know it sounds silly but I really gotta go," she said pleading with them.

This was getting out of hand. "Look Essie, let's go to the food place next door. They're still open. If they don't let you, then there are plenty of trees behind the building."

Every one was laughing. They walked over to the restaurant but their bathroom was out of order. Looked like she was going to have to make do with a tree. They walked around the corner with her to pee. Desi had to go to. Shine couldn't believe that they had all that money and wouldn't just pay to go use the one in the club. She was still wet behind the ears. The toilets in that place were a breeding ground for bacteria. Honesty would take her chances with the great outdoors anytime.

A bug was crawling up Des's leg when she squat down to pee. It was so funny. She was moving around all crazy. Shine told her that she better be still before she ended up with pee in her shoe. Then she would be stinking. That made her laugh all the more.

The four of them were walking back around the corner laughing so hard. Des was on the phone with Devan. He said that they were standing by Shine's truck. They were on their way to meet them. Someone cut them off on the way.

"Hey, excuse you bitches," Shine said. It was a group of girls who blocked their way. From the middle of the group of them, one emerged. It was Shanequa.

"Well, well, well, what do we have here? If it ain't the bitches of Eastwick," she said. This bitch was about to catch one to the dome.

"What the fuck are you jabbing your jaws about, po ho? Don't you have anything better to do?" Essie said.

"Yeah I have something better to do. Right now I plan on kicking your ass."

"Baby, it ain't that much ass kicking in the world. Stop talking and make it do something ho. As-a-matter- of-fact, I'll make it do something." Essence reached her little as up and swung out on Shanequa. Her fist caught her upside the head. The girls stood around to make sure that none of those other girls got involved. This was going to be a one on one fight.

Shanequa never stood a chance with Essence. What made this girl think that she could phase Essence? People just naturally assumed that Essence wasn't a threat because of her size. She showed them time and time again that big things came in small packages. She was lighting that girls head up. She must have thought that her friends would help her, the reason she came at Essence sideways.

Someone from the crowd screamed, "He got a gun!" The crowd broke left and right. The fight was still going on though. Nobody came forward with a gun.

"Baby come now! The commotion on the other side of the parking lot is Essence and Shanequa. They're fighting!" Desiree said frantically to Devan.

"Me and Lo are on our way!"

Shanequa was screaming "shoot this bitch!, shoot this ho!"

When Honesty heard that, she started mean mugging the other girls. She wished they would pull out some heat on her girl. This was going to be a fight. Not a shoot out at the O.K. Corral. Desiree had her eyes trained on them too.

They were looking at the wrong people. Out of the crowd came Dante' wielding a pistol. The girls stopped fighting just in time to see him point the gun at Essence.

Shanequa kept screaming, "shoot her now. Do it now nigga!"

His eyes focused on Essence. He looked from her face to her stomach back to her face again. The sound that came out of his mouth sounded like an injured wolf. With his arm lifted, he trained his gun on Essence. Everything was moving in slow motion.

Devan was trying to reach Dante' before he fired. He dived on his cousin just as the first round was discharged. The gun fired so quickly, it was empty by the time Devan and Dante' hit the ground.

Honesty's heart stopped as she saw both Essence and Shanequa fall. Blood was pouring out like water. She ran over to Essence but Lo wouldn't let her touch her.

"Don't move her, babe. You could do more harm than good."

Essence was lying so still on the concrete. It began to rain.

Next to her friend Honesty dropped to her knees. The rain poured down her face as she looked toward the sky.

"Please call 9-1-1. Somebody please call them."

Lo dropped down behind her and held her. There was nothing that she could do for her friend. She was just as powerless as Essence was at that moment. Desiree and Shine were crying hysterically. Devan was on the phone. Dante' had ran away. In the distance was the wail of sirens approaching. They were too late.

"Baby, I'm here for you," Honesty heard Lorenzo say. The tears had begun to mix with the rain.

The paramedics lifted Essence carefully onto the stretcher. No one saw them take her away. Their eyes were downcast that whole time. Lo had to help Honesty get up off the ground. Devan took Desiree with him. The others rode with Shine. They headed towards the hospital.

No one said a word. The ride over was quiet. Only tears could be heard falling . Lorenzo held his woman in his arms. He was always where she needed him to be when she needed him.

The police were at the hospital when they arrived. Ebony was there and so were Kim and Leo. It also appeared that Shanequa's people were there. A woman who appeared to be her mother was breaking down. Ebony followed suit. The doctor was talking to them both. Ebony let out a death cry and fell to the floor. Kim raced over to comfort her friend. Her eyes told Honesty what she already knew. Someone would be attending a funeral.

CHAPTER TWENTY- TWO

The soloist was singing 'His Eye is On the Sparrow' when they walked into the church. So many people were there. Honesty saw many faces that she knew and more that she didn't. Her heart was so heavy. This should not be happening. In four days, Desiree was getting married. They should not be at a funeral.

Everyone was crying. Honesty was too. She couldn't stop. Her grief enveloped her. Too many bad memories were coming back. When she looked up front and saw that casket sitting there, she was a little girl again. All the pain she had felt *that* day, she was feeling all over again. She sat perfectly still on the church pew the entire time she was at the church. Her eyes stayed forward. Head never turned.

Lorenzo was rubbing her hand. Tears steadily streamed down her face. She was mourning for lives lost. For a child who would never have a chance at life. For a mother who lost her daughter and her granddaughter in one fell swoop. She lacked understanding.

Why would that man want to take a life so precious? He plotted and planned and premeditated all that had gone down that night. That man had allowed jealousy and rage to eat at him. Until he was consumed with a passion deeper than love. Hate. Shanequa had intentionally picked the fight with Essence. It was all Dante's idea. He had told her to start the fight and once it got going he was going to start shooting at Essence. The only thing that he didn't count on was Essence kicking her ass the way she had. He figured that since Essie was small she would get beat up. He thought wrong.

No one was supposed to know that he was the shooter. He was going to fire from under a car. That's where he was when Shanequa called him. Hiding under a car. Only when he heard her voice did he come to her rescue. If he didn't love anybody else in his sick, twisted, little world, he loved Shanequa.

The funeral progressed . Desiree grabbed Honesty on one arm and Lorenzo grabbed the other. The funeral was over. It was time to walk around and view the body. She wasn't ready for this. This wasn't ready for her. Her legs wouldn't move. They couldn't.

Honesty's heart caught in her throat. She couldn't breathe. Tears began to stream even harder. "Come back!" She screamed in her head. "Please come back to me. I need you. I've always needed you." Up front, she almost fainted. "Look into the casket" her mind screamed. "Look! Look!" She wanted to. She needed to.

Lorenzo held her up when her legs started to give way. He held her close to his chest. 'I'm here for you baby. I'll always be here." His lips grazed the top of her head. That gave her strength. His love gave her strength. Her head turned toward the casket. She looked down.

The woman who lie there was beautiful. Her daughter was going to look just like her. They were being buried together. Chyna was the baby's name. She looked like a porcelain doll. A shaky hand reached down to touch mother and child. "Good-bye," Honesty said to them. She was saying it to her parents too. Finally she had closure.

Her head lifted up. She looked at her friends who were there and they all linked arms. Healed, Honesty walked up out of that church. The dreams would stop. All nightmares cease. Her heart was fixed. She was free to love again without fear of loss. Stepping out into the afternoon sunlight offered her the cleansing she needed to complete the healing process. Lorenzo hugged her.

"I love you, Lorenzo."

The rest of her friends walked over to her.

"That could have been me."

They all nodded "yes" in agreement. It could have been. Thank God it wasn't. Their arms wrapped around Essence and her unborn child. They would never let her go again. Troy had brought Shine's boys down to see her. She was leaving the funeral and going to see them. It had been almost four months since she had seen them but they talked on the phone all the time. She said if Troy gave her another chance, she would not mess it up ever again. This was from a woman in love.

Essence was overwhelmed with relief. Her life had been spared. Although, she was sad for Shanequa and her baby, she couldn't help but feel blessed that it wasn't her. It was hard for her to think that anyone hated her so much to plot her death. Dante' had had a hold over Essence she realized. But none so strong that she would help him kill anyone.

Lorenzo took his eyes off the road long enough to look at his girl. She smiled. For the first time in her life she was in love and could proudly admit it. This was a new beginning for her and the man she loved. Nothing would be able to separate them again.

Devan and Lo got calls on their cell phone at the exact same time. Lo's call was from Troy. Dev's was from Delante'. Both of them had news. Shine was speeding and got pulled over. When the officer had asked her for her license and registration, she gave him one of her check writing I.D.'s accidentally. He searched her purse and found several different pictures. After running a check on her real name, he found that she had a warrant. She was in jail. So was Dante'. That's what Delante' called to tell Devan. It was a bittersweet moment for all of them.

Troy didn't remember how to get to the county jail so they all said that they would meet him at the hotel. He was staying downtown anyway so they could park and walk over. He was sad. This trip was supposed to be a reconciliation trip for him. He came here to take Cheyenne back with him. To take her home. The county jail was packed. There were bondsmen milling around. Some of them were not even there to get someone out. They were there drumming up business in case someone needed a bondsman. Desiree had already called Mykelti. He was like their family bondsman. By the time they got there, he would have already had the paperwork drawn up. He came from the back of the county and had everything done.

Troy was happy about that. His boys would be too. They were ready to see their mama. Desiree had stayed at the hotel with them so that they wouldn't have to be at the jail. It was no place for children. Mykelti didn't tell Troy what he wanted to hear though.

"She hasn't been booked in yet. The paperwork is done on my end but until she's booked they can't start the release."

"That's fucked up! What's taking so long?" Troy was frustrated.

"They take their time on these things," Mykelti said. With his end of the deal done, he was ready to go. Troy paid him and they waited. Before he left, Troy stopped him.

"Did they say how long it could be?"

"Yeah. Up to sixteen hours."

Today was sweeps day and they had over one hundred people to book right now. And the officers just kept bringing them in. This was ridiculous.

"You guys go on ahead. I'll wait here," Troy said.

Lenora Campbell, Dante's mother walked in the jail. Honesty saw her getting ready to go through the metal detectors. She looked at her and then looked at Essence. Her eyes shifted to her belly. Uh-oh, it was going to be some more shit.

She walked over and started talking to Essence. "My son said that that was his baby you were carrying. I will expect to see it when you have it so that I can tell if he really is a Campbell." No this bitch didn't. She had her nerve.

Essence stood with her back straight and lifted her head. "I don't know what Dante' told you but it's not the truth. This baby doesn't belong to him, it's mine. I was married a few months ago. This baby belongs to my husband, Morris."

"If you's just now getting married, then how come yo belly so big? I know you wasn't stepping out on my baby now was you?"

"Your baby? Your baby beat me in the head and blacked both of my eyes when I confronted him about cheating on me. Your baby was plotting to kill me and in his rage he killed the mother of his two children and his unborn child. Your baby, Ms. Campbell is not a baby at all. He's a coward ass man."

"Chile no you didn't. After all he den done for you. You's an ungrateful little hussy. He should have left you when I told him too."

"Your son did nothing for me. I took care of his ass. Nothing that he had or did was done on his own. It was me. All me. You need to stop believing everything he tells you. He's a liar. A liar and a cheat. Now if you'll excuse me, my husband is at home waiting for me. Good day."

Essence walked off leaving that old battle ax standing there, stewing in her own juices. It could have gotten loud and ugly but she controlled it. The audacity that woman had. She was crazy.

Ten hours later, Shine was released. She looked no worse for wear though. Just a little shaken up. Troy was the first to see her when she walked through the door that said inmate release. He ran over and hugged her so tight and picked her up doing so. She was crying. They were a pair of saps. But happy saps. Back at the hotel Shine was going to stay at the hotel with Troy and the boys. Everyone was getting ready to leave and give the couple some privacy. Lo and Devan gave Troy some dap.

"We'll see you tomorrow man."

Out at the car, Essence hugged Shine but when Honesty went to hug Shine she backed up a bit. When she asked her what was wrong, she said that she was sore. Honesty didn't say anything about the fact that she had just hugged everyone, including the guys, but her. But she let it go. Her mind was troubled over that but she didn't want to call attention to it right now. She would wait until she got with Desiree. She would understand where Honest was coming from. Lo might. She would run it past him tonight when they got home. For right now, all she had could do was wonder.

It was a long ride back to the Ranch when a person was tired. Streets got longer. Red lights stayed red forever. The whole drive was tedious. And someone always had to pee. That someone was Honesty. There were some flowers sitting on the front porch when they pulled up to the house. Three bouquet's. Lo and Devan were looking confused. They didn't send them. The looks that they were giving one another said so.

It was one bouquet for each young lady. All of them were from Leo and Kim. They had something different to tell each of them.

Essence's card read: *We are so blessed that you are here with us. Rejoice in the life that you have been given. Look up for all your help from now on.*

Des's card read: *Congratulations on your upcoming nuptials. Don't let anything come between the love that you and Devan share. It is priceless.*

Honesty's card was the last one: *God blessed you to be our baby so long ago. Today, you got what you have been seeking… closure. Close the door on the past and look toward the future. It is yours for the taking.*' All the cards were simply signed Land K.

The fellas looked at them like they were crazy because they had tears in their eyes. They were standing on the porch hugging. Lo and Devan went into the house. The girls walked into the house sniffling and giggling.

Honesty pulled Desiree to the side and told her about what went down after Shine had been released. Neither understood why she would do that. Desiree told her that Shine probably just felt weird having been in jail and didn't want to face her. Sounded good but that still didn't make any sense.

In the room she looked at Renzo for answers to her question. She asked him the same thing that she asked Des.

"Don't you think it's weird the way she brushed me off?"

"Babe, I didn't even see the interchange between you two. I'm sorry. But I'm sure it's nothing."

Am I making something out of nothing?

"Baby, if you tell me that I'm tripping then I'll leave it alone but I just don't feel that I am. When Shine got released she didn't even look at me. It was like she was avoiding me. Then when we were getting ready to leave she hugged everybody but me. Tried to hand me some bull about being sore or some mess."

"Maybe she was, Hon."

"I would believe that had she not hugged you and Devan. And think about the way Troy held her. I'm telling you the girl was not in any pain."

"Honesty, I don't think that you're making something out of nothing. But I do think that you're reading more into this than you should. You guys have gotten closer and things have been going so well for you two. Just ride this out and see how she acts in the next few days.

If she continues to avoid you then, you'll know something isn't right between you two."

That sounded like some sound advice. She took him up on it. If in a couple of days things were still strained then Honesty would know something was up. Right now, she was going to make love to her man and go to sleep.She was tired.

It didn't take a few days for her to figure out something was wrong between her and Shine. The next day would be more accurate. She had just finished washing her face and brushing her teeth when she heard a knock at the door. There were some men's voices up front. Desiree knocked on her door. She said that there were some people there to see her. A tear rolled down her face.

Honesty put on her sweat pants and a tank top and went up front. It was two detectives. The taller one handed her a piece of paper. It was a warrant for her arrest. She was on my way to jail.

Desiree called Lorenzo's name. He came running up front. Honesty was crying. The officers were putting her in handcuffs.

"What's going on here, man? Why are you taking my girl to jail? What did she do?" All the questions started to roll off his tongue.

"Step back, sir. She'll have a chance to go before the judge and hear all the charges against her."

"Well can you tell me if she has a bond?"

"Yes sir she does. It will be ninety - five thousand dollars."

"Da-mn, who y'all think she killed?" Lorenzo was tripping. But not more than she was.

This whole thing was unreal. Honesty didn't read all the papers they had given her. When they had grabbed her arm the papers fell out her hands. They said that she was being charged with five counts of first degree forgery and twenty one counts of second degree forgery, multiple counts of false impersonation, and conspiracy. She was in big trouble.

As they were escorting her away she was shouting instruction to all of her friends. She told them to call Leo and Kim. Mykelti for sure. Bernard Coleman because they had an appointment today. It was apparent that she wouldn't make it. And she told them to call Shine.

Something told her that she would know exactly what was going on here.

And she did. While little Miss Muffett was in jail, she dropped the dime on Honesty. Because she was caught with all those I.D. cards, the cops wanted to know what she was involved in. Rule number one that they told her was to keep all business items at the office. She was caught with every I.D. that she had been assigned. Rule number two was keep your mouth shut no matter what. That didn't happen.

Honesty did not know what they told her. She didn't know what they asked her. But she did know that her cousin sold her out. That was unforgivable. Honesty thought that they were better than that. That they were family for real. But what she just showed her was the exact opposite.

The detectives drove her to the county jail. When they got down there, they drove through a secured gated entrance. There was a keypad that the driver used and punched in a code. The gates opened up and they drove through. They ended up in what looked like an underground tunnel. Everything in there was steel.

The short detective, who had read her rights, opened the door for her. The whole time he was at the house he looked sad. This was not the job for him. He took the cuffs off her and told her to stand by this sliding steel and glass door. His weapon had to be put up in this cubby that they used for weapons.

The morning was busy but it went slow for Honesty. She finally made it through the whole booking process. Fingerprints, photos, and demographics. Then they sat her in a cell that contained at least fifteen other women. Some of them were sleep on the hard concrete floor and others slept on the metal bench that lined the wall. There was one toilet that sat sixteen inches off the floor. It was connected to the only sink and drinking unit in the room.

There wasn't any tissue in the place. Someone had put a bloody pad next to the toilet. This place was horrible. There were only two phones in the room and both of them were currently being occupied. When one became available, she hurried up and jumped on it. She called Leo. Ms. Louella answered the phone and accepted the call.

"You all right baby?" She asked with concern in her voice.

"Yes, granny. I'm cool. Are they coming to get me out?"

"Yeah, honey. They's already down there right now. You should be home soon. Just keep ya head up and pray."

"Yes ma'am. Will you click over and call Lo for me, Granny? I really need to hear his voice."

"Sure, hold on." She clicked over and dialed his number. While she was waiting on him to pick up, this woman was pulling on her arm.

"Hey, do yo' people got three way? See if they'll make a call for me. I need to tell my old man I'm in here so he can come get me out. He don't even know I'm here." Honesty told her to hold on. Lo had answered his phone.

"Ms. Louella, what's going on?" He said.

"Oh, baby. Honesty is on the phone and she wanted to talk to you. She said she needed to hear your voice."

"I got it from here, Granny. Thanks."

"So you miss me and needed to hear my voice?"

"More than you know."

"Ask him to make the call," the lady said again. "I'll give you my dinner tray."

"Who is that?" Lo asked.

"This young lady in here. She wants you to make a call for her. Her man doesn't know that she's in here and his phone doesn't accept collect calls."

"Give me the number. But this is the only call that I'm making. I know how things can get up in there."

"What's the number? He said he'd make the call for you." She gave Honesty the number and she repeated it to him. Her man, Mo, was at home and she told him what happened. He told her that he was on his way. She got off the phone happy.

"Thank you, thank you. Girl you just saved my life." The lady crossed the room and sat down.

"Where are you baby? I'm ready to come home." Now she was pouting.

"I'm up front waiting on them to release you. Mykelti said they should be bringing your papers to you to sign soon." No sooner than he said that a smart ass lady jailer called her name.

"Hold on babe. They just called my name." She sat the phone down and ran to sign her papers then ran back. "Lo, is Mykelti still out there with you?" He said "yes."

"Then ask him how long I have to wait once I sign the papers." He told her that he said within the hour. She was getting impatient.

"Calm down, Hon."

"You tell her baby," Ms. Louella said. They had forgotten that she was on the phone.

"I will. I love you Gran. I love you, Lo. I'll see you when I come out." They hung up the phone. The lady that she had made the call for would not stop staring at her.

"Yo hair show'll is perty. Is it real?"

"Yes ma'am it is."

"Can I touch it?"

"You wanna touch my hair?" This was getting weird.

"Uhn, huh. It look so soft."

"Umm, sure. I guess that's okay."

"Ooh this is soft just like it looks. What kind of perm you have?"

They talked about hair until they finally called her name. Lo was the first person she saw upon release. When he walked over to her, she started crying immediately. Lorenzo took her home and she had a good bath. Her skin felt she had little bugs crawling underneath. They didn't make love that night. Only held one another close. Tomorrow morning before she left the house to go to the church for Desiree and Devan's wedding, she would have to call her lawyer. It was time to start fighting her case.

CHAPTER TWENTY-THREE

Dear Diary: I have spent the past eight months fighting a case that I now believe I'm not going to win. Since October of last year I have been to court at least twice a month. Each time the district attorney comes with some crazy offer sillier than the first. She is new to the county and very eager to make a name for herself. It looks as if I'm to be her example.

Karla's son, a known pimp and drug dealer, took the county sheriff's and the city police on a three county high speed chase. While he was speeding down the street he ran a red light. A mother and her five year old son were hit. They survived. Charles was throwing dope and guns out the window while he was driving. He finally got caught when he drove over a device that blows your tires out. In the end, he ended up with a ten year sentence. On paper.

These bastards are trying to give me fifteen years for the five checks they could prove that I had a part in. Fifteen years. Justice might be blind but the bitch can see the difference between men and women. And the shit just ain't right. I am pissed the fuck off!

With that Honesty closed her diary and sat back. It was a known fact that in the State of Oklahoma a woman could commit the exact same crime that a man did and end up with more time than that man. The state was biased towards sex and then color. A woman didn't stand a chance at a fair shot in court. Women of color got the shortest end of the stick. They might as well hang it up because they were going down for real.

A white man named Finch Howl was convicted of murder and rape. He killed and raped four women around the state. Two were elderly and two of them were high school students. The man had cut the big toes off each of them and burned half of their faces. The judge sentenced him to nine years in prison.

And yet, they offered Honesty fifteen. Offered. Like fifteen years was a gift. Today she had another court appearance at nine. It was almost eight o'clock in the morning. She was getting familiar with this routine. Mr. Wall, her attorney, played hardball. If her going to court for the next decade meant a fairer, lighter sentence then she would keep going.

The only reason that the district attorney's office even found those checks at all is because those were Honesty's 'before' checks. Checks she wrote with her right hand before she started to use her left. Most of them were just practice checks anyway. Cheap shoe stores, grocery stores, places like that. All of her big licks were lefties. Luckily, they could not prove that she had anything to do with the credit card or payroll check scams. The D.A. didn't know she was ambidextrous.

Neither did Shine. Honesty was sure that had she known these folks would have been trying to hang her up by her toes. The feds were thinking about picking up the case and taking it out of the state's hands. That's only because they heard she was involved in credit card fraud. None of those accusations were proven. Her petty checks didn't interest them enough so they left her alone.

Shine got off with a three year deferred sentence. It wouldn't even go on her record. Honesty had a chance to talk to her about why she told on her. She said that the cops asked her what was going on.

"They told me that I was going to get life in prison and never see my kids again. They said that they would send them to an out of state orphanage where they would get lost in the system."

Honesty believed that she feared for her children. When they were 'working' together she saw another side of Cheyenne. A side that was trying to be better than her mother, Karen. Shine really did love her boys. *Hell, I would have done the same thing to protect my kids,* Honesty admitted so she forgave her. They still spoke often. Her and Troy did get married. Lo said Shine was going to have another baby. A girl. Troy told him that when he talked to him the other day. Honesty was happy for her. For once in her life, Shine was truly happy and she deserved it.

Honesty knew that everything she was going through right now did not have anything to do with Shine at all. It was about her and the choices that she has made. The life she was leading could have only ended two ways. Jail or dead. Smart people quit the game while they are ahead. She wasn't one of them. And now she was facing jail.

Lorenzo was back in Atlanta for the rest of the week. He has been her rock through it all. She told him that he needed to check on his home and make sure that his businesses were doing what they were supposed to. If she hadn't made him leave he would still be by her side. A person can only be there for you for so long. Sometimes a person needed to stand alone. This was her time. For far too long she had people coming to her rescue. That's why her ass acted the way she did now. Never had to take responsibility for her actions and always blaming someone else.

It's been like that a long time too. When she was in school and she didn't do well on a test it was the teachers fault for not giving her all the information she needed. If she didn't get something that she wanted at home, it was one of her family's faults. Someone was always her scapegoat. Even the Shine and Marco situation was something that she could have prevented had she wanted to.

She knew that Shine was feeling him. And given half the chance Marco would have liked her too if Honesty was not leading him on, making him think that they could be together. Not! Her ass was so damned cocky thinking that no dude would want another female if she was the other option. Hell, she felt like she was the only option. That day Marco asked her what time she was going to be home so that he could come over. She gave him a time but blew him off. She was at the next nigga's house letting him lick her pussy. Marco was the last thing on her mind.

Lately she has had to take stock of her life. Things have been fucked up for far too long. It was time for her to make a change. Last year she had gotten the closure with her parent's death that she had been seeking. But since then she hadn't done anything to make any real changes in her life.

Lo wanted her to move to Atlanta with him. Kim and Leo thought it was a great idea. She told him that she would think about it. Moving has been at the forefront of her mind for a long time. Oklahoma did not have anything to offer her anymore. It would always be home but she couldn't live there and be happy. Her life needed to change like everyone else's.

Desiree was going to have a baby. She and Devan were moving. They were going to Atlanta. She thought that Honesty should take Lo up on his offer. Of course Honesty wanted to be where her sister was. It would be hard to live so far away from her. They had been tied to the hip for years.

Sitting in the courtroom caused her to reflect on so many things. She remembered a conversation that she had with her daddy right before he died. He had told her something about people in Oklahoma being like crabs in a bucket. Back then, she was young and was just listening to what he said. But she lacked understanding.

Now, she was a grown ass woman and she knew exactly what he was talking about. People who were trying to come up couldn't do it in Oklahoma. If you had something and another person didn't, then they would do all that they could to bring you down. Just like a crab in the bucket. Honesty was at a grocery store the other day when she finally saw what he was talking about.

A woman wanted to buy some crabs. The meat clerk took the lid off the crab tank and was finding the ones she wanted. While the lid was off, the other crabs tried to climb to the top. One crab was on its way. He had almost made it when, bam, he was back in the tank. Another crab had pulled him down.

Honesty didn't think that she was the crab that got pulled down. Rather, she was not the only one. There are many trying to come up and do better in Oklahoma. But it was not only the cops that kept people down. It was the people that the hustlers were the closest too. Those who were supposed to love them.

A person finds out how many true friends that they have when they are fighting a case. People who used to call Honesty for no other reason than to see if she was going to pull a caper, had stopped calling her. When she used to go out to the club nigga's and bitches would flock around her trying to be on her team. They would treat her like royalty. But now that they believed she was no longer the head bitch in charge, they were cool on her.

Regardless of what they thought she was still the one. There were others before her and she was sure that there would be others after her, but there was only one her. Everybody knew her name. She was more popular than Norm from Cheers.

Just as she thought, Mr. Wall came in to the court, walked over to her, said a few words, and went over to the D.A. But instead of him coming right back like he usually did, he stayed for a while. Not only did he set his briefcase down, the man took a seat. Something was going on. He looked back at Honesty and winked. Something was definitely going on.

Her head was starting to pound thinking about being locked up. The county jail was a horrible place and before she hit any prison yard, she would have to be there. It was taking the prisons a minimum of sixty days to move people from the jail once they have been sentenced. That place was from hell. Nobody should have to be there.

Hank got up from the table. Her stomach began to jump when she saw him coming. He had a smile on his face. In his hand was one sheet of paper, his briefcase was still up front. The prosecution team had made an offer. Two years. She knew she had to take it. He told her that she didn't have to accept that offer. That he would fight for something else. Even with the words that she heard him speak, it was the one's he didn't utter that were the most important.

"Take this deal. It ain't gonna get any better." She told him that she would take the deal.

Before he went back to the table she wanted him to negotiate time for her to turn herself in. She needed to get her affairs in order. The prosecutor gave her forty-five days. If she didn't turn herself in, he said, they would put out a fugitive warrant and file escape charges against her.

"She'll be here even if I have to bring her myself," Mr. Wall assured them.

The judge called her to his bench and read the charges and plea agreement. He also wanted to make sure that she wasn't coerced or threatened into accepting this deal.

"Of course I was!" She wanted to scream. *You all aren't giving me any other option. This is do or die for me.*

After court was over Hank said that she would do about a third of the actual sentence For him, that didn't seem that long. Maybe it wasn't for some, but for her, it was. Any time spent away from her family involuntarily would be a long time. She cried all the way home. Lorenzo called to find out what happened in court. He was going to take the first plane back to her.

Instead of going straight to her house, she drove to her parent's place. Ms. Louella came to the door as soon as she saw her pull up in the drive way.

"I'm always here for you baby, just you remember that," she said, holding the door open for her. Honesty hugged her and told her "I know." She had always been her granny. The only one she has known. Kim was lying in the bed with the baby when she came in. Amethyst was a year old.

Honesty looked up and saw that Kim had her arms outstretched to her. Without saying any words she just walked over and crawled into bed and allowed Kim to wrap those arms around her. Kim rocked her while she cried. This is what she had been warning Honesty about all those years. She should have listened.

"I'm so sorry, mama. I really am. I should have listened to you. I don't want to go to prison." She said through tears.

"I know you don't baby," she said, "but don't worry too much about this. Things are not as bad as they seem. You have to look at the good instead of the bad. Don't think of this as a jail but as a jewel. The things that you will learn here will be gems. Take those things and apply them to your life. Make it a point to come out a better person than you were when you went in." She said encouragingly.

"That's what Desi said too. Well, something similar to that. But she was encouraging too. I'm just gonna miss you all. This is so horrible. I promise that I was through. We were all through."

"I'm aware of that. But do you remember when you were having all those bad feelings about letting Shine in? Well, this is why. You didn't know that she was going to do what she did, but you did know that there was something up with her."

"I had forgotten about that. It seems that I had wanted us to be family for so long that I was willing to believe that my gut was wrong. That's my fault. Leo told me to trust my instincts. I'll never doubt them again."

"That's my girl. I need you to be strong right now. We are going to come through this as pure gold. Look at me." Kim lifted Honesty's head to face her. "You need to hear this. There has never been a moment in your life that I haven't been proud of you. No matter what it was that you were doing.

I should have told you this a long time ago. Your parents didn't want you to build an empire like theirs. Just the opposite. Don't you know that you were created for greatness? Everything your parents were doing was so that you could have the best and be the best.

Why do you think you went to all those private schools? Girl that wasn't my doing. That was Mr. Golden Mitchell himself. That's why he named you Honesty. All things about you were supposed to be good. I'm afraid that because of what I was doing, that may have rubbed off on you. I love you and have always loved you as my own. Your mother was my sister.

There is not a day that goes by that I don't miss her and mourn her death. But going forward, we, you and I, need to stop mourning her death and start celebrating her life. You think we can do that?"

Yeah. But how do I do that? I mean us."

"First off, you have to stop thinking that your parents wanted you to continue their legacy. They wanted to get out of the life. That's what your dad was working up to when he got killed. Let this life go. You have enough money. Get your ass a job when you come home. Lord knows you have enough clothes and shoes to last you for two years without having to wear the same things twice. Go back to school. Get your life together. You wanna do something to please your parents? Do something that they really wanted to do with their own lives. "

"What's that?"

"Live within the legal parameters of the law. Hell, write a book. Your mom loved to write. Do *something*. Just live your best life now."

Honesty heard every word and took it to heart. It was time for her to make a change in her life. A significant one. That night, she decided she was going to write in her journal every day. Not just when the mood hit her. Each day she was free and even after she got locked up she was going to write down what she did that day and what she was thinking. Her life was going to count for something.

Lorenzo came in the next morning and along with her family and friends surrounded her with as much love as she could stand. Essence's baby girl, Innocence, was clinging to her like never before. She was so precious. They had bonded so much since her birth.

The days came and went fast. The night before her surrender was sad. Everyone was trying to make light conversation but it just wasn't working. She told them that they didn't have to. They could talk normally and she would do her best not to cry.

Lorenzo and Honesty made love like this was their last time together forever. She didn't want to let him go. He cried on her shoulder. Had that happened two years ago, she would have said he was gay. But now she knew that this was a sign of love. He was going to miss her as much as she was going to miss him.

She didn't want anyone to go to court with her. Mr. Wall came to pick her up. It was easier for her to leave them at home versus at the elevator in the courthouse. Maybe she took the easy way out. It took fifty-six days for her to leave the county jail. While she was in there, she did crunches and lunges. Her abs and legs were tight. *My man ain't gonna recognize me when I come home.* Because the county was so understaffed, they stayed locked down in their cells most of the time. Honesty read and wrote letters to pass the time. She was happy when she finally left.

The corrections department has an assessment facility that all incoming inmates have to go through before they make it to any prison yard. The staff will screen all inmates for diseases and health issues. Also they performed mental and academic tests to see what was going on in their head. Some of the people coming in didn't have an education so this helped determined who needed to go to school.

All of Honesty's tests came back negative as far as diseases were concerned. She scored high on all the battery tests they gave her. With all her assessments complete, she was ready to leave. Her sentence began day one at the county and she was ready to end it. Honesty was ready for a new life.

CHAPTER TWENTY-FOUR

She knew it was going to be some shit in the game as soon as she hit the yard. It was almost eleven at night and the yard was closed. But a feeling rose up in her that let her know she needed to beware. The women she was about to meet were treacherous. All the ladies that were going to that facility got off the bus. They were escorted to a concrete room that was painted white. It had a bunch of ugly green mats in it. They looked like they had been in a war. And lost. Those were their beds.

An inmate came around the corner with a large laundry barrel on wheels. It contained bed rolls; two blankets, two sheets, one pillow case, two bath towels, and two wash cloths. This was all the linen they would see for months, maybe years. Then she gave them what was supposed to be a pillow. It matched the green mattress that they had given them but it was flatter than a pancake.

Before they left the assessment center, they had already been assigned their housing units. The officer who processed them in told them to get their stuff and follow him. He was going to take them to their assigned units.

Honesty and this one chick were assigned to the same unit. The woman had been trying to make conversation with her on the bus but Honesty tuned her out. This was neither the time nor the place to be making friends. If she did, then great but she wasn't looking for any. She must have gotten the point from earlier because she didn't say anything else to Honesty once they entered the unit. The officer told them to check in with the guard on the unit and she would tell us where to sleep. When they walked into her office she was on the phone but got off to show them to their bunks. Honesty got a bottom bunk.

The unit was an open dorm room. It was one giant room that contained bunk beds that were lined up next to one another. Underneath the bunks were large footlockers for storage. Each lady had two foot lockers. The lockers were only big enough to hold the few clothes you were assigned and some food items. Everything you bought had to be put in those lockers.

The unit bathroom also served as the shower room. There were sixteen toilets that had green long curtains for doors. Eight on each side. The same went for the showers. The green curtains were made of the same material that the mattresses were covered in.

I need to find out who their decorator was.

They couldn't take a shower because the showers were closed. Actually the bathrooms were closed period. You could only get up to pee. Nothing else. Honesty wasn't trying to be disrespectful on her first night there but she needed to brush her teeth. The guard would have to be mad. When she came out the bathroom, Officer Locke, was back on the phone. She didn't appear to care about anything other than what was going on on the other end. Before Honesty brushed her teeth she had found out where her bunk was located. She had put her mat down and made it up.

For the first time in years she got down on her hands and knees and prayed. She didn't even know what to say. She and God hadn't been cool for a minute.

"Lord, I don't really know what to say, but um, thank you Jesus for blessing me to see another day. I know I'm the reason I'm here but please watch over me. Amen."

After praying she got on her bunk and stared at the bottom side of the top bunk and hoped her 300 pound bunkmate did not come crashing down on her. The next day at around six in the morning, the large overhead light came on. Women were up milling around. Some were making beds while others went into the bathrooms to groom themselves. Honesty got up and made her bed. People were looking at her like she was crazy or something. This one girl, who was about four feet tall, came over to her. She looked crazy for real.

"Hey look everybody, we got an alien. Welcome alien. How many came with you?" She asked.

"There were about twenty one of us on the bus total but only thirteen got off the bus with me," Honesty replied.

"What county did you fall out of? Do you know if Big Boom was on the bus with you?"

"I'm from Oklahoma County and I don't know any one named Big Boom."

"Damn yo ass is fine. You wanna be my woman? I'll buy you shit from canteen."

"No, but thank you. I have a man. And I don't need you to buy me anything; I have money of my own."

"Well, can you buy me something? My ass is broke." This girl was crazy but cool. Honesty liked her sense of humor. Another woman, who looked like a fine ass man came over.

"Don't pay any attention to Small Fry. She always fucks with the new chicks that come here."

"Oh, don't worry; I wasn't paying any attention to her at all."

"Awe man, girl I loved you and you just broke my heart," Small Fry said.

"I find that hard to believe considering you don't know me." Honesty said before laughing.

The other chick introduced herself as 'Conflict.' It was obvious she was gay. So was Small Fry. If Conflict was a man she would be fine as hell. As a woman she was fine as hell. *I'd better watch myself. She could be dangerous.*

Both of them walked Honesty down to property to pick up the rest of her prison issue and belongings she bought while in the county jail. They showed her around the yard and took her to the relevant places. Chow hall, law library, the education building, mailroom, and canteen. They ate breakfast and lunch together. Honesty opted out of dinner. The food wasn't that good.

For the next several days she got situated in her new surroundings. Things were routine there. The yard opened at five forty- five in the morning and closed at nine at night daily. This included weekends. An inmate could not be on the yard when it was closed. There were some places that inmates could not be without permission. If they were caught there they could be issued an out of area citation that could cause them to lose good days or be charged with an escape.

Surprisingly Honesty had seen some women that she knew from the streets. *No wonder I hadn't seen them in a minute.* They were locked up. They talked a little but she didn't tell them how much time she had been given. It was no one's business. The chicks she knew told people about what she used to do and how much money she had. Some of the other women didn't believe them, until she came with her fly ass kicks and started buying lots of food and things off canteen. That made a believer out of them ho's.

Lorenzo and all her friends and family came to visit often. She had a visit every weekend. Her family would rotate so that she could spend equal time with all of them. She didn't want her parents to come on the days that Lo came because that would be hard dividing the time between them.

As much as she loved visits, she hated them too. After every visit inmates were strip searched. The visiting room officer, a woman, would make them take off all their clothes. Once naked they would have to spread their butt cheeks, squat and cough. The whole process was humiliating.

No inmate could be in prison without doing something. You either had to go to school, if needed, or get a job. Honesty got a job. Most people ended up working in the kitchen. Manual labor and Honesty didn't agree. She looked for another job and ended up being a staff assistant. For a penitentiary job, it was pretty decent.

She helped the unit counselor with clerical duties. All the papers she worked on for the inmates she filed for her. When she needed something typed Honesty did it. Ms. Grist, the unit counselor, and Honesty got close. The lady was cool. She let her do whatever she wanted to. It was a pleasure working with her too. The woman spoiled her. She would buy her things and let her use her phone to call her family, even though she could call them collect.

She wasn't the only one who took care of Honesty. There was an officer named Mr. Christian who used to let her shower when she wanted. This may not sound like much but washing your ass when you want to is an honor. Prison staff called it a privilege. Mr. C, liked to visualize her showering naked. He told her so.

The man was fine. After she had been locked up four months he had started coming on to her. She was horny. Some of the girls were getting their grooves on in the visiting room with their men but too many were getting caught and being sent to lock down. Honesty wouldn't take that chance. The price was too high.

Lo wrote her these nasty ass letters but couldn't finish what he started. Honesty was tired of masturbating. It gets boring after a while. She needed something more.

Fuck a finger I need a man.

On one of her canteen days, Ms. Grist let her do a special count at the education building because it was close to canteen. Mr. C was the yard officer. He was in charge of going from building to building picking up the count sheets. When he came into education, he stopped short when he saw her. Surprise.

He went into the principal's office and picked up the count sheet and told her that after he turned them all in, he would be back. It took him ten minutes to return. She was upstairs in an empty classroom when he came to her. He led her to this door that said 'keep out' and unlocked it. It was a staff lounge that looked like it hadn't been used in quite some time.

He started kissing her on the neck and rubbing her. It felt so good. She wouldn't let him kiss her on the mouth though. He wasn't that fine. She couldn't believe what she was doing. This was so risky. Maybe that's why she was overly excited. He unbuttoned her gray shirt and pulled her titties out of her bra. His mouth was hot on them. Her nipples were hard. With one hand he rubbed her pussy through her pants and the other one caressed the breast that he didn't have in his mouth. Lorenzo who? This was all about Honesty and Mr. C.

Her pussy was throbbing so hard she thinks he felt it. He unfastened her pants and pulled them down with his thumbs. Kneeling down he licked her panties. His hand moved them to the side and his fingers entered her. She stood while he did that. Her knees were getting weak and luckily there was a sofa in the room. Walking backward, he guided her over there and sat her down. She threw her legs over his shoulders and he began to go to work. His tongue felt like it was electric. Shocks kept running through her. Clamping his lips over her clit, he gently sucked on it until she came in his mouth. He continued to love on her until they were both satisfied.

They hurried up and got dressed to prevent getting caught. If anyone came in the room, dressed or not, what they had just did would be evident. The room smelled of sex. He went out the room first then she went out. There was no one in the hall. She watched him go down the back stairs outside the building. To keep suspicion down she waited about five minutes then went down the steps inside the building. No one knew she had been gone. She was downstairs less than a minute when she heard "count is clear, yard is open."

She could not share her life in prison with her friends. They both knew that Lo was in love with her and wanted to get married and they would not understand her cheating on him. She felt guilty but she loved having sex with Mr. C. She was beginning to like him though. Their sexual relationship was turning into something more. The man was writing her under an alias name and sending her money.

They used to sit and talk about all kinds of things. His co-worker Mr. Graves liked to come on the unit when Mr. C. was the officer. They would sit in the office and talk about crazy shit with Honesty and some other cool chicks. But when the two of them were alone, he would tell her such wonderful things. He said that he was in love with her.

Honesty was so confused. Although she didn't love him, she really did have feelings for him. It was possible that it was one of those 'if you can't be with the one you love, love the one you're with kind of things'. One day an inmate saw Mr. C. rub Honesty's ass and filed a grievance secretly. The warden launched a full scale investigation. Mr. C. couldn't work her unit anymore. They searched all Honesty's property looking for contraband and letters or anything to substantiate this claim. There was nothing found.

They decided to cool it. He had been cleared of any misconduct but they still wouldn't let him work that unit again. She was still battling with what to do about him and Lorenzo. It was a weird triangle. Her heart told her Lo. Her body wanted 'C'. Two weeks after working a new unit this girl told Honesty that she was fucking Mr. C. She gave her too many details to be lying. He had made the decision for Honesty. Lorenzo it was.

It was almost time to go. The last two months were crazy before she left. Conflict started liking her. She went off on Honesty one day like she was her woman because she was talking to Small Fry.

"Hey Honesty, have you seen Linda," Small Fry yelled across the dorm.

"Yeah. She's down here between my legs," Honesty was greasing her scalp.

"Shit, then can I be there too?"

"Sure, why not Small Fry." It was all in good fun.

Conflict came over to her bunk raging mad. Telling her how fucked up it is that she was talking nasty in front of her like that. Linda looked at them like she didn't know they were together. Honesty gave her a look back that said 'bitch please.' Calmly, Honesty let her know that although she was fine as hell, she was not interested in her or any other woman.

Women were getting caught fucking around every other day. This one couple was caught naked in the shower together. Smart. A sexual misconduct was a class 'A' write up. The penalty was lock down and good days taken away. No bitch was worth that. No man either. *Glad I didn't get caught with Mr. C.*

A lot of the women were fighting, stealing, doing drugs, and many things that got them there in the first place. All of the women who were in prison with her were unique. There were a few common factors in all of them. They were mothers, daughters, sisters, wives, and nieces. Some were once cooks, homemakers, and nurses. They became forgerer's, prostitutes, robbers, and addicts.

Many of their lives had suffered irreparable damage because of lust, greed, lack of self control, and even necessity. They were a distinct group of women who bear a cross so different than the average 'Jane'. Suffering a degradation and humiliation not experienced since concentration camps. A separation which is capable of killing the body and mind. A separation that *has* killed the body and soul.

They were in prison. Incarcerated within the Oklahoma correctional system. A legalistic place which stripped women of all ages of their pride, joy, peace, self-worth, and self-love. This place made many women age before their time. Bitter before they have had a chance to be happy. Dying before they had an opportunity to live. But it didn't defeat Honesty, nor could it. She was going home. The time had come for her to say good-bye to the place that was her temporary home for seven months and twelve days. Here, she learned how to trust herself and listen more closely to her heart.

The day she was to leave she had to take this paper to all the department heads on the yard. They had to sign off on a form clearing her from that department. She had already changed into the street clothes Desi sent. She hugged everyone who showed her love while she was locked up. They would be getting letters from her soon. That was a promise. They would be missed but she didn't want to stay with them. Honesty left everything she had purchased off canteen to Small Fry. The two of them had become good friends. Honesty promised her friend she would write and send her some money and she would.

Lorenzo came to pick her up in a beautiful silver Mercedes Convertible. She couldn't believe that she was going to screw up her relationship with a lovely man for a lame prison guard.

When they drove off from the prison she didn't look back. Her future was ahead. A big part of it was sitting beside her. She rested her hand on the console. Lo put his on top of it. He gave it a light squeeze. Her storm was over.

EPILOGUE

Honesty had been out of prison for six months when she and Lorenzo started to pack her things to move. She was going to Georgia. Desiree and Devan had moved four months ago. Essence and her baby left last week. Honesty was the last of the crew to go. When she got out they all threw her a welcome home party. Her family was so excited to see her. Kim was shocked at Honesty's stomach. She had a six pack.

"With a little hard work and a few years, you can have one like this too." Honesty joked. Things were fabulous.

Kalif was going off to school in the fall. His singing had gotten him a few commercials and local gigs. But he wanted to take it further. It would be easy for him to do since he had chosen a performing arts academy in Atlanta. The couple was packing things out of the garage when Lorenzo noticed a door about three feet high. Honesty had never seen it before. It was padlocked. Her nosey butt wanted to know what it led too. Lo, took a hammer and knocked the lock off. There was a trunk inside.

He pulled it out. It was an old footlocker that was covered with dirt and cobwebs.

It also had a lock on it. Again, he knocked the lock off. Honesty pulled up a chair and sat down when he lifted the lid. Eureka! The trunk was filled with thousands of dead presidents. Rubber band stacks of cash by the hundreds. There was also uncut dope, guns, and various knives inside. *This was my daddy's stash.* The money that D-Snake had been looking for all those years ago. It was almost a million dollars in the trunk. Honesty's heart was beating so fast. Lo looked at her. She looked at him. They smiled. He pulled the trunk inside the house and they counted the money. This was a financial windfall. They had both seen things like this happen on television but never thought that this could happen in real life. But it just did.

Lo leaned over and kissed Honesty full on the lips. She kissed him back. He stood up and removed his shirt and took off his pants. They both knew what time it was. She got on her knees and took her shorts off then sat back on down. With her knees lifted in front of her chest, she spread her legs open to reveal her pussy. Lo, liked it when she didn't wear any panties. Right there on the floor next to the treasure trunk, he gave her the business.

When they finished and their breathing returned to normal, they continued to lay there on the floor. They were in a spoon position. Her ass was backed into his dick. He was getting hard again. The way he stroked her hair felt so good to her. She moaned. He kissed her neck. She groaned and smiled. His arms held her tightly. Without using any words the couple had come to an agreement. A decision had been made. The more things changed, the more they stayed the same. They were back in business.